4

STARTING OVER

Recent Titles by Tessa Barclay

THE CHAMPAGNE GIRLS
DAYTON AND DAUGHTER
OTHER PEOPLE'S DREAMS
THE PRECIOUS GIFT
THE SATURDAY GIRL

Foreword

This novel was first conceived in the late 1970s. Women's Lib had brought about some important changes in career openings. But, as recession began to bite, it was women who were more likely to be made redundant from high-profile jobs.

I wanted to make a portrait of a woman who had become the mainstay of her small family. What would she feel when the economic climate turned against her? How would she cope, who could she turn to for help? As I thought about it, it seemed to me that far from freeing themselves, some women had taken on even heavier burdens than before, burdens that they couldn't shed.

So this book is an attempt to portray the struggle to be at the same time career-woman, loving wife, and devoted mother. It's a role that almost no one can bring off – and Margaret Durley is no exception. I hope my readers will agree that the subject is as relevant today, in the early years of the 21st century, as it was when the book was first published.

© Tessa Barclay, November 2000

Chapter One

The change of angle in the big Boeing's flight was just enough to tell Margaret Durley that the long descent towards Heathrow had begun. She stretched a little in her seat without disturbing Jack, who had fallen asleep after the meal – whichever meal that was. Collapsed against him like a jointless beanbag, Laurie was asleep too, as he ought to be at this hour of the evening.

She'd enjoyed the holiday, but was pleased to be nearly home again. She'd have a good report to write on Monday once she'd distributed the obligatory presents to her colleagues at Hebberwood. Mombasa was a super place to send upper echelon staff on reward holidays, or to hold a top level unofficial conference; it was so hot there, so langorous, that people simply had to relax. Plenty of maids and waiters to do every slightest task, drinks at the snap of a finger, and in the hotel Margaret had been 'tasting', two swimming pools as well as seemingly unlimited expanses of golden beach. She'd taken plenty of notes in the intervals of unwinding from the tensions of a winter's hard work for the firm. Despite the fact that the holiday was one of her officially permitted expenses, she was glad she could justify it further by recommending it as a Hebberwood perquisite for those trying to keep their tax liability down.

The stewardess came to clear away glasses that had held vodka and lime. It was just enough movement to rouse Jack. He opened one eye and said: 'We there yet?'

'Almost, I think. You'd better wake up.'

'I got into the habit of it in our wooden hut. God, it's going to be difficult getting down to work again after three weeks of Lotus-land.'

Margaret laughed. Her husband was fond of talking about the pains of his work, and she never argued back that he had it easy compared with herself. Jack was a sculptor – quite a good one, she thought, but then she was biased. A few other people shared her view, but not enough to make it viable as a real career for Jack. But that didn't matter because, as he was fond of saying when called on to explain their domestic set-up, 'I've got a rich wife to support me.'

She wasn't rich, she was well paid. When she joined the huge brewing combine's headquarters staff about eighteen months ago, rumours had gone round over the salary she'd negotiated but she in her turn had fended off inquiries with the laughing comment: 'I've got a starving artist to support.'

'Try not to wake Laurie,' she warned, as Jack sat up and wriggled his shoulders in the unaccustomed jacket. For three weeks he'd gone around in a short-sleeved, open-necked shirt, and at home he generally wore a sweater in winter and a T-shirt in summer, but on journeys he felt he ought to wear a jacket so as to have pockets for money and travel documents and permits and passports. They had found it easier to let Jack be in charge of all that kind of thing because officials at airports expected it.

'He weighs a ton,' Jack complained, shifting the three-year-old so that he leaned against the other shoulder. 'What were they feeding him in that toddlers' group at the hotel? Whole coconuts?'

Laurie made a snuffling sound, put his arms octopus-like round his father's neck and went more soundly asleep.

6

'He had a marvellous time, didn't he?' Margaret remarked, brushing back soft fair hair from the little boy's forehead. 'He had such fun with those other kids to play with.'

'Well, he'll have kids to play with when he gets back to play-group – '

'But he's the youngest there, isn't he?' She was thinking about the little plump two-year-old who had staggered round after Laurie in the hotel play area under the palms. It would be nice to give Laurie a little sister like that. A couple more months, and she'd see her way clear to putting out feelers about maternity leave starting, say, in December. That would mean the new baby arriving three months later, in spring – a good time to have a baby because it meant the whole summer stretched ahead for her first difficult weeks. Of course it would be a girl, she was sure of that. Emily, she would call her. Or Portia, perhaps?

From this pleasant day-dream she was summoned by the need to fasten seat-belts, straighten chairbacks, and otherwise begin to think about the world that lay below them at Heathrow.. They were delayed very little at customs; Jack's collection of wood carvings from the markets of Mombasa and Nairobi were looked at with tolerance but considered of almost no value.

'Shows how much they know, the idiots,' Jack grumbled, when at last they were in their car heading for Sussex. 'Those carvings had more real worth than all the bottles of gin and brandy from the duty-free shops – '

'Oh, I don't know,' Margaret said, stifling a yawn of real weariness. 'Don't you feel they sort of knock them out by the score for tourists like us?'

'Of course they do, but they do it by hand – it's real craftsmanship with real wood. That tribal god, the bigger one – that's a beautiful piece of wood, the grain's just right, you know. The carver – '

'This car smells like the inside of a vacuum's dust bag –'

7

'What d'you expect after three weeks in the long-stay car park?' He looked in his mirror, signalled for the turn off the motorway, and drove on to the lesser roads he preferred except when very pressed for time. Jack liked to drive without hassle. In fact, that was the way he preferred life to be – without hassle.

After a few minutes of silence, during which he took in the small leaves on the birch trees and the primroses in the hedges, he gave a huge sigh. 'It's nice to be home,' he murmured.

'Yes, isn't it?' She was surprised how much it pleased her. The Tokoni Beach Hotel with all its splendours, the sparkling blue of the sea, the golden warmth of the sun, seemed a lot less important now as she sat beside her husband in the gathering dusk of an early April evening watching the budding trees slip by and conscious of the easy, capable movements of his big hands on the wheel.

He glanced at her. His teeth gleamed white in the tanned face. He sported a short, carefully tended beard, all that remained of a bushier growth from the Bohemian days when she'd first met him.

'You look like one of those Arab merchants we saw in Nairobi,' she remarked.

'Do I? Turns you on, does it?' His grin grew wider.

From the back seat, where Laurie was carefully wedged in and sound asleep, came a little snorting snore. 'We're all exhausted,' Margaret said. 'Including you.'

'I hate to admit it, but you're right. Lord, I'm having difficulty keeping my eyes open. Travelling narrows the eyes, that's the truth of it. But it was good, Meg. I liked it there. Hotel a bit too posh, perhaps, but I saw a lot that'll come back to me when I start work again.'

'Thinking of doing a group – "Black Fishermen Mending Nets"?'

'Not for a bit. Needs time to simmer. Not like you – straight in on Monday, isn't it?'

8

'Yes, well, I've left Lena doing all the donkey work for the Antigua conference, but I dare say there'll have been problems.'

She leaned back in the seat and thought about them. The travel arrangements bringing the firm's advertising men together from various parts of the world had been almost completed before she left for her Kenyan holiday. Provisional itineraries had been sent out to each of them. The biggest problems were likely to come from the Japanese contingent for they had the most awkward journey and, in any case, would rather have held the conference in Macao. It had made no difference to Margaret – she could have arranged a get-together for Macao as easily as for Antigua. But the heavyweights at the directorial level had let it be known to her that Macao didn't suit them. She was almost sure that was because they thought the conference members would spend too much time in the casino. So the Antiguan venue had been approved. But Margaret knew she would have to take the complaints of the Japanese as if it was all her fault.

Still, that was of little important. The aim was to lay on a meeting in which, once they were there, they met with no annoyances, no obstacles. She'd made a flying visit to Antigua the previous December to vet the hotel, and since then had been on the telephone to ensure everything was perfect. Flowers in the rooms for the women, with spray cologne in the centre of the bouquet. Cigars for the men who smoked, champagne on ice for each conference attender. Programme in a limp leather binder by each bedside bureau. Buffet supper the first evening, a casual get-together. A trip round the island for the whole party, eighteen in all, at about ten next morning. Lunch and introductory pep-talk at one. An afternoon session to explore the advertising problems of a multi-national brewing combine from three to five.

Study groups to take up individual points – four rooms reserved for these. Afternoon tea at five, to please the British contingent and amuse the others. Drinks at six-thirty. Dinner at eight, speech from Paul Dickerman of Dickerman & Proud on 'Image in the Present Climate'. The hotel had no dance-band or floor show but she had arranged for cars to take any pleasure seekers to the nearby Club Plantana – although she was fairly sure no one would do so on the first night of a four-day conference because it would look too flighty. Later, when they'd got to know each other better, they might make sorties to find what turned them on.

As far as Margaret could remember – and she had almost total recall where business was concerned – she had covered everything in her first plan. During the three weeks of her own holiday, one or two things were sure to have gone wrong but nothing of a crisis rating. She was quite looking forward to going in on Monday, to sign the letters authorising payments. Then it would be launched, and she'd turn her attention to the next Hebberwood conference, which was to take place in Quebec the following month and would require facilities for a party of twenty-three scientists from the brewing laboratories.

'Doesn't it ever scare you, spending all that money?' Jack had once asked her. 'It's a hell of a lot that passes through your hands – and trying to give people a good time is such a chancy business.'

'That's why I'm where I am,' Margaret replied. 'I know how to do it so that there's a ninety-nine per cent success rate. So, people relax, business is done, things go well, and I'm worth every cent they pay me.'

'Right,' said Jack.

Her job had given them both a life-style that most people envied. True, a few of their friends and many of their acquaintances thought them a peculiar pair. A career woman – yes, everyone accepted that these days. But most career women had career husbands, bright, clever men as eager to get on in the world as their wives. Margaret Durley's husband was quite different. He seemed to have no ambition in the business sense of the word. He wanted to make good as a sculptor – that was shown by his working almost every day in the little extension cleverly built on to their goodlooking house near Ladhurst and his submitting pieces to judging committees for exhibitions. But he never earned a penny nor seemed to have much interest in doing so.

Both Jack and Margaret were aware of a faintly patronising tone that would come into a friend's voice when talking of Jack's work. Luckily they had learned to live with that. Their life-style suited them, was based on what they saw as sound commonsense. It had become imperative for Jack to find a more tolerable life rhythm about four and a half years ago, when a serious operation for a stomach ulcer had warned him the film industry wasn't for him. His talents as a special effects constructor were no longer in demand; as a freelance he'd had a precarious income over several years, dashing all over the world as he was needed to construct miniature mediaeval monasteries, or models of Rome-as-it-was-in-Christ's-day. He had been a background-constructor, at the top of his profession while the fashion had reigned for big-scale 'historicals'. He could make anything architectural – Viking castles, Saxon camp-grounds, Japanese harbours – all to scale as required. But film styles had changed, job opportunities diminished, anxiety grew, and his doctor had told him: 'Give up this life or I give you up.'

It had made sense to Margaret and Jack when they talked it through. They had had a long relationship, at that time spanning eight years of more or less complete faithfulness but without the bond of marriage. Now

11

perhaps it was time to try matrimony. Margaret thought she would like to have a baby too. For the sake of the child or children, it was better to be legally married, and how convenient it would all be: Margaret would take maternity leave, then, afterwards, Jack would be there to look after the baby. With plenty of help, naturally: Margaret's job brought in enough for them to hire a nanny and a daily and whatever else they needed.

Because of Laurie, they had found a house with plenty of ground around it. Jack's cleverness with his hands had been a great asset; with only occasional help for the more technical bits he had remodelled it, built on the extension, laid out the garden. In the intervals he had worked on his chunks of wood and stone. Other people could say he lazed around at home while Margaret went out to do the breadwinning; Margaret had a different view of him.

Almost two years ago now, Margaret had been offered this job with Hebberwood's. Without a husband like Jack, she couldn't have taken it on. It meant swanning around the world on short trips to ascertain that Hebberwood's various small properties were being looked after so as to be ready for instantaneous occupation by travelling executives. It meant surveying hotels, peeping into new restaurants, reading extensively about new resorts, new airline facilities, hire car firms, credit card uses, leisure activities, business centres, and any other aspect of life for high-powered businessmen and women on the move. In a word, she was in charge of the Travel and Accommodations Department of the huge international company. Moreover, she foresaw that quite soon she would move up to something bigger and better yet – a new department she was planning to put before the board of directors in a month or two. Hebberwood owned so much property scattered here and there, and had one or two resort hotels; it had seemed to Margaret that these were neglected, and she hoped to persuade Hebberwood's to give her the job of exploiting them to the full. She even had a name for the new department: Entertainments Property Management.

Almost inevitably her thoughts had turned to this as Jack drove them home from the airport. The new department could be launched in perhaps a year or so; it couldn't be done at once, of course, there had to be preparation. It was quite convenient, really. She could have this new baby, the little sister for Laurie, and during her maternity leave she could go on with the planning stages, and then when she returned to work she could probably walk straight into her new office.

'How d'you think you'd like to have more than one junior family member to look after?' she murmured, exaggerating her sleepiness to make the question sound less serious.

'Eh?' Jack said. 'What d'you mean, more than one? If you're thinking of inviting the play group to meet in our house – '

'I wouldn't inflict that on you. No, it was just that . . . You know, that little girl in the sun bonnet who staggered round after Laurie – she was rather sweet, wasn't she?'

Jack expelled a long breath through pursed lips. 'So that's what you're thinking about.' He gave her a momentary glance.

'It's a thought, you know. Laurie's three. If we're going to give him a brother or sister, it's time we got on with it.'

'I'm all in favour. You know I think you missed a lot by being an only child.' He was silent a moment, thinking it through. 'What about the job, though?'

Sometimes, in the midst of the most ordinary conversation, Margaret had an impulse of love for Jack

13

that was like a warm tide flowing through her. This was one of those times. No other man, she felt, could have asked that question so totally without rancour or ulterior motive. She knew Jack wasn't having a little sense of triumph over the fact that womanhood imposed its own conditions. She knew he wasn't enjoying the notion that she would have to step back from her career for three months or so. It was a simple question: What about the job? What would it entail for her? Would it cause an upset? Could she afford the break in concentration, the understandable though hidden irritation of her male colleagues?

'It's quite a good time to be doing it,' she replied. She didn't confide her plans for the new department and the prospective profits she was going to offer Hebberwood. Though Jack would listen with interest to chat about her work and its problems, he never could take in money details; book-keeping to him was a mystery as hermetic as the Rites of Isis. But she knew he would hear in her voice the confidence she felt, and be satisfied.

By the time they reached Sussex, the light had gone from the sky and they could see the windows of the house gleaming through the trees. Their 'treasure', Mrs Prior, had been in today to dust and tidy up so that there would be no chores awaiting them. Thoughtful as always, she had left lamps alight. As Margaret unlocked the front door she could smell the wax polish, the freshness of the place. One glance at her precious abutilon in the hall showed it had been kept watered. The post had been picked up and ranged in date order on the hall table. An appetising odour greeted her as she went into the kitchen: the indicator on the cooker showed that something was being kept at a low heat in the oven.

'God bless Mrs Prior,' Margaret thought with gratitude. But then, she added to herself, Mrs Prior knew when she was on to a good thing. Margaret paid her over the odds for her services as a cleaning woman and the old girl enjoyed coming every day to the house to carry on a flighty friendship with that nice Mr Durley. On the council estate where Mrs Prior lived on the other side of Ladhurst, the affairs of the Durley family were no doubt discussed at length, Margaret thought. But it was a small price to pay, in either money or involvement, for the services of a totally reliable help.

Jack carried Laurie upstairs and popped him into bed with only the sketchiest of face-washings. Margaret brought in the lightest of the luggage then headed for the kitchen to serve the food. Even as she did so, her phone began to ring. She knew it was her mother before she picked up the receiver.

'Oh, darling, there you are, safe home,' Mrs Grant cried as soon as she said hello. 'I thought you might ring but as you didn't, I felt I ought to just make sure you got back all right.'

'Yes, Mother, we've just got in, haven't even put the car – '

'How are you? Didn't pick up any of those nasty African ailments?'

'No, we're fine, all three of us. Jack has a beautiful tan, I was just telling him he looks like an – '

'You didn't do too much sunbathing, did you? You know it brings you out in freckles, dear. I hope little Laurie came to no harm through sunburn, I always think this fetish about getting brown is a mistake. You find it cold now you're back, I dare say.'

'Yes, but I had sweaters to put on when we got off the plane – '

'You wrapped Laurie up well, I hope. You know he has a tendency to take a chill. You were the same when you were small, you know, dear.' Margaret's mother was obsessed about health. The one good thing in Jack, so

15

far as Mrs Grant was concerned, was that he provided an excellent example of what happened when you neglected to look after yourself. His ulcer of nearly five years ago was continually being discussed by her, even sometimes with a tinge of hope that it might reappear.

Margaret spent ten minutes assuring her mother that they were all well and in the end got her to put the phone down by murmuring that they were very tired after their journey and ought to get some sleep if they weren't to be under the weather.

'Quite right, Meg, you be sensible about that, don't go into the office on Monday if you haven't got over it. Take a hot toddy and go straight to bed. Father sends his love.'

'Mine to him,' Margaret said, and turned to find Jack closing the front door for the night. 'That was Mother.'

'You do surprise me. Is she sending you a remedy for beriberi by special delivery?'

Margaret laughed. 'If Lhasa fever didn't exist, Mother would have invented it. She was suggesting they should come over and see us next weekend but I've put her off by saying it'll take that long for Laurie to settle down again. I promised to send her present by post – though whether she'll put up that bead curtain I very much doubt.'

They went together into the kitchen to eat. Travel fatigue made them both disinclined for talk. The familiar house lulled them, and tomorrow the familiar routine awaited them: brunch with neighbours and then an informal meeting with acquaintances who were hoping to launch a local arts festival. Jack might have chickened out of the brunch date, but he was too interested in anything to do with the arts to give up the exploratory talks.

He said as they got ready for bed: 'Nice to be home. Africa was interesting, even from a luxury hotel, but it's good to be back.'

'Back to the old routine?'

'It's a good routine. Even when we've added Baby Jane to it, it'll still be great.'

They kissed and got into bed, and with arms about each other fell deeply asleep.

The Sunday brunch at the Cooper-Watts' was always a very elegant affair, requiring clothes casual yet smart. Although it was still very cool English spring, Jack put on a white safari suit to show off his tan, just to give the Cooper-Watts something to envy a little. Margaret chose a pale pink shirt dress and low-heeled black patent pumps. It was true, as her mother said, that she freckled in the sun, but her skin had a tinge of gold which went well with the shell-pink of the dress and, after a moment's consideration, instead of using the sash as a belt she tied it around her taffy-coloured hair.

'You'll do,' Jack told her. 'Now what about Laurie? Are we going to present him as Little Lord Fauntleroy today, or Tarzan?'

Laurie settled the matter himself by insisting on a jersey he hadn't seen since before the holiday, and Ladybird jeans. For a touch of fantasy – for in this social circle even children were part of the dressing-up process – Margaret added a small shady straw hat bought for him in the Tokoni Beach hotel.

'Why does Patty Cooper-Watts always remind me irresistibly of Margo in *The Good Life*?' Jack asked.

'Jack, don't be unfair!' Margaret felt bound to spring to her defence. 'She's not *that* bad, she can be a very generous person ... '

Jack supressed a smile. 'Did we bring them back a present?'

'Reed mats. The kind of thing you pay a fortune for in Habitat, and they'll be able to tell their friends they were brought back specially from Africa.'

'Ho-ho. Who else are we giving mats to?'

'Practically everybody, unless it's bead curtains. Well,

17

it's not my fault,' Margaret chuckled, 'I didn't start this business of bringing back presents from holidays.'

'Whoever started it, I hope he gets all the curliest bits of glass from Murano,' Jack said in disgust, and started the car.

The Cooper-Watts lived in a very large house about two miles off. The Durleys were neither late nor early and were pleased to see four other cars already in the drive. Patty Cooper-Watts came hurrying out to welcome them as they parked. 'Darlings! Let me look – oh, how brown you are, Jack! Give me a kiss, handsome – you look like Omar Sharif!'

'Is that a compliment?' Jack said in his wife's ear as he got out.

They were ushered through the house with loud cries of explanation heralding their arrival. 'Isn't it marvellous of them to come out, the very morning they get back! And don't they look marvellous? Stan, here are Margaret and Jack. Solveig, take Laurie to the playroom.'

The au pair girl collected Laurie and bore him off. Everyone advanced on them to hug and kiss them, or shake hands and stand back in approval. Caroline Keppler admired Jack's tan, showering them with questions. 'How was Mombasa? Did you like the hotel? What kind of flight did you have? You flew Kenyan Airways, did you?'

In the flood of questions Jack brought forth the package containing the reed mats, which were unrolled at once to be walked upon and exclaimed about. Drinks were pressed into their hands: Buck's Fizz, Stan's speciality, and then red wine to go with the food. There was a bewildering selection of cold meats, hot quiche and continental sausages, cheeses, and six different kinds of bread. Fruit was always served as dessert: 'We always stick to simple food,' Stan would explain with a casual air, well knowing that the fruit on his buffet table was beyond the reach of most people. He was the owner of a fruit importing business.

After a three weeks' absence it was taken for granted that the Durleys would need to be brought up to date. Maurice Attins had bought a Ferrari, the Grimbles had found a house in the Dordogne at last, Julie Lessinger had been accepted for Lady Margaret Hall, there had been a flooding at that corner where the B2181 met Mow Lane, Sir Roger had made a deal to sell that lower paddock after all, and Joan Spadwell was talking about divorce.

'No!' Margaret exclaimed, as she knew was required of her. She had no real interest in whether Joan Spadwell divorced the adulterous Frank. She glanced about the big, elegant room and out towards the guests lounging on the patio. 'Isn't Martin here? I haven't seen him around in a while.'

'Oh, Martin ... ' Stan Cooper-Watts said with a significant nod of the head. 'My love, nobody ever invites him these days.'

'No? Why not? Got something infectious?' Jack inquired.

'Thank God, no, it isn't catching. But all you hear from him these days is a hard luck story. It's a bit boring, you know, when you've got friends in for a bit of a good time.'

Patty Cooper-Watts came by with a tray of freshly baked rolls. Jack took one, buttered it, then said: 'I don't recall Martin Lesswith ever boring me, particularly?'

'Oh, well, he wouldn't, would he? *You* can't do him any good. Whereas I ... '

'You can do Martin some good?'

'Well, as a matter of fact, no. How can I use a half-trained management consultant in a fruit-importing firm? I ask you! Just shows how desperate he's getting when he starts throwing out his line that far.'

'Oh,' Margaret said, understanding at last. 'He's looking for a job?'

'His firm's retrenching. It's hard luck, I know, but after you've sympathised and listened to the tale a couple of times, what more can you do?'

'It's awful,' Patty put in. 'I don't know what to talk about when I meet Sally.'

'Well, then, stay out of her way.'

'I can't altogether do that, Stan. We collect the children from school at the same time. Besides,' Patty said with a sigh, 'I feel sorry for her. It's such terrible bad luck, if your husband is chosen to be put out of a job. I mean, he's just a victim of the present times – '

'Don't you believe it,' said Maurice Attins, who had joined them to fetch one of Patty's fresh-baked rolls. 'They don't choose people to dismiss by lot, you know. You can take it from me that Martin had been found wanting. They had a look at their staff and decided Lesswith was the one to go ... ' Maurice paused for a moment as a bon mot simmered. 'Lesswith-it than others, that must have been the reason.'

'I say, that's good!' Stan laughed, slapping him on the back. 'Damn good!'

Some of the guests at the Cooper-Watts' were going on to Sir Roger Filmore's for the meeting about the proposed arts festival. Patty offered to keep Laurie to play with her three children until the Durleys could collect him on their way home. 'He'll nap, probably,' Jack said. 'He usually does, from about three to four – he'll just keel over and fall asleep, but let him, he's okay.'

Patty gave him a wide smile. 'Yes, of course, you're the one who knows all his little habits like that. Stan wouldn't know whether Poppy takes a nap or not ... But then you're unusual in more ways than one, Jack. And very fanciable with that dark suntan. You keep an eye on him, Margaret, or I'll snitch him.'

'Should I say, chance would be a fine thing?' Margaret inquired as they drove off.

'You're quite safe, she's not my type.' Jack was almost absentminded. Already he was looking ahead to the meeting about the arts festival.

This was the brainchild of Sir Roger, the local landowner and something of an old-style squire. His family had only been in the Ladhurst area for a couple of generations but he enjoyed the role of lord of the manor and, to give him his due, tried to further the good of the local inhabitants. It was on his land that the local flower shows and pageants were held, it was to him secretaries of societies turned for speeches at annual dinners and treasurers turned for handsome donations. Now, in emulation of Hastings, Sir Roger wanted a festival to enliven the drearier part of the year. He had fixed on February as a month that needed cheering up, and was hoping to get the festival launched in a small way the following year.

'The year after, we'll increase the categories,' he explained in his opening speech. 'But as a beginning I suggest we have competitions for the visual arts, a craft market with displays of work in progress, and a choir competition. Strikes me, y'see, that those are the things people are already involved in so we'd get lots of entries. We might add drama later – I don't know what sort, you might come up with ideas but don't let's offer a prize for the best one-act play, for Pete's sake.'

'You're proposing to use Ladhurst Village Hall, are you?'

'Yes, and the old Assembly Rooms. The damp's getting in, I know, and it'll need money spent on it, but if we run some money-raising events between now and the autumn, such as a donkey derby or even a golf tournament, we ought to raise enough to do it up

21

sufficiently well for the craft market. And I thought, we might have a restaurant there – so that folk coming from, say, London, could get a cup of coffee and a snack.'

One or two of those present groaned inwardly. It was well known that catering was always the most difficult part of any event. If you got a firm of outside caterers to undertake it, the profits dwindled. If you asked amateurs to do it on a rota basis, standards were tremendously variable.

The discussion went on until Sir Roger hospitably offered drinks. It was then felt good manners to bring business to an end. Sir Roger was elected chairman, Delia Cuggins secretary, Maurice Attins treasurer. A committee of six was suggested. 'I feel it would be an excellent measure to ask both Jack and Margaret to serve, if they will,' said Sir Roger, turning a broad and benevolent smile on them. 'Jack of course because of his artistic interests, and Margaret for her business ability.'

Margaret was in no doubt the invitation had come because of her connection with Hebberwood's Breweries. There would be no problem over catering for the festival visitors, no matter how successful the event became, if someone with her resources was on the committee. But for the moment Margaret declined. She felt that if they had Jack, that was enough; he could pass on their hopes and suggestions and she, if she felt so inclined, could take them up. But it was better not to be committed to it.

She was always aware that the men of the neighbourhood were a little in awe of her. There were plenty of 'good women' in Ladhurst, willing to take on the chores connected with the village's social life. It was women who ran the gymkhanas, the play groups, the pageants, the flower shows, the debating society, and the various church activities. Margaret was recognised as being as capable as these organising geniuses – more so in fact – yet no one ever felt easy in approaching her. Her position in Ladhurst society was tinged with something like alarm. A small Sussex village was so different from London. It was known she handled vast sums of money, travelled on business throughout the world, had 'influence'. She had reversed the normal order of things; she kept her husband, her husband didn't keep her.

Yet at times like these she had her uses. They knew they could fall back on her for help over such things as cheap catering for their festival. It made her more understandable to them.

'I suppose you'll ensure that one of the categories of the visual arts is sculpture,' she remarked to Jack as they drove home.

'I certainly will. Quid pro quo – the quo in this case being the sausage rolls and iced fancies that you'll get for them at cost price, not to mention my hours of devoted committee work.'

'Have you got anything on the stocks that you want to show next February?'

'Mm ...' he murmured. 'By then, maybe I'll have got something going from our African safari. If I can just find a good piece of wood ...'

'You can start looking tomorrow. There's a place over by handcross where they have seasoned timber –'

'Huh! Tomorrow I'll have to spend at least an hour listening to Mrs Prior's yarns, and sort through that pile of mail, and get Laurie to and from play group, and deliver our films to be developed, and spray the roses against aphids and mildew ... I've left out something, I know I have.'

'It's a rich, full life.'

'Whereas you, my love, will be sitting in an air-conditioned office, dictating letters to your secretary and dispensing the gifts you brought back to your admiring cronies. I bet you've even got a posh-nosh lunch laid on.'

'No, as a matter of fact, I haven't. I thought I'd better

leave Monday free so I can work straight through and clear anything that's been lying in my in-tray. But I dare say Lena and I and a few others might have a glass of wine at lunch time. First day back, Jack – you can't expect me to buckle to straight away. I want to tell them all about Mombasa.'

Jack grinned and said, with a certain edge of truth, 'If you want to know what I think, I think we only went to Mombasa so you could size it up for your precious Travel and Accommodation reports.'

She said nothing to that. If the truth were acknowledged, she'd already been drafting the report inside her head. Instead she suggested, 'Let's get something easy out of the freezer and have a big meal and an early night.'

Jack grinned. He didn't even say what seemed to follow on from that.

But it wasn't to be. Laurie, his routine still upside down, refused to settle down to sleep. He wasn't being naughty, he just couldn't understand what time of day it was. The Durleys were thankful to fall into bed at eleven-thirty and sleep, themselves still not quite sure that their life rhythm had caught up with them across the African continent.

As Margaret drove into London next day she was rehearsing some of the comments she would make about Mombasa. It had its disadvantages; it was perhaps too relaxing, and the humidity was higher than she'd been led to expect. But if it was viewed as a 'reward' category venue rather than as a business setting, it had its value. Moreover, she sensed potential there for investment. If Hebberwood were to build a resort hotel there, they might do well, besides earning goodwill from the Kenyan government.

It always gave Margaret pleasure to run her car into the big underground garage at the skyscraper building in the City. She glanced along the rows. Mr Hughes, her immediate boss, was already in, and so was Gantry of accounting and Amabel, the personal assistant to the chairman. She collected the packages from the back seat and went up in the lift to the sub-penthouse floor where the higher executives had their offices. The penthouse contained the suites of the chairman and the managing director. The floors below housed the huge organisation that ran the breweries; one whole floor was taken up with the tied public houses, another entire floor dealt with sales. The place hummed with life even at night, when the computer staff were still on duty and certain key personnel to deal with anything urgent from overseas.

Her secretary, Lena, wasn't in the outer office but was in the building, for her handbag was on the desk, and her telephone showed by its keying that she was already switched through for the day's work. Margaret put one package on Lena's desk, then went along the corridor, laying little parcels here and there where the owner would see them, or dropping them casually in front of colleagues already at their desks.

When she got back Lena was undoing the bright paper Margeret had brought back specially from Mombasa. As she took out the beaded necklace, her face lit up. 'Oh, it's lovely, Mrs Durley! It's handmade, I can see! It'll go beautifully with my cheesecloth dress.'

'Yes, I think it will. It was what I had in mind when I bought it.' Margaret went into her own office, followed by Lena inquiring how she'd enjoyed herself and thanking her for the postcard. 'Lena,' she said when the first flush of talk had subsided, 'Is there anything wrong this morning?'

'Wrong? Nothing that I know of. Why?'

'I don't know exactly. It just struck me one or two people were a bit quiet as I passed by.'

25

'Well, goodness, first thing in the morning, Mrs Durley! And they haven't just come back from a fabulous holiday!'

'No, I suppose not. But I'd have thought they'd have wanted to delay me for a word or two about a place like Mombasa ...'

She was disappointed. She herself felt that having been to a place so new and far away deserved a little interest from her colleagues. But then, she supposed they had been fully occupied with their own affairs. She reminded herself how perfunctory her own inquiries had been about other people's holidays.

'Well, what's on the diary?'

'It's clear, more or less, as you told me. But you've an appointment first thing with Mr Hughes – he asked me to make sure you saw him at ten.'

'Something bothering him?'

'I expect it's about that Antigua thing. Oh, come to that, it's probably Mr Hughes who's put a damper on everybody. He's been a bit grouchy all last week.'

Erewyn Hughes was Margaret's chief, the head of Establishments and Property. It was he who had hived off part of his work a couple of years ago and then come looking for Margaret Durley to take it on as a separate department. 'My wife doesn't like me to go travelling so much, and with all the leases of all our property to look after I simply haven't time to deal with travel arrangements and conference venues. I've heard good things of you, Mrs Durley. How would you feel about joining me?'

It was a dream job, almost exactly tailored to suit the experience she'd built up. Moreover, as she listened to Mr Hughes talk about Hebberwood, she'd understood that the prospects were almost unlimited to a woman of ability.

But though Mr Hughes had given up direct control of

26

Travel and Accommodation, he still had a tendency to fuss at times. With a sigh, Margaret accepted the folder about the Antigua conference from Lena at a few minutes before ten, and made her way along the corridor to the small suite of offices at the far end.

Mr Hughes's secretary gave her a welcoming smile then buzzed through; 'Mrs Durley is here, Mr Hughes.'

'Send her in.'

Margaret nodded and went into the main office. It had a wide expanse of window running along one wall and facing the door, so that Mr Huges was always to some extent in silhouette. He swung his chair a little and waved her to another, and as the cool April light caught his features it struck her he looked rather drawn.

'Good morning, Margaret. You look well.'

'Yes, thank you, the holiday was just what I needed.'

'Your family enjoyed it?'

'Oh, yes, especially my little boy – he absolutely lived out of doors all day. I'm doing a report on the hotel for the files.'

'Er ... no, don't bother about that, Margaret.'

'No –? Oh, but it has some good points, although it's not ideal for –'

He gave a wave of the hand, almost impatient. Margaret stopped in mid-sentence. He had never treated her opinions like this before.

'Has something gone wrong over the Antigua conference, Mr Hughes?' she asked with alarm. It seemed the only explanation.

There was a long pause. Then he sighed. 'There's no easy way to say this, Margaret, so I'll just jump right off the deep end. We're having to dispense with your services.'

Chapter Two

The words were so totally unexpected that they made no sense to Margaret. For a tiny, disorientated second she thought Hughes was speaking to her in a foreign language she didn't know.

She stared at him.

'Do you understand, Margaret?' Hughes said.

'What ... what did you say?'

'We're having to let you go. I argued against the decision but it makes financial sense.'

'Argued? Who ... Whose idea was this?'

'Sit down.' She had strolled into the room, holding the file on the Antigua meeting, and had begun a conversation with him while still on the move. His announcement had stopped her dead on the spot she had reached. Now at his command she took a step or two on the deep, rich blue carpet, turned the chair a little, and lowered herself onto it, all awkward and at an angle. Hughes got up suddenly and came round to take her hand and lead her to a more casual area of his office, where a sofa and a couple of chairs were grouped round a coffee table. He drew her down beside him there.

'You have to understand that there's been a lot of anxiety behind the scenes here for six months now, Margaret. Sales of beer and lager have gone down because of the recession – the shortage of money took a long time to reach the licensed trade, as it always does, but in the end it caught up with us. We might have decided to tough it out, except for that proposed purchase in France.'

Margaret was trying to get a grip on herself. The terrible sensation of cold that had seized her at Hughes's first words was receding, her brain was beginning to function again. 'The thing they're going to discuss in Quebec?' she ventured, to show she was understanding his words.

'The Peyroc Vineyard and bottling plant. It's a big outlay, worth it in the long run because it helps us further our marketing in France, which is one of our stickiest areas for trading. The directors have wanted to get into the wine production business for a long time now, rather than just carry on as retailers. It's been a long time getting settled because of the "wine lake" – quite a faction on the board was against having anything to do with wine production but now it's arranged and the Quebec meeting will work out the details of the contract, and the use the various parts of the Peyroc firm are to be put to.'

'But how does that ... concern me?'

'The books have got to be balanced, Margaret. To finance this new project economies have to be made. One of them is your department.'

'My department?' She drew in a breath. 'You mean, everybody?'

'Yes, everybody, not just you. Some of your staff can be transferred elsewhere – the typists, the word processors. But we've no place for specialists in travel arrangements or hotel bookings –'

'But someone will have to do that!' she interrupted, at last beginning to see a chance to fight back. 'Our executives will still travel –'

'They can travel without the help of a T&A Department. We're handing all that over to an outside travel agency –'

'But there will be a terrible hiatus –'

'No, we've been negotiating for six weeks now and settled on one last week.'

'Negotiating? Behind my back?'

Hughes sighed, gave a tiny shrug, and leaned back in his armchair. 'That's just a phrase, behind my back. It was a confidential business negotiation. Why should you be informed?'

'But, Erewyn –! Surely I should have had warning that my job was on the line!'

Her use of his first name was a plea for help. Because he had originally come to her and offered her the job, she had always felt it important never to let it be thought there was anything between them. So in business hours she always referred to him as Mr Hughes although he, easily, called her Margaret. Now that barrier had gone on her side. She needed his help, on any terms, and if there had been some friendship on his side she needed to call on it now.

'You were on holiday when the final decision was taken. I thought of telephoning you in your Mombasa hotel but ...'

'But?'

'What good would it have done? It would have wrecked your holiday. You might have packed up and come rushing home –'

'Of course I would –'

'And it'd have done no good, Margaret. It was settled, finished. It seemed kinder, really, to let you have your holiday out in peace.'

'But this ... this is so ... It's like falling over a cliff, Erewyn! I came in this morning so full of plans ...'

'I'm sorry. I know.' His round, Welsh face was creased with concern, his brown button eyes were unhappy. He was hating this. He longed for her to accept the dictum and go, so that he could know it was done, was over.

'No, you don't know,' she objected. 'I've had this idea on how to exploit the various properties owned by the firm – build them up as an asset that will bring in a profit, rather than just using them occasionally. A small department to –'

He shook his head. 'No. No more empire-building –'

'But this is a *good* idea, Erewyn –'

'Good or bad, it makes no difference. There's a moratorium on new projects for the next two years at least, and longer if profits have failed to reach a certain level. The accountants have been through it all backwards and forwards. You know what Byers is like.'

Byers was the Chief Accountant. Young, hard and clever, he had reached the top at Hebberwood by being utterly dispassionate. Friends he had none. He told the absolute truth about money and what he advised was done without appeal. No one could deny that under his guidance, Hebberwood Brewing had become one of the most sought-after investments in the market. Even now, with the Exchange nursing a bad chill, brokers were still looking out for Hebberwood shares.

Seeing that Margaret was momentarily silenced by the mention of that unassailable name, Hughes went on: 'Don't think it's just you. Your department is going entirely, but others are going to contract with some speed. To fill vacancies in office staff we're going to transfer people, not take on new employees. The Scientific Department is going to be cut down because the board has decided there's no point in launching new brands for the foreseeable future. The advertising firms meeting in Antigua are in for a big shock – the budget is going to be decisively cut at the end of such programmes as are in the pipeline now. So you see, it's an all-round siege situation.'

When he stopped, Margaret made no reply. She sat for some seconds listening to the echoes of his words.

31

She heard finality in them. It was no use to plead or protest. She had been first class at her job, but the financial climate made her job unnecessary. The ideas she'd been about to put forward were still good, but the tortoise had withdrawn into its shell, so that it would be useless to knock, hoping its head would emerge – it would stay in suspended animation until warmer weather.

'I hate to do this to you,' Hughes burst out as she sat in silence. 'I can't say I think it's unjust because I truly believe it's a logical step – from the business point of view. But it just seems ... I don't know ... brutal.'

The words of a long-forgotten song came into her mind: 'Awaiting the sensation of a short, sharp shock, from a cheap and chippy chopper on a big black block.' Perhaps it was better this way, to have it descend unexpectedly, like a thunderbolt.

'What happens next?' she asked in a faint but steady voice.

Hughes looked at her. She had gone dead white when he first gave her the news but now she had regained a little colour. All the same, above the rich brown of her thin wool dress her face was pale. 'Let's have a drink and I'll give you a pointer or two,' he began, getting up.

'No thanks, it's too early for me –'

'Oh, hell, Margaret, you need a drink if ever anybody did.' He ignored the protest and opened a cupboard among the wall shelves of books and delicate pieces of china. He sloshed brandy into a glass and brought it to her, waiting until she put it to her lips before returning for his own. He was glad of it. Thank God he didn't have to go through a thing like this very often; it could turn him into an alcoholic in no time.

'Your next step is to go and see the personnel manager. He's got your file out and done all the paperwork, so he'll be able to tell you what your entitlements are. Briefly, what I know is this: you're on an agreement that calls for three months' notice on either side, but Hebberwood's won't insist you stay right through that if you get another offer – as you surely will with all your contacts, Margaret.'

'Three months,' she repeated, letting the brandy bring a sensation of warmth and comfort. Three months seemed a long time. Within the first few weeks of that, she'd find something else.

Something else! Already she was coming to terms with it. She was having to go elsewhere, she was being sent away. Talented and efficient though she was, Hebberwood no longer wanted her.

'I think you'll find, when you talk it over with Twillan, that Hebberwood's aren't being stingy. The board of directors regret having to close down your section and want to let you know they've appreciated you work, so there's a pretty generous ex gratia payment –'

'Ex gratia?' she said. She felt like a parrot, repeating his salient points. But this suddenly seemed important. 'Ex gratia?' she said again, with more emphasis.

'Yes ... well ... the fact is, Margaret ... you haven't been with us a full two years.'

'No, of course I haven't, I know that. I joined the firm in the June of ...' Her voice trailed away. She had two months to go to make up the two years necessary before she was entitled to redundancy pay.

It had never seemed important to her before. She had never imagined herself being redundant. She had been *invited* to join Hebberwood – she had always imagined she was a valued, treasured member of staff. She had got to know the members of the board of directors personally through her work, had learned their foibles and preferences, had made herself indispensable – or so she had thought.

And even without that total personal involvement she

33

had given them, she was so well qualified. Fluent in three languages besides her native tongue, expert in handling travel arrangements on a first-class basis, familiar with several foreign terrains and the facilities available there, tactful with VIPs, foresighted, unflappable ... Who could ever want to dispense with her services? How could such as she ever become redundant? It had never even occurred to her to ask what redundancy pay consisted of.

Suddenly it seemed as if a great black abyss had opened in front of her. For the first time since childhood she felt totally vulnerable. The room seemed to recede from her. She thought: I'm going to faint. I'm going to make a fool of myself.

Some strength from somewhere outside her seemed to bring up her hand with the brandy glass. She got a big mouthful and made herself swallow it, breathing deeply as it went down. She leaned back in the buttoned leather chair.

After a moment she became aware that Erewyn Hughes was speaking to her. ' ... never be un-generous in a situation like this. So you needn't fear you'll have no cash in hand when you go. And you'll find Twillan has made arrangements that you can take advantage of, if you need advice or information. But I myself don't think you'll be calling on a consultancy service. I think you'll land something good the minute you let it be known you're available.'

'Yes,' she said, almost at random. She looked up. Hughes was standing by her side but looking at the windows, reciting the information he had to pass on to her. She knew that the longer she stayed, the more he would suffer. And she couldn't afford to make anyone suffer. She needed the goodwill of everyone she knew. She might need to call on people for help – and into her mind came the phrase Stan Cooper-Watts had used yesterday: all we hear from him is a hard luck story.

People didn't like to be in the presence of those with problems. It made them uneasy. She'd been with Hughes long enough. If she wanted his unstinted help later, she mustn't put him through any more now.

She put the brandy glass on the coffee table and got to her feet. She tried to do it with assurance, but sensed her own unsteadiness. Shock and brandy-at-ten-in-the-morning ...

'Thank you, Erewyn,' she said, smoothing her skirt before picking up the file she had brought into the room with her. 'You've been very kind.'

'Oh, I –' He didn't know what to say. Kind? He felt like an assassin. He had tempted her away from a good post with Paracelsis Travel to this fiasco. 'I know you'll get something else in a minute, Margaret. Let me know if I can be of any help.'

'Yes, thank you. There might be the business of references –'

'Oh, that!' His wave of the hand dismissed the idea. For the kind of job Margaret would get, fame would have gone before her. To talk of references was simply a symptom of the stress she was under. 'Just give them my telephone number if you feel it necessary.'

'Yes. Thank you. I'll ... I'd better get on.'

'Just give Twillan a buzz when you're ready. He's expecting you to drop by.'

'Of course. Thank you.'

She went out. Mr Hughes's secretary looked up as she walked through the outer office. Her face was puzzled, distressed. The news, it appeared, had not yet leaked out. All that Miss Templar could tell was that there had been trouble. Big trouble, or Mrs Durley wouldn't be looking like that.

Margaret sensed the girl's curiosity. Her face must be giving her away. She couldn't walk along the corridors looking like this. She bent her head, opened the folder as if she were reading something in it that held her undivided attention, and headed for the ladies' room.

It was a pleasant room, with a spacious area lined with mirrors and shelving before which stood stools covered with pink Dralon. She sank down on the stool nearest the door. She would have liked to lean back but there was nothing to lean on. She put her arms on the shelf, lowered her head on them, and closed her eyes.

For a few minutes it almost seemed as if she had gone very fast asleep, or into a deep trance. Everything receded. Traffic in the street far below seemed to be miles away. Voices and the opening and closing of the lift doors were like faint calls from another world. Some protective system came into action, giving her a spell of blessed relief.

She was roused by someone coming in. A voice said: 'Are you ill, Mrs Durley?'

She raised her head. In the mirror she saw the anxious face of one of the junior secretaries.

'I'm all right,' she said. 'Jet fatigue.'

Of course. The girl's face cleared. Everyone knew Mrs Durley had just got back from a fabulous holiday in Mombasa.

'It'll soon be coffee time,' she offered by way of comfort.

Margaret glanced at her watch. Ten-forty. She'd been here almost half an hour. Lena would be wondering what had happened to her.

She got up, feeling oddly light and disconnected. With a smile at the girl, she went out.

Lena jumped up as she came into her own outer office. 'Mrs Durley! you've been wanted on long distance. I didn't like to interrupt your meeting with Mr Hughes...'

'It's all right, Lena. Who was calling?'

'Danshibu from Tokio. I said we'd call back.'

It was about ten o'clock at night in Japan. Courtesy required that she return the call quickly so that whoever was anxiously asking for her could get home to his wife and family. It turned out to be a query about the connection at New York. Could the representatives from Danshibu travel a day earlier and stay overnight in New York? She guessed it was a shopping expedition for a wife. She agreed the overnight stay and made a note to arrange accommodation. It would cost Hebberwood extra money, of course, which wouldn't have perturbed her at all yesterday. Today it ought to have been important. Economy was the order of the day. But she couldn't cope with it for the moment. She had more important things to do.

She put her head round her door.

'Lena,' she said, 'tell the switchboard not to put any more calls through for the next half hour. You and I have got to have a talk.'

Her secretary gaped, went red with surprise and embarrassment, but picked up her phone without comment. Margaret went back and sat down. In a moment Lena came in with her notebook, although she had guessed this wasn't the usual letter session.

'I have to tell you what Mr Hughes has just told me,' Margaret said in a low, steady voice. 'Hebberwood's are closing down the T&A Department.'

'What?' Lena's reaction was more immediate and direct than her own had been. Some warning had been conveyed to her by the morning's events so far. Even so, she was astounded.

'It's a big economy drive. The recession has caught up with the brewing trade. Mr Byers has –'

'But they can't do that!' Lena cried. 'You mean the whole thing? You and me and eighteen people?'

'I'm afraid so.'

'But ... but ... We haven't had notice?'

'I think that will come at the end of this week.' She should have asked Erewyn Hughes before she left his office. She should have made inquiries on behalf of her staff. What terms were they to get? Who was to be transferred, who dismissed? She said: 'I believe you're to be offered something in another department. Some of the others, too. But that will be the girls who know how to use the processors. The filing clerks, the messengers – they're the ones who'll have to go, I think.' For the first time she felt tears pricking behind her eyes. She had failed them at this very first point: she didn't know what their fate was supposed to be. 'I have to see Twillan in a minute,' she went on. 'I'll ask about who's going where, and what they get by way of notice and redundancy if they're leaving.'

'Oh, some of them will fight it,' Lena flashed. 'Hebberwood can't just throw them out –'

'I think, in fact, they can, Lena. They're dissolving the department. The entire staff is redundant. I haven't gone into it but I imagine the personnel department has a plan to offer replacement jobs to those who can be fitted in, and those who can't – those who have training specifically for the travel side of the work – will get the push.'

Lena gone red with defensive anger. 'They can't do this! I'll go to the union for –'

'That's another thing I haven't asked, but I feel sure there have been consultations with the union – perhaps not at local level, because I got the impression Mr Byers had kept it all under wraps until Mr Hughes could give me the news. But the unions must know. Hebberwood's wouldn't make a mistake like trying to dismiss a whole department without having put out feelers to the unions.'

Lena burst into tears. 'I just ... I can't seem to ... It's so *unfair*!'

Of all the reactions Margaret had momentarily envisaged when she invited her secretary into her office, this was the last. Lena was the kind of woman you referred to as a 'tower of strength'. It had never occurred to Margaret that Lena would cry. She had chosen her, out of many applicants, for her stability, her maturity – she was about four years older than Margaret. Yet here they were now, in the relationship of mother and child, with Lena unbelievably playing the role of the child. Margaret came round her desk, put her arm round her secretary, and let her head rest against her shoulder. 'There, there,' she said. 'There, there.'

And as she soothed, she was thinking, '*I* mustn't cry. Anybody else can break down into sobs, or throw things about, but I have to keep my cool. Because in the first place I owe it to the staff, and in the second place, it wouldn't look good to the directors if they saw the super-efficient Margaret Durley blubbing like a baby.'

After a few minutes the other woman straightened up. She rubbed at her nose with the back of her hand. Margaret reached over to her desk drawer and produced a box of tissues. Lena dragged several out, scrubbed herself dry, sniffed, and said: 'What a fool! Crying isn't going to do any good. And in any case, it's just dawned on me – this is a lot worse for you than it is for me.'

'Well, it's no fun,' Margaret agreed drily.

'They must be out of their minds to let you go!' Lena said. 'There must be another department they could give you?'

Margaret shook her head and shrugged. Now wasn't the moment to go into the total economy drive nor the fact that her talents were specific to the work she did. The same, in fact, was going to prove true of several of her staff. Old Patrick Hyde, for instance, who knew the rail timetables of the continental services like the back of his hand, who could arrange the transport of an 'air-scared' executive from London to Belgrade without even opening a reference book. Or Jim Tares, who seemed to carry a street map of almost every American city inside his head. Or Fanny Carruthers, whose knowledge of gourmet restaurants all over the world had proved invaluable in arranging the entertainment of jaded directors.

At present she had to get from Lena an idea of what they would need to know. She made notes as they talked. Then she said, 'Right, buzz through to Mr Twillan. Tell him I'd like to see him – though it's quite untrue, I've never looked forward to anything less in my life.'

'Shall I tell the others?'

'No, I'll do it when I come back from the Personnel Department. She glanced at her watch, the Longines watch she had treated herself to when she started at Hebberwood. Its smart bland face seemed to mock her. Coffee time was over. In fact, she'd probably prevented Lena from having hers, though neither of them had thought of that. She supposed she would need half an hour with Twillan, perhaps more. That would bring them to more or less midday. Was it better to tell them before their lunch, or after? If she told them before, it would take away their appetite pretty conclusively. But if she held it over until afterwards, they might hear rumours and be anxious and a little resentful. Besides, during their respective lunch breaks they might want to talk and think things over.

'Try to have everybody in the main office at about twelve –'

'High noon,' muttered Lena.

They looked at each other and gave a shaky laugh.

'At noon, then. I'll tell them the news and pass on what information I've gathered from Twillan.'

Eugene Twillan was ready for her. He had been

preparing for this meeting since last week, and had even had schedules of benefits and entitlements photocopied, together with examples of his own calculations to show the financial positions. He had seven unsealed envelopes lying before him: these were for the members of her staff who were being asked to transfer to other departments. On top, she noticed, was Lena's.

'You'll want to glance through these before you seal them up and hand them on,' Twillan said after he had plunged into the subject. 'You need to know which departments they are going to so as to be able to hold discussions with them on whether they wish to take up the offers.' He paused. 'I strongly urge you, Mrs Durley, to persuade them to accept. This is not the time to be going out onto the job market.'

'No,' she said, looking down. Her hands closed convulsively round the sheet of notes she had brought with her.

'I'm sorry,' Twillan said with a sigh. 'I decided not to commiserate with you on your own situation – don't think I'm unsympathetic but you're better off than some of your staff. Mr Hyde, for instance – he has almost no chance at his age. But you, Mrs Durley, will be snapped up at once, the moment it's known you're free.'

'It's good of you to say so –'

'Oh, I mean it! Believe me, after you joined the firm, I had several hints from outside sources to the effect that if you ever wanted to make a change they would like to be given first refusal.'

'Really? Who –' She broke off. For the moment that wasn't the point. She was here to get the picture about her staff, that was the first priority. She started again. 'Would you just take me through the general situation, Mr Twillan? After I've delivered these letters to the seven being offered other posts, what do I say to the twelve others?'

41

'I'd advise you to say as little as you can. They'll be in a state of shock.' He hesitated. Unspoken were the words, As you are yourself. 'Tell them to come and see me as soon as they feel like it. Hand out these leaflets and photocopies. The official notice will be issued on Friday, which is the usual day for the dating of employment. That's to say, according to the terms on which they were signed on, they have two weeks' notice or a month's notice, plus the extra days from now to Friday. They are free to take as much time out of the office as they wish, to look for another job. The work in your department is of course being wound down so there's no need for them to stay at their desks in the ordinary way – all they need do is tidy up what is already in the pipeline. They'll have no new work to initiate so they're more or less at leisure apart from that.'

'I see. That makes sense. They should ask for appointments to see you?'

'As for today, no – they can drop in just as they please. I've cleared my desk of everything else to deal with their first queries. They can come singly or in groups – it's up to them. But from tomorrow I'd like them to come and see me by appointment, and I've set aside the hours from two to four in the afternoon all this week. After that they must just fit in with the rest of my work schedule because, as I suppose you know, yours isn't the only department that's losing staff.'

'But mine is the only one being closed down,' she protested. 'It's different –'

'Only in degree.'

She looked at him. 'Am I the only executive being cut off?'

'I can't discuss that with you, I'm afraid. The board of directors have a comprehensive plan but I'm sure you can understand it wouldn't be a good idea to broadcast the details.'

'But what you're saying is that I'm the only one so far.'

'Yes, I'm afraid so.'

She wanted to jump up and run out of the room. It was like being told she had leprosy. She alone, of all her peers, had been singled out to go. What had she done to deserve it? She was better at her job than most of the others were at theirs, knew more about her subject, took greater pains, received more approval from those she dealt with.

The sheer indignity of it was like some rough surface scraping against her skin – as if she were in a hair shirt. She wanted to put her arms about herself for protection against the humiliation. But she forced herself to sit calmly in the elbow chair across from Twillan because it wouldn't help to make a spectacle of herself, and there were nineteen people whom she would have to face with some facts and figures in a little while.

'Have you put out any feelers with other companies about vacancies for my staff?' she asked.

'Not yet. Hebberwood's didn't want to leak their plans in advance. But I can start now, making inquiries of a quite wide circle of contacts. The only thing is, Mrs Durley, those left on the list are specialists, recruited mostly by yourself to deal with special aspects of the travel work. It seems to me that you yourself have better contacts to put at their disposal.'

She thought again of Patrick Hyde and his timetables. Who would want him? Aged sixty-one, an expert in a form of travel that was unpopular now – most people took package holidays including air travel or, if they wanted to save money, went by coach. How was she going to find Patrick Hyde another job? She had lured him away from an old-fashioned travel firm in Wigmore Street. They certainly weren't going to take him back two years later at her suggestion.

She checked through all the queries that she and Lena

had listed. Then, when she felt she had asked every question that would come first to the lips of her hearers, she turned to her own problems. 'Mr Twillan, can I talk about myself now? Mr Hughes pointed out . . . that I've only been with Hebberwood's for twenty-two months.'

He nodded his silver-grey head. 'I'm sorry. That is the fact. You fall short of the statutory requirements. I . . . er . . . It did seem a pity that the axe had to fall at this precise moment . . . '

She stared at him. A thought had come to her from his embarrassment. Hebberwood's had decided to close down her department now because by doing so they could minimise the financial compensation she would have claimed. In her contract high rates had been offered, much higher than the legal requirements – it wasn't a point to which she had paid much attention at the time, having decided when she took the job that she would stay with Hebberwood for at least five years and get at least three steps up the ladder before she left.

But now she understood she was being cut down to size. She had no rights to redundancy payment, none at all. The special golden-handshake clause in her agreement was nullified.

'I had a long discussion with the salaries department on this point,' Twillan went on, pushing papers about his desk. 'You'll want to go through it with them, I've no doubt. But I thought you'd like to know that there will be money due to you.'

'An ex gratia payment, Mr Hughes said.'

'Yes. I . . . er . . . believe it will be in the region of one thousand pounds.'

'A thousand?' She was appalled. She'd been imagining about six times that amount. 'But that isn't even a month's pay!'

'I . . . er . . . haven't the details of your salary, Mrs Durley. That is confidential between you and the

44

salaries department. But I believe the amount was calculated on the basis of what would have been due to you under the Act – I have the tables here, if you'll just look ... You'll see that supposing you had indeed completed two years' service, at your age, you would have been entitled only to two weeks' salary. The management's offer is somewhat more generous than that ... '

'But nothing like what was written into my original contract, Mr Twillan!'

'Quite,' he said, defensive but firm. 'But your contract does stipulate that you're eligible for the severance payment only at the end of two years. I'm afraid the calendar doesn't support any claim you might feel like making. The ex gratia payment is in line with what we hear other employers are doing in similar circumstances. And of course, you must remember, Mrs Durley, you're likely to find a new post within a week or two. So you'll be able to take three months' salary in lieu of notice. All in all, you'll be leaving with a fair sum in hand.'

'I can't believe that Hebberwood's will take a stand over those two months,' she insisted. 'I have a much larger sum due – '

'You must take it up with the salaries department,' Twillan cut in. 'It's outside my jurisdiction. All I'm asked to do is to put the services of the personnel office at your disposal, which of course I do. I don't expect you'll need my help, but if there's anything I can do, let me know. I'll make a list of the names of firms who expressed an interest when you joined us, if you like. But you have your own contacts ... '

She knew she was being dismissed, and guessed he had a lunch date for which he wanted to be in good time. It struck her as ironic. A few weeks ago, Twillan would never have dreamed of ending a conversation with her by his own initiative. In the pecking order at

Hebberwood, Margaret's importance had been much greater than Twillan's. Sic transit, she thought with wry amusement as she went back to her own office.

It was now a quarter past twelve. She had a sheaf of government pamphlets and information leaflets in her hand. Lena got up as she came through the outer room. 'They're all here. Only Mary Walker was about to go out – she wanted to go shopping but I asked her to hang on a bit. I didn't make a big thing of it.'

'Yes. Well ... '

'How did it go with Twillan?'

Margaret showed her the envelope with her name on it. 'You and six others have got offers to go into other departments. The leaflets about where to go to find a new job, and so on, are for the others.'

'Dear lord,' breathed Lena. She hesitated. 'I rang my mother. I thought I ought to warn her something was brewing. She was upset.'

'I don't think there's much need, Lena. You'll be all right.' But the thought occurred: ought she to ring Jack?

Not yet. First she must make the awful announcement to her staff and talk it through with them. After that, she would ring Jack.

The hour that followed was the very worst she had ever experienced. Not even the arguments with her parents over Jack, over her marriage – nothing else came near the misery she underwent. Mary Walker, engaged to be married, had hysterics. Victor Spence was taken ill because he missed lunch and his ulcer played up. Between these two events there was dismay, disbelief, argument, anger, rejection of the facts, and finally acceptance with bitterness. 'Well,' Jim Tares said, 'they've picked their day for it. My wife just told me this morning she's expecting another baby.'

His colleagues expressed sympathy. Yet most of them, Margaret knew, felt they had problems just as great.

46

Patrick Hyde said nothing. He had seen too much of life to cry out against this new stroke of fate. But he was pale with distress.

In the end they dispersed, Jim pointing out with acid humour that if they didn't go out soon the pubs would be shut and they'd be too late to drown their sorrows. He and a couple of the women went to the White Unicorn. A group of girls went out together to compare the letters offering them transfers. The senior clerk looked up a number in the phone book and hurried away looking determined. By and by only Lena and Margaret were left.

She was about to send Lena out for coffee and a sandwich. But then she thought it might look like hiding in her office. She said: 'Want to come out for a meal?'

'I'm not hungry, thanks, Mrs Durley.'

'But it's after two – '

'If you don't mind, I'll sit down at my desk and ring Mother. She'll be worrying.'

'You'll be able to put her mind at rest. You'll take the offer to go to maintenance records, won't you?'

'I suppose so.' Lena looked unhappy. 'It means not working on a one to one basis. I hate just being a face in a room with a lot of others.'

'But it's interesting work, I imagine. And the money'll be the same.'

Lena shrugged. 'I better take it, I suppose. At least until I can look around and find something I like better.' Lena wasn't unduly troubled, when it came down to it. A good secretary, with her speeds and experience, could always get a job.

'Right then, I'll leave you to it. Before you make your own call, will you get my home for me, Lena?'

She went into her office and sat at the desk, waiting for her phone to flash. But after a time Lena put her head round the door. 'No answer from your house, Mrs

47

Durley. I suppose Mr Durley is out.'

In search of the piece of wood for the carving. 'All right, Lena, I'll try later. I'm going out to lunch now.'

She ate at her club, a quiet, elegant place in a turning near St Paul's. She was rather late in arriving so the diningroom was almost empty. A few women greeted her but when she opened her newspaper and retired behind it no one approached her. Businesswomen all, they understood the need for a quiet interlude in a hectic day. The waitress tried to tempt her with the dish of the day but she ordered an omelette and a glass of wine. After the first few mouthfuls, she felt she was choking. She pushed her plate away, got up, went into the restroom, and lay down on a chaise longue.

Scenes from the morning passed in front of her. Lena's flushed face, the headings on the pamphlets Twillan had given to her; 'Summary of Information for Employees', 'Leaving Your Job' . . .

How was she going to break the news to Jack?

She bathed her face and put on fresh make-up before she went out to get a taxi back to the office. It was now half-past three and the tea lady was coming along the passage with her trolley. As people came out of the offices to queue for tea, she could see by the way they looked at her that they had heard. She found a group of her own staff waiting to talk to her. Others were in with Twillan. A long afternoon crawled by in which she hadn't a moment to herself, being either in conversation with someone about the dismissal notices or attending to the business for the Antigua and the Quebec meetings – which must go ahead despite retrenchment because it was easier than explaining a cancellation. She had found a memo to that effect on her desk, signed by the managing director.

It was later than usual when she drove out of the underground car park. Traffic in the City had died away considerably so that she threaded her way south with less difficulty than she expected. She handled the car automatically, hardly noticing her journey.

Her mind was busy with the evening ahead. She was going to tell Jack that she was out of a job. And in all the time she had known him, she had never had to admit such a humiliation.

Chapter Three

She found herself adopting delaying tactics when she got home. She ran the car into the garage, although often she went indoors first to say hello. She pushed the button to close the door then stood watching it come down, as if it was important to ensure it fitted against the ground. As she made her way up the sandy path – they had intended to gravel it this year – she looked with interest at the plants, noting their growth since they went away on holiday. Since they went away! Only three weeks ago, but it felt as if it had happened in another existence.

When an end had come to all the things she could find to linger over, she put her key in the door and went into the hall. Immediately she could hear wails from the living room. Smitten by conscience at her own neglect, she hurried in to find out how her little boy had settled down to his ordinary routine again.

Laurie was sitting on the floor, surrounded by toys, but ignoring them while he cried in longstanding misery. Margaret snatched him up. 'Laurie! What's the matter, precious? Oh, Laurie, don't cry – Mummy's here –'

'So I see,' Jack said, emerging from the kitchen. There was a certain grimness in his manner. 'You're late, aren't you?'

'Yes, well, it's been a terible day, Jack, I –'

'Yes, first day back, I can imagine, but you might have

rung me to let me know what time to expect you.'

'I did ring, Jack, but there was no –'

'If your day's been bad, you should have tried mine! Mrs Prior didn't turn up, she phoned to say her nephew had broken an arm –'

'Oh, darling, I'm sorry! You've just left the house-work, of course –'

'It wasn't that so much, but I wanted to go to the sorting office to collect those parcels we got cards for, and then to Handcross after a block of wood –'

'I thought probably that's where –'

'But the worst thing was that Penny wouldn't accept Laurie for the play group today. He's got a bit of a temperature –'

'Oh, God,' Margaret groaned. 'Mother was right after all, then. He's got a chill –'

'I think it's more like a tummy upset. I asked Dr Threlfall to come, but he couldn't fit it in today –'

'Couldn't fit it in? What on earth do we pay him for –'

'I know, I know, you feel when a kid's not well a doctor should drop everything. But he explained he was up to the eyes in house calls and said he'd like to leave it till tomorrow unless it was urgent. And I thought Laurie wasn't all that bad – are you, lad?' he inquired, coming to Margaret's side and giving the boy a playful punch on the chin.

Generally Laurie loved that. But today he burrowed his face into Margaret's shoulder and wept.

'Why didn't you put him to bed, Jack?'

'Why didn't I put him to bed, Jack!' he mimicked. 'Because he wouldn't go! He's been used to having you around all the time for three weeks and he insisted on staying up till you got back. If I'd known you were going to be this late, I'd have come the heavy father with him.'

'He'd better go now, then –'

51

'Sure thing, you do that while I get this meal on the table. It's only cold meat and salad, I haven't had time to do the bon viveur bit tonight.'

'It's all right, I'm not hungry, Jack.'

Jack shrugged, as if to say, That's all I need, and turned back towards the door leading to the kitchen. 'By the way, your mother called. She wants you to ring her back.'

'What on earth for? Did she say?'

'Oh, she won't talk to *me*, you know that. It'll be nothing, as usual. For God's sake don't tell her Laurie's under the weather or she'll be here with her calves' foot jelly and iron tonic before you can say "colic".'

'Mummy,' sobbed Laurie, 'where have you *been*? I wanted you!'

'Yes, precious, I know, I know. Come on upstairs and have your bath and I'll tell you a story until you're ready to sleep. Come on, stop crying, you'll feel better when you've had your bath.' Murmuring soothing words, she went upstairs with Laurie leaning heavily into her, moist hands clutching her dress.

He took no pleasure in being bathed, although generally it was one of his favourite moments of the day. He allowed himself to be dried and put into his sleeping suit with a listless air. He had only a slight temperature but he clearly felt unwell and moreover, was angry with her for not being there when he wanted her. She was being punished, she knew. But she talked gently to him and he lay down without complaint. Asked which story he would like, he asked for Tom Thumb. This was one of the longest, as they both knew, so she understood it was his intention to keep her with him as long as possible. But sheer weariness defeated him. He fell asleep around the point where the peasant woman was making a cradle out of a walnut shell.

'Right,' Jack said. 'What's my standing?' He was still

frowning and looking very fed up. 'Am I still the ogre who wouldn't let him see you all day? Or am I to go up and say goodnight?'

'He's asleep, Jack. Don't be annoyed. He's not feeling well, that's all.'

'Oh, I know that! I've had him all day, remember. Well, come on, let's have a drink and get over it.'

He mixed gin and tonic. As he handed hers he said, 'It means Penny won't take him tomorrow either – not until Threlfall gives him a clean bill of health.'

'It'll only be a day or two. His tum is queasy.'

'We know that, and he knows that, but everybody else I've met today has taken it for granted he's got Lhasa fever.'

'Jack!'

'Oh, I'm sorry. It's been a bloody awful day, that's all.' He stretched out long legs in front of him, let his head retract into his chest, and grunted. 'Those seedlings I left in the greenhouse have all damped off –'

'Oh, Jack, what a shame. Didn't Mrs Prior –'

'It's nothing to do with Mrs Prior. They were all in a propagator, should have been fine. It's a fungus – I meant to sterilise that compost before I used it but I didn't have time. Means I've got nothing to put in the front of the border, though.'

'Can't you sow some more –?'

'Too late to start again now. I'll have to buy something in – but I wanted those coleus, they'd have made just the right contrast to the bells of Ireland behind them. Damn nuisance – and it's all my own fault so I've no one to get back at.'

Margaret sipped her drink and felt it doing its work of reviving and relaxing her. She was trying to sense what moment to use for her own announcement. Not just this precise minute – Jack was still too irritated to want to hear the tidings she was bringing.

He went upstairs to peep in on Laurie before they sat down to eat. 'Tossing about a bit but he's okay,' he reported. 'Shall I open a bottle of wine?'

'Not for me, thanks. Jack, I –'

The phone rang. He cast up his eyes. She rose, sighing. She knew it would be her mother.

'Margaret, I wanted to say to you, get extra prints done of your holiday pictures. You know Father and I are longing to see them, so put them in the post since you can't spare the time to –'

'Yes, of course, Mother, I'll make sure you get copies.'

'I would have explained all this to Jack, but he seemed in a bit of a state when I called. Is anything wrong?'

'No, not a thing, Mother.' Now what had made her say that? She should have taken that opening and told her mother that she'd just been fired.

But no – she had to tell Jack about it first. He'd never forgive her if she talked about it to Mrs Grant before she told him. There was a tension between Jack and her mother that nothing could eradicate. Although it must be obvious that they were happy, that their marriage, however unorthodox, suited them, Mrs Grant was convinced her daughter had made a terrible mistake. She would have distrusted any artist, but an artist who was prepared to let his wife support him while he 'fiddled about' with bits of wood and stone – that was unforgivable.

'Little Laurie all right?' Mrs Grant inquired.

'A bit tetchy – overtired,' Margaret said, offering a partial truth.

'Of course he is. All that long journey by plane to Africa and back – I know it was a very glamorous place and all that, dear, but don't you think a mother should put her child first and not go on such long trips for holidays? There are plenty of nice places –'

Margaret knew that her mother was about to suggest,

for the thousandth time, that they all took a cottage together for the next part of Margaret's holiday allowance. They had done it once, when Laurie was in his first year: the supposition had been that it would be more of a holiday for Margaret and Jack, since Grannie would look after the baby. But it had been such a miserable experience that Jack would have wrapped Laurie in a blanket and taken him to Australia by steerage rather than go through it again.

'Mother dear, we're just back from this one and it's my first day back at work. I'm a bit tired. I'll ring you in a day or two, and I'll certainly send you copies of the pictures.'

'All right, darling, I understand. You have a nice bowl of soup and get to bed. Get Jack to bring you a cup of hot chocolate before you put out the light. That'll build up your energy again.'

'Yes, Mother. I'll do that.'

When she got back to the dining room Jack was pouring coffee. 'What was it she refused to tell me?'

'She wants us to get copies of the holiday snaps.'

'Oh, hell. I took them in today, never thought of it. I only ordered one print of each.'

She sighed, sipped coffee, scalded her tongue and put it down, gasping.

'What's wrong? It hasn't gone bitter, has it?'

'No, it's too hot –'

'Good lord, of course it's hot – I wouldn't serve cold coffee.'

'No, I meant . . . it took me by surprise . . . oh, it doesn't matter.'

Her husband jumped up and went into the kitchen. He returned with a wine bottle. 'I don't know about you, but I'm going to get sloshed. I'm just in the mood for it.'

'No, Jack, don't. There's something I want to talk about –'

'Save it. It's just not been my day today. Whatever your high-powered friends at the Hebberwood Tower have been wishing on you, don't tell me about it.'

She pushed her chair back and got up. It was no use trying to communicate with him when he was in this mood. 'I'm going to have a bath,' she said. 'Perhaps we'll both feel a bit more civilised in an hour or so.'

He paid no heed. He was opening the wine bottle.

When she came down later, in a silk robe and with her hair damp so that it lay close to her head like a brown velvet cap, Jack was in the living room listening to Jacques Loussier on stereo. The wine bottle was two thirds empty.

'Jack –'

'Eh?' He turned his head to look at her. The throbbing beat of the piano and drums blotted out her words.

'Turn it down a bit, Jack.'

'No, I feel in the mood to be filled with Bach-on-the-beat. Conversation isn't in my plan for the rest of the evening.'

'We won't be able to hear Laurie if he calls –'

'Oh, God.' He got up, lowered the volume, and sat down again. 'I came back from Mombasa so full of ideas – now I feel like the wrath of God.'

'I'm not feeling all that sunny myself, love. And there's a reason. At the office today –'

A thin wail came from upstairs. 'Daddy, Daddy!'

'Christ *Almighty!*' roared Jack, and rushed out and up the stairs.

It was no use. The moment just never seemed to be right. Perhaps later, in bed ...

Although Laurie was restless he slept at last. Jack got into bed with a groaning sigh. 'Today has been what I would describe as sub-standard,' he muttered. 'Me too, I think. Sorry, darling.'

'Oh, Jack!' She put her arms round him and hugged

him. When he kissed her she responded almost despairingly.

He was mistaken in the quality of her response but she was glad to find release in love-making. They were good partners, always had been, and although tonight there was less lightness and good humour in their approach she found happiness as always at the climax. As they lay afterwards in a twine of arms and legs he said against her shoulder, 'I was a swine earlier. I shouldn't visit my disappointments on you, Margaret. I apologise.'

'I'm the one who should apologise. Coming home expecting you to pay attention to what I want to say –'

'But I had a good reason for being so beastly.' He sighed. 'One of those cards from the Post Office, for parcels to be collected –?'

'Yes?' she prompted, with a sinking heart.

'It was my entry for the Colfax Arts Festival.'

'Oh, poor love!' She held him tight.

He returned her embrace then slid out of bed and went to his clothes. From a pocket he retrieved a small square of paper. In the light of the bedside lamp she read: 'The Colfax Arts Festival Committee thanks you for submitting your work but finds it unsuitable. This is no reflection on the standard. Our artistic aim is specific.' Under it someone had written: 'A more adventurous approach as to method or materials might have gained more favour. Try again next year.'

She glanced at her husband. His expression was sombre. 'If I'd known they wanted something made of tinfoil and dust from the vacuum cleaner, I wouldn't have sent carved oak!'

'But they liked your work, Jack. You can see they did. They wouldn't have bothered to write a comment if they hadn't.'

'"Try again next year." Dear God, I'll be twelve months off my fortieth birthday by then! I tell you,

Margaret, it's frightening. The years are going by and I'm getting nowhere as a sculptor. Perhaps it was a mistake to think I could ever make a go of it.'

'Nothing of the kind,' she comforted. 'We both know you've got talent. Didn't your group get awards for the models they made for *Aucassin*? And didn't Di Veronchi ask for you specifically to do the village sets for *A Peasant Life*? You were one of the best special effects technicians in the industry – if only British films hadn't ground to a halt you'd be head of a huge department by now.'

'Instead of which I'm playing about with bits of oak and granite, kidding myself I'm saying something more important than miniature buildings for film scenics. It's a joke, Meg. I'm just another fellow who's good with his hands, that's all. I'm not going to be the next great British sculptor, and we may as well admit it.'

'But I don't admit it! I've got more faith in your abilities than you have! It's just that fashion is not in your favour at the moment, there's still echoes of all the fads – pop art and high tech and all that rubbish. When the critics get back to appreciating the surface values on materials –'

'When pigs fly,' Jack sighed. 'Well, I've moaned at you enough. Goodnight, love. I'll try to be more fun in the morning.'

In the morning . . . As she listened to Jack's breathing become deeper and steadier, Margaret tried over some introductions she might use in the morning. 'I wanted to tell you last night but the moment never seemed right. But the fact is, Hebberwood's have given me the push.'

The electric clock made its little clicks as its digital display changed. The night wore on. She found that for the first time she had the chance to look ahead to her own future. All day she had been in a state of modified shock, and such strength as she had available was put to the service of her staff. She'd had only one or two intervals to herself, during which she'd tried to renew her defences against breaking down in public. But now she could think things through.

After all, it was a terrible blow, but not a fatal wound. As everybody kept saying, she would get another job within a day or two, before the week was out.

What, in fact, was the point of inflicting bad news on her husband? He was smarting from the rejection of his work, and worried about Laurie. What good would it do to tell him the state of play at the moment? In a few days she would have a new post, and she could tell him then. In fact, make a better showing by telling him in that way: 'Hebberwood and I decided to part so I've taken this job with Whoever . . .'

Yes, that was far better. Less panicky, less humiliating, less likely to spread momentary gloom and despondency. She would tell him as soon as she had fixed up alternative employment; with any luck, she'd be reporting an increase in salary with the new job.

Her whole body relaxed. There was no need to tighten herself up into defensive attitudes ready for the questioning that would follow an announcement of her dismissal. She could put it off until the questions would be about the new job, the new prospects.

She put an arm round her sleeping husband. He made a sound in his sleep and a hand came up to touch hers. She ran her fingers between his and leaned her head against his back. Comforted, she went to sleep.

Chapter Four

The rest of that week taught Margaret a bitter lesson. It wasn't going to be easy to get another job.

From her office she rang her business friends. They were shocked at her news, commiserated with genuine distress, but shied away from promising immediate help. Even her best friend, Rosie Chaney, ended by sounding unhopeful.

Margaret and Rosie had been friends since university days. They had both been reading modern languages, from which springboard Rosie had gone into the career of teaching English to foreigners, after taking a special certificate. A genuine taste for business had brought her to the stage where she now owned several small schools, taking élite students from abroad; she had two schools in London, one in Eastbourne, one in Bath, and another in Canterbury.

'If you were thinking of going into teaching . . . ?' she speculated as they talked on the telephone.

'God forbid, Rosie. I haven't the temperament for a teacher.'

'No, but your German is good, and we get a lot of German students in the summer. Our busy season is just coming on.'

'I've no qualifications for teaching, Rosie – even English to foreigners.'

'And that's the main problem. I could only take you

on as a temporary assistant, and the money's nothing – well, you remember, that's how I got started, doing it as a job in the vac. It's really only suitable for students.'

'I wasn't really asking *you* for a job, love, I was wondering if any of your rich Arab students had fathers looking for intelligent British executives.'

'Oh, I see. Well, of course, we do get on friendly terms with some of our students ... But I don't know that I'd like to fish for a favour as big as that, Meggie.'

'I see.' It was the answer she had expected, but she had felt she must try this avenue. She had been down so many, and turned over so many stones in the past few days – only to find nothing. Even Twillan's list had provided no openings.

'Have you rung Charles?' Rosie asked after a pause.

Margaret lifted her chin, as if her friend could see her. 'Charles is the last person I'd ring, Rose.'

'Don't be dumb. So what if he used to fancy you and still does? Charles is *rich*, Margaret. All merchant bankers are rolling in it. And he must be even richer now than when he was trying to stop you marrying Jack.'

'Don't you see that's just it. I can't go to him and say, I didn't want you, but I want a favour from you.'

Rosie made no reply, as if the words that had sprung to her lips would be sharply argumentative. After a moment she said: 'All right, then, I'll put out a few feelers among my rich kids. At what level am I to pitch it? I mean, you don't want to be invited to go out to Ryadh and manage an oil company's office – not that that's likely. Where should I lay my snares?'

'Anything in travel, hotel company offices, property management – that kind of thing.'

'Okay, Meggie, leave it with me. But I don't think it's likely to do any good.'

'You're a love, Rosie, you always were. We'll lunch

soon to catch up on everything.'

'Sure thing,' Rosie said in a worried voice, and broke the connection.

Margaret had less time than she had envisaged to go fishing on her own behalf. Of the twelve members of her department who were looking for jobs, three found something in that first week – two of the women and one of the men. Jim Tares had decided to emigrate; it had been in his mind more than once, he said, and now this job had folded he'd decided to go to Canada. Relatives there were helping clear the way, his wife was in favour. So that left eight still without prospects, and they took it for granted that Margaret would help them. 'With all your contacts,' they would murmur when they came to sit in her office and report their failures.

Moreover, though the department was closing, there was still work to be done. The Antigua meeting was due to take place in two days time, lasting four days; during that four days Margaret would be expected to stay near a telephone in case any hitches occurred. It was necessary not only to get people to the hotel in Antigua, but to get them back to their home bases again, without trouble. The Quebec meeting was also still to take place; although it was three weeks ahead and less difficult to arrange, it needed attention. She didn't want it said that she'd gone to pieces in the last few weeks of her employment and made a hash of things.

Allowing for the time difference between London and Quebec meant being available for telephone calls until mid-evening. She found herself making it an excuse to stay at the office. She was avoiding Jack's company – because the longer she didn't tell him about the situation she was in, the more impossible it became to tell him. She found she couldn't admit to him that pride had kept her silent in the first place, that vanity had made it impossible to say, 'I've fallen flat on my face.'

62

She'd never thought of herself as vain before. But then, vanity was usually thought of as being about your looks, your physical attractions – and those she'd always taken for granted. She knew she was good looking, if not beautiful, with rich glossy sherry-coloured hair, hazel eyes in a pale, clear-skinned face, and a decent figure. She had dress sense, always knew what to wear and how to wear it. She'd never thought about herself – her *self*.

Now she was beginning to understand that part of her store of good looks depended on self-assurance. When she looked in the mirror in the morning now, she saw that anxiety was taking away something from her clear-eyed glance, from the tilt of her head. Now and again she caught glimpses of herself in shop windows as she walked by and discovered she was carrying her head forward as if in a hurry to meet and detain someone – and she was, that was the horror of it. She was tense with the need to talk to people, to ask for help in putting her career back on the rails.

But she'd found that people didn't want to talk to her. It had become known on the bush telegraph that she was job-hunting. Those who had nothing to offer avoided her. She even saw one man, a business acquaintance of eight years' standing, cross the road to avoid their paths crossing. She stood in Cornhill watching his retreating back and thinking that she would never know a more bitter moment.

She had had two more conversations with Twillan and learned the full horror of her prospects. She was supposed to be on three months' notice but having still three weeks' holiday due to her, would leave at the end of nine weeks. Two weeks had now gone by, including two weekends at home with their usual social engagements which had fretted her so much she could hardly bear it. Yet, until she explained everything to Jack, she couldn't give any reason for not going to barbecues, drinks parties, outings to the theatre in Brighton. It scared her to notice that on one or two occasions she and Jack had been called on to use their two cars to ferry friends around. One of their two cars, Margaret's car, belonged to Hebberwood's. When she left, she would have to give up the car.

Medical attention, too, would be withdrawn. It was one of the perks of the job, to have herself and her family registered with a private medical insurance firm. Special credit cards issued by Hebberwood would be called in – no more meals at certain famous restaurants without payment, no more stays at certain hotels on the most favourable terms. She and Jack had always been a bit lavish about entertaining people – that would have to be cut down drastically without the wines and spirits she had been able to order through the Hebberwood Staff Club.

It was coming home to Margaret not only that she wouldn't get a job with so many peripheral advantages – she might not get a job at all for months. The recession was hitting everyone. And when, towards the end of the second week of her job-hunting, she went to talk to a firm who had a vacancy, she found another barrier.

'Your qualifications are excellent, Mrs Durley,' the establishment officer told her. 'But you are a little younger than we had in mind.'

'When Frank put me in touch with you, there was no mention of an age requirement?'

'No, perhaps not – Frank's a good chap, but I hadn't talked it through with him. We had in mind a man of forty or thereabouts, you see.'

There was nothing she could say to that. She couldn't add six years to her age even to get a job like this.

It was only afterwards, as the taxi took her back to Hebberwood Tower, that she heard the other echo: 'a man of forty or thereabouts'.

It was understandable, of course. Men interviewing people for a good job were likely to think of other men as being most in need. Men, after all, were fathers of families, providers, breadwinners. She could hardly launch into a description of her marriage, so as to prove to a prospective employer that she was just as deserving as a married man.

She realised she was going to have someone else put these points for her. Commonsense told her that her 'contacts' weren't going to be enough in the present financial depression. She went to a head-hunting firm and put herself on their register.

'Well, great,' said Joe Brunskill, co-partner in Executive Selection Limited. 'I'm honoured that you've come to us to find you a new post. Just tell me your present circumstances – talk me through it as you would a friend, if you will.'

Margaret made allowances for his over-effusive manner. He was accustomed to people who had been hurt by rejection; this was his way of saying, Somebody loves you. It also accounted for the rather garish decor – sunbright yellow paint and many green plants, more suitable to a hairdresser's, she felt.

But she had come not to praise, but to bury her own shortcomings as a job-seeker. She explained to Joe (Call me Joe, he insisted) about her complete success so far in her career, the unexpectedness of her dismissal, and the fact that it was she who earned the family income.

'I *see*,' Joe replied in a tone of deep thought. 'Now that is a little unusual. I don't believe I've met that particular set of circumstances before. Your husband is a sculptor, you say? Er ... forgive me, I'm not up on art – is he known at all?'

'No, not at all.'

'Ah.' Joe tapped a pencil on his desk. 'What did he do before he went over to full-time sculpting?'

'I wouldn't exactly say he does full-time at it,' Margaret objected. 'He runs the house.'

'Ah,' Joe said again. It was clear he was baffled by everything she told him. 'He ... er ... does the housework?'

'No, of course not – we have a daily. But he looks after our little boy, takes him to play group, sees he's amused and happy when he's home, gets a meal for the two of them at midday, sometimes whips up gourmet meals for all of us in the evening.'

'Oh, he can cook?'

'Like an angel – when he feels like it.'

'Temperamental, is he?'

Margaret frowned. 'Not more so than anyone else,' she said. 'Why are we talking so much about Jack?'

'Well, you see, generally, when I'm interviewing a man, I have to find out if the wife is supportive, capable – whether she has a job or is just a housewife. In this case ... er ...'

'You're trying to find out whether Jack is just a house-husband?'

'Well,' Joe Brunskill remarked, trying to gloss it over. 'I'm always saying ... you learn all the time at this job ...'

'I'd prefer, Mr Brunskill, that you don't "learn" on my case. I came here asking for help in presenting my credentials to prospective employers. I don't want to start every interview explaining my domestic circumstances. It is no one's business but my own.'

The co-partner of ESL raised his eyebrows. 'I hope you don't lose your cool so easily in an interview situation, Mrs Durley.'

'I hope not. Can we stop talking about my husband and get on with my own qualifications?'

'What I think would be best,' Brunskill said, 'is if you fill out this questionnaire for us. You can put down all

66

your details, and where it says dependents you can enter ... er ...'

'Husband and one child?'

He looked divided between disbelief and amusement. 'Well, I suppose those are the facts. Yes, you'd better put that.'

'Thank you. Then what happens?'

'Well then we'll put it through our computer and come up with any matches in the job arena. You'll hear from us in about a week. Okay?'

He rose and held out his hand. He shook hands with unnecessary firmness; she guessed it was one of his bits of role-playing, the honest, dependable friend. But all it did for Margaret was to crush her garnet ring painfully against the fingers on each side.

'Good afternoon, Mr Brunskill.'

'Good afternoon, Mrs Durley.'

She knew it was a bad sign that they were back on surname terms. She had antagonised him. She must stop being so touchy about Jack. But it was so hard to start all over again, putting up with the patronising amusement of strangers – and from a position of vulnerability now.

Nevertheless, if ESL had any job openings that suited her, she felt she would hear from them. It would be something to crow about to potential clients: We found a post for the most extraordinary woman ...

The trouble was, she was extraordinary only in having a husband who was hale and hearty. Thousands of women had dependents for whom they had to make a living. If she had said that Jack was disabled, sick ... If she had lied, then, Joe Brunskill would have been all sympathy and kindness. But why should she conceal the truth? What essential difference was there between a man needing a job to support his dependents, and a woman needing a job to support her dependents? If a man applied to ESL, he wouldn't have to pretend his wife was ailing; it would be enough to say he had a wife and children. The Joe Brunskill's of this world took such a blinkered view – they were pitifully narrow-minded. And how could she respond to them with anything but anger?

It was simply that other people didn't understand. To alter their view, it would have needed a long explanation – the facts about Jack's past health record, his need for a quiet life, his talents as compared with her business ability. How could it improve matters if they conformed to the usual pattern of marriage – he going out to work and getting another ulcer, and she staying at home fretting in domesticity? It would have been a recipe for disaster – but how could she expect anyone else to believe that, viewing it from the outside?

Margaret tried three other agencies, and forced herself to be more controlled and circumspect. Women with wide glossy smiles oozing charm and self-confidence built up her hopes and convinced her that they had just the job she wanted. She went to four interviews over the next few days for jobs that were totally unsuitable. Either she was over qualified, or else the posts demanded skills outside her experience – facts she invariably discovered only once the interview was under way. She would return to her office fuming with suppressed anger, determined never to be conned by employment agency hype again. If she had examined her anger she would have known it had several causes. She was angry with her employers for the wreck they had brought down upon her, her staff for draining away so much of her strength with their own problems, and even Jack for not sensing, not guessing, the turmoil she was in. How could he be so blind? Didn't he feel how tense she was? Why didn't he take her in his arms and ask what was wrong?

The fact was, Jack had his own miseries at the moment. Mrs Prior couldn't come to do the housework so instead he had to rely on a substitute who could only 'oblige' two days a week. Laurie's upset had been diagnosed by Dr Threlfall as a tummy bug picked up in Mombasa, and though his temperature returned to normal the doctor insisted he should stay on a special bland diet. Laurie found milk pudding and steamed fish boring, and Jack didn't blame him, because he had had to live on a diet of the same kind when recovering from his ulcer op. But so long as he had to stay on the diet, the play group's organiser felt she couldn't accept the child : 'I don't want to be sticky but the doctor wouldn't be insisting on special treatment if the kid was a hundred per cent, Jack – so let's say we'll take him back after Whitsun.'

Beset by these mainly domestic problems, Jack was unable to get to work on the block of wood he had so carefully selected at the wood merchant. He had made sketches, done a preliminary cut on some balsa wood, could feel the sculpture aching in his fingers – but couldn't get at it. If only Margaret would get back from the office a bit earlier in the evenings, he could have done more then. But it was often after eight by the time she came in, and that meant working by artificial light, and he didn't want to do that. He'd decided that he would cancel out of their weekend engagements this coming Saturday, and spend two days in the studio – Margaret could take over the care of Laurie.

It would be as well to ring and tell her so. She'd probably want to ring round those friends they would have been visiting, to explain that she'd be coming alone. Besides, he thought, getting up off his knees in the middle of a flower-bed, he ought to ring her anyhow. Over the last couple of weeks or so they seemed not to be in touch so closely.

He rinsed his hands under the garden hose, dried them on the backs of his jeans, and went indoors, pausing to take off his clogs on the doormat. Padding through the kitchen, he fetched himself a glass of milk. Laurie was taking his afternoon nap. He glanced in on him, curled up on his bed with his snuggle-rug clutched against his cheek. Nodding in satisfaction, Jack Durley went into the master bedroom to use the bedside phone.

'Hello, Lena?' he said when he was put through. 'Is Mrs Durley available?'

'No, she's out, Mr Durley.'

'Out?' He glanced at his watch. It was four o'clock. Surely couldn't be a business lunch; even the longest lunch and the most free-loading client allowed you back to your office by four. 'Where is she, then, Lena?'

'Job-hunting, of course, Mr Durley.'

It took his breath away so completely that he couldn't say anything. Lena said: 'Hello? Hello? Mr Durley?'

'Hello, Lena.'

'Oh, you're still there. We got cut off for a minute.'

'You say she's out job-hunting?'

'Yes, but she'll be back soon. Shall I ask her to ring?'

'No, thanks, Lena. It wasn't important.'

'Any message?'

'No message, thanks.'

When Margaret came in, smarting from an interview with a firm of wine shippers who had really been looking for a marketing manager, Lena was about to mention Jack's call. But her boss seemed so down, and after all Mr Durley had specifically said it wasn't important. So she said nothing about it but instead set about making tea.

Late telephone calls kept Margaret at the office until after seven. It was dark when she got home and, of course, Laurie was in bed. She felt cold and tired, almost a stranger in her own house. The weekend was ahead of her, two days during which she would have to act as if nothing was wrong, so that her friends wouldn't begin whispering about her when she wasn't there. And as to Jack ... It was time to tell him. She couldn't go on alone any longer.

He was in the living room when she came in. Tempting smells came from the kitchen – her husband had had one of his cordon bleu inspirations. The table in the dining alcove was set with a certain elegance. For a moment she was bothered: had they invited anyone to dinner? But no, her memory hadn't played her false – she had on purpose made no invitations on weekdays during the time of the Antigua and Quebec meetings, because she might be summoned to the telephone for a transatlantic call.

So it seemed to be a celebration of some kind. It wasn't anybody's birthday, and it certainly wasn't their anniversary because they'd been married on a cold day in early December.

Some special event must have occurred. Something to do with Jack's sculpture, perhaps. Thank God, in that case – some good news to give a lift to her spirits. Very well, she'd let Jack play it his way; he'd make the announcement when he was ready.

'Smells gorgeous,' she commented as he put his head round the kitchen doorway.'

'Lamb chops à la Provençale,' he announced. 'Strawberry and Curaçao mousse to follow.'

'Good lord! Luckily I only had a sandwich for lunch.'

'Want a drink first?'

'Pour me a sherry. I'll just change my shoes and wash my hands.'

She looked in on Laurie as she went by. A pang of loss struck at her as she studied him, sound asleep, his lashes lying like strands of gold silk on his pink cheeks. She'd scarcely seen him since last Sunday – only in brief

71

glimpses in the morning, while she dressed and had breakfast. She must get home earlier in the evenings. What if they wanted her across the Atlantic to deal with some hitch – the hell with them, she owed them nothing now.

The meal was marvellous. She was hungry, and perhaps for the first time in a month she recovered her sense of taste. It dawned on her that ever since she was told she had lost her job, she'd lost other things too – her enjoyment in food and wine, her ease of conversation, her ability to put her work behind her at day's end.

Her husband chatted about the day that had gone by – putting bedding plants in the flower border, repairing the washing machine when it broke down, getting estimates for the gravelling of the drive.

She made only enough response to keep the conversation going. She wanted to hear his voice moving easily among the thoughts and memories of the day. Jack's voice was one of the things she loved most about him – deep, rich, a velvety baritone. She had once told him he had a voice like plain chocolate and he'd laughed and said that in his schooldays in the choir they'd called him the Bournville Baritone.

When the meal was over they went to relax in armchairs in the big sitting area, where Jack brought the coffee. After he'd poured and given her a cup he said: 'Now.'

'Ah,' she replied with a smile, 'now you're going to tell me what the occasion is.'

'Occasion?'

'For all the good food and special trimmings.'

He considered that for a minute then said 'I suppose it was a way of saying that *I* am keeping my end of the bargain. Why haven't you been keeping yours?'

She looked up, startled. Her hand jerked so that

72

coffee slopped over into the saucer. She put down the coffee cup.

'I don't understand,' she said.

'We agreed, didn't we, when we got married, that we'd be a totally open partnership – everything on the up and up, everything discussed and voted on. The idea of the new baby –'

'There's a new situation –'

'So I gather, and I want to know why you didn't tell me –'

'I meant to, Jack! I meant to, and then it began to get so complicated –'

'What's complicated about it? All you had to say was, I'm changing my job.'

'How did you find out?'

'I rang you this afternoon. Lena said you were out job-hunting. Now I want you to understand, Margaret – I've nothing against you leaving Hebberwood's, if you have something better lined up. But I think you ought to have discussed it with me before you started out on it.'

She stared at him. In the soft light of the table lamps she couldn't read his dark features, but what she could descry was reproval, irritation – nothing like the alarm she would have expected.

'I don't think you understand,' she began. 'I haven't –'

'I understand that you've had some sort of plan you haven't even bothered to tell me about. Look, I'm not being petty, if you want to take the next step up the ladder, okay. But your career is part of the way we live, Margaret. I need to know what's going on. Don't become so much a career woman that you forget the human side –'

'Jack, Jack, don't! You've got it all wrong! Do you seriously imagine I've been angling after some super job and keeping it from you because ... because it might

73

upset our household, or . . . or mean some trivial change? It's not that at all!'

'What, then? I wouldn't understand the considerations? Or you've been told to keep the whole thing secret? If you're telling me that embargoes like that apply to me, then all I can say is, you've changed a lot since –'

'Jack, I'm not in line for a big promotion. I'm not seeing people about taking two steps up the ladder. Not at all.'

He leaned forward in his chair. Echoes of her secretary's words came back to him, lost until now. 'Job-hunting, of course.' Of course? Why of course?

There could be only one reason.

'Margaret, you mean you've –'

'I've got the sack.'

'What?'

'Made redundant. I was out at an interview when you rang.'

'Redundant?'

'They're giving us all the push. Economy measure.'

'Oh my God!' He got up, threw himself on the sofa beside her, and took her in his arms. 'Poor love,' he said, holding her close.

'I . . . I don't know what to do, Jack,' she whispered. 'I thought it would be easy to get something else. I thought I knew so many people in the upper echelons of business. But . . . but . . .'

'You mean you've been trying?'

'Oh yes, I contacted everybody I knew, that I could think of. But nobody –'

'What do you mean, you contacted everybody? Who?' He had taken hold of her by the shoulders and held her away from him as he gazed at her.

'Anybody I thought might know of an opening. And Rosie –'

'You told Rosie Chaney? When was this?'

'About ten days ago. But though she said she'd put out feelers I haven't –'

'Ten days ago?' A dark flush was creeping up over the skin above the carefully-trimmed beard. 'How long have you known?'

'Almost a month.'

'A month!' He jumped up, glared down at her. 'You mean you've had all this on your mind for a month, and talked to folk like Rosie Chaney, and never told *me?*'

'I meant to, Jack. I really meant to. But . . . I got off on a wrong foot . . . and I couldn't . . .'

'You lying bitch! What the hell do you mean, you got off on a wrong foot? All you had to do was say, I've lost my job.'

'I couldn't. I . . . the time never seemed right . . . you were upset –'

'I was upset? What the hell are you talking about?'

'It was the day you got your sculpture exhibit back –'

'Are you telling me that because I'd got a piece of work back from a judging panel, you thought I was too beaten down to hear your news?'

'But I was upset too, and I . . .'

'You must see me as a knock-kneed fool,' Jack snarled. 'Too fragile to be told the bad news because his precious little sculpture was rejected? Is that it?'

To her own dismay, Margaret began to cry. Tears, unthought-of until now, spilled over on to her cheeks and ran down to shine on her skin. Sobs suddenly racked her. She turned away from her husband's accusing glare and buried her face in her arms against the back of the sofa. In the secure darkness there, she let her world come to pieces, a jumble of dark fragments without pattern or purpose. She wept with the painful shuddering of one who is unused to tears, her whole body shaking, her inner being torn with clawing wounds that seemed almost physical in their agony.

75

It was a long time before she became aware that Jack was trying to lift her, to prise her away from the sofa. At first she resisted, but it took too much energy. She let herself be turned so that her face lay against his chest. He held her close.

'Stop it now, stop it. It's all right. Everything's all right. I'm sorry I lost my temper. Stop crying, Meg. I've never seen you like this. Don't cry any more, sweetheart. It's all right.'

He soothed her as if she were Laurie. She let the voice work its charm, so that presently the tears stopped and the sobs subsided except for an occasional shudder. By and by he set her gently into the corner of the sofa and moved off. When he came back he put a glass to her lips. She sipped. Brandy. She took a mouthful, felt better.

'I'm going to make fresh coffee,' he said. 'Stay there, drink the brandy.' He clasped her hands round the glass, and she obeyed. When he came back she had finished it and felt strange, dizzy, light as a feather.

'I'm drunk, I think,' she said.

'No wonder, after all that emotional storm.' He sat beside her, took the glass and replaced it with coffee as he knew how to make it – as the Germans have it, black as coal, hot as hell, strong as love.

When she had drunk most of a cup he said: 'Now – calmly. What has happened?'

'Hebberwood's have made me redundant. I'm on three months' notice. Taking in my unused holiday allowance, I've five more weeks to go. And, Jack ... I can't find another job.'

He made no reply. He took the coffee cup from her after a glance at the clock.

'We'll talk about it in the morning,' he said.

'But, Jack –'

'In the morning.' He drew her to her feet, put his arm around her, and led her to the door. There he paused, still holding her, to switch off the lights. He brushed her hair with his lips.

As she went upstairs with him it was like the very first time she went to bed with him. There was the same light-headedness, the same tremulous need, the same linkage of sensation and sensitivity. He treated her with the same gentleness. It was like falling in love all over again.

Chapter Five

They woke early, but took their time about starting the day. For a while they lay in bed talking now and again. Then Jack padded downstairs to make early morning tea. It was still not six o'clock. The world outside was glistening with rain that had fallen in the night, and which they had heard in moments between their long, intense love-struggle. He watched a blackbird snatch up a worm that had come up to breathe. 'Poor old sod,' he said to the worm. 'I know just how you feel – your world's gone all to pieces.'

When he got upstairs with the tray, Margaret had drifted off into a doze again. She roused as he came in, and at last sat up against the pillows. He twitched her dressing-gown from a nearby chair. She draped it round bare shoulders.

He gave her the tray then climbed in beside her. They balanced the tray between them while she poured tea. Then he pushed it to the far end of the bed. They linked an arm about each other and with their other hands, held the tea cups.

'Well,' Jack said, 'so much for that.'

'How much for what?'

'I've often wondered how I'd react if your job really got in our way. Now I know.'

'You couldn't have foreseen that I'd act like such a nutcase.'

'How d'you mean? You didn't actually invite dismissal, I suppose.'

'No, not that – I mean about not telling you. I'm sorry, Jack, I really am. I seemed to lose touch with myself. I can't explain it. I just . . . couldn't bring myself to say the words to you – I've got the sack.'

'Well, I'm sorry too. Sorry I jumped to wrong conclusions about empire-building, sorry I got huffy over not being told, sorry I shouted at you.'

'Hmm . . .' She drank the remains of her first cup and clambered down to pour another. She looked over her shoulder. 'You ready for more?'

'In what respect?' he asked, pulling at the silk dressing-gown so that it slithered off.

She smiled at him. 'In any respect you like.'

But they could hear Laurie stirring in his room, asking drowsy questions of Paddington Bear who sat at the end of his bed. Although they didn't have any deep feelings about it, they preferred not to be found in the act of love by their three-year-old. And as they never locked their bedroom door, he might trot in at any moment.

When Margaret was settled again beside him, Jack went back to the real issue. In answer to his questions, out it all came – the weeks of suppressed but growing panic as she understood she wasn't going to walk into another job, the financial juggling she'd been doing. As she explained, Jack's dark features became grave.

'Allowing for the fact that I've no head for figures,' he said, 'it's not looking good, is it?'

'No, we're going to lose a lot. Even if I were to find a job within the next month – and I'm not so optimistic as I was, darling – they'd scarcely take me on at once. The kind of job I want isn't easy to come by, in any case.'

'Not the kind that gets advertised in the Sits Vac, you mean.'

'Exactly. There are three ways it could happen.

Somebody is promoted and leaves a vacancy, someone retires, or they create a new post. The first and the last are less likely in the present financial circs. The last, perhaps, isn't going to happen at all.'

'So you're left with the one in the middle.'

'Somebody retires – yes. But you see, Jack – the kind of work I do isn't normally a thing of long-standing. I don't think anybody aged sixty or over would be doing it. So even that possibility is a bit dim.'

'Um,' Jack said. 'What you're saying is that we've got to think of the job-hunting as a long-term affair.'

'Unless I have a stroke of good fortune. And the funny thing is, Jack – ever since Hughes handed me the bad news, I've stopped feeling lucky.'

'Feel a bit of a loser, do you?'

She nodded. 'And I'm not used to it. That's what makes it so bad. I don't want to sound smug, but I've done well up to now. Perhaps I should have been wary about how well I was doing ...'

'Rubbish.' He hugged her briefly. 'You know what Willie says.'

'Willie?'

'Shakespeare. Some are born great, some achieve greatness, some have greatness thrust upon them. I always feel you achieved success. You had talents, and you got good breaks, but you knew how to take advantage of both. And the same applies now. You've only to wait for an opportunity and you'll know how to take advantage of it.'

'Oh, you're such a comfort!' she cried, leaning her head against his shoulder. 'Why didn't I tell you all about it at the outset? I could have had you to tell me this twice a day to help keep my morale going.'

'Oh, I'm not just a pretty face, you know.' He was thinking hard about keeping her spirits up. It had surprised him to see how shattered she was by the blow at her self-esteem. She almost never cried. Last night's storm of tears had been a revelation to him. It brought out in him a protectiveness he'd never felt for her before. He wasn't one who believed in protecting others, except children, who needed shelter in which to become personalities. But as for the rest, he felt they had to take their knocks and come to terms with themselves, as he had.

Art college had led him on to the design department of Furnival Gilms when British film-making still had some impulse behind it. He had deliberately chosen to go into the rather restricted area of model-making and miniature construction because he was so good at it, so deft with his hands. It left his deeper creative instincts at call for his own work, which he did between film contracts. But when the British cinema took a nose dive he had had to hurry around the world, leaving Margaret in the flat they shared or having her join him when she could and when he was in some interesting place. He had done a lot of work at Cinecittà, had found it wonderful when she was there with her easy command of the language to help him find his way around. He'd spent a lot of time in the States too during a fashion for big-scale historicals. Nothing he liked better than having to construct a miniature medieval castle for back projection.

Then came the pains in his stomach. Nerves, he said. Freelance contracts became fewer and jobs less frequent. Money was going to a different kind of film, the violent, contemporary ciné-verité shot on location. He got work in television but the pains got worse, until he collapsed and was carted off to the casualty department of Charing Cross Hospital.

Perforated ulcer. It seemed his insides were in a mess. An emergency op to clear up the immediate damage, then another later to tidy up little ragged edges. A long convalescence, on a boring diet. But he had had long sessions with a therapist who at last argued him into a different view of life. 'It's either adopt a different way of living, or you'll be back in hospital again in a year or two. You can't live out of a suitcase, eat sandwiches and snatch a glass of beer or, when you feel extra tired, a whisky, without doing yourself a lot of damage. You haven't been getting proper rest, proper vitamins, proper fresh air and relaxation. When you first came in here, you were as pale as a corpse and that wasn't only because you were so short of blood. You'll have to get outdoors, do something less demanding. Either that, or you're heading for disaster.'

When Margaret heard the therapist's verdict she put on her thinking cap. It was her idea to make a complete change.

She had put her proposition boldly to Jack. She was twenty-nine, and if she wanted children, now was the time to have them. They should turn their permanent partnership into a marriage. They could buy a house, in the country. And Jack should be the one to look after the baby. She could continue her career and he could escape from the pressures and stresses of a job he'd grown tired of – give his sculpture some real time, do some serious work. It could be a perfect arrangement.

They had talked it over again and again. The consensus had been that they knew each other well enough to believe they could make it work. The only real problem was how their friends and relations would take it. Jack's were surprised at first but accepted it before long; not that their opinion meant too much to him because he had struck out on his own from the moment he went to art college fifteen years previously.

Margaret's parents were harder to convince. At first when she explained her plan, they thought she was joking. When it dawned on them it was a genuine solution to a genuine problem, Mrs Grant became indignant. 'Haven't you wasted enough of your life on that man?' she cried. 'You've been more or less living with him ever since you went to university. Now he wants you to support him while he lounges about at home –'

'It's not going to be like that, Mother –'

'Oh, nonsense, don't tell *me*! I've seen the way he sponges on you, coming back to live with you whenever it suits him, when he hasn't got a job to go to. And it's been so *embarrassing*! I've never known how to introduce him to our friends –'

'You'll know in future. He'll be my husband.'

Long and bitter the arguments had been. In the end Mr and Mrs Grant had had to accept that they couldn't stop their unruly daughter from doing what she liked – and in this case she seemed to like to saddle herself with a husband who wouldn't take a job and assume his proper responsibilities. A coolness had descended on their relationship after the Register Office wedding. But the birth of their first grandchild had thawed the Grants. For three years now they had been not exactly approving, but at least tolerant of the strange marriage.

'I haven't told Mother and Dad,' Margaret said now to Jack. 'I'm dreading having to break it to them. I have this awful feeling Mother will say, I told you so.'

Jack stretched down the bed and regarded his toes, which appeared from under the duvet. He couldn't help thinking that Margaret was right; his mother-in-law was exactly the sort to say 'I told you so'.

'Are you going to tell anybody else?' he inquired. 'I mean, hereabouts – friends and acquaintances.'

'Well, I'm not thinking of making a public announcement. But it'll become known.'

'I don't see how?'

'People talk to people –'

'But your kind of people in the City don't know our

kind of people here in Ladhurst. I mean, Cooper-Watts is in importing, Sir Roger only knows departmental civil servants and JPs and so forth, Maurice is in cars, the Goshalls are in antiques, Bernard buys and sells shares – who that you know in London is going to tell them?'

'I suppose ... not many of my London friends have any contact among the Ladhurst set.'

'Exactly. So if you want my opinion, I don't think there's any need to let it be known here.' He eyed her. 'If you remember, Stan was pretty bitchy about that poor bloke who was looking for a job – who was it? – Martin Lesswith.'

She remembered and coloured at the remembrance. 'Less-with-it than the others so he lost his job' – that had been Stan's quip. Of course it was silly to mind, but she didn't want them saying things like that about her.

'It makes sense to keep it quiet,' Jack went on. 'In the first place, you'll find something else fairly soon, even if not quite as quickly as you at first thought. So when that happens it might have been an awkwardness to let them know our problems.'

'Ye-es ...'

'And then there's the way they might start to shie away from us. Not that I give a damn,' he interjected, with a shrug. 'But we want Laurie to have friends to play with, to be invited to birthday parties, just as usual. It might make a difference if they knew about your job.'

They could hear Laurie now, singing to himself as his day got under way. He had a few nursery rhymes in his repertoire but it was mostly made up of advertising jingles learned from television. He was now rendering the Smarties tune.

Margaret listened for a moment. How awful if he suffered, by however little, because of her failure! She said quickly, 'All right, we needn't say anything to anyone else, if you think that's okay.'

84

'I certainly won't say anything,' Jack remarked. 'I can just imagine the *Schadenfreude* in Sybil Goshall's face if I mentioned it to her.'

'Yes, all right. It's agreed.'

'And we'll go to our usual engagements, and act just as normal.'

'But Jack, we'll have to economise a bit. I mean, I've only a month or so to go, when I'll be bringing in any salary. We have to look at it sensibly ...'

'What are you saying – that we should give notice to Mrs Prior? Stop using the family car?'

'Well, so long as we still have the company car, all its expenses are covered from the office. It makes sense not to use the Renault if we can use the Metro.'

'Okay, agreed. What about Mrs Prior?'

'That would mean you'd have to do everything – the house and all the cooking as well as the garden and looking after Laurie ...'

'I don't mind that.'

She hesitated. 'We'll keep Mrs Prior for the time being,' she said. 'I do think it would be wrong to ask you to run this place with no help at all –'

'Oh, I'd manage, love,' he laughed, and flexed his biceps. 'I'm not exactly a seven stone weakling, you know.'

'But you're not used to it. And housework's a bore.'

'I'm with you on that. While she's been tending the nephew with the broken arm, I've found sweeping and dusting to be the two most tedious undertakings in the world. Let's see how it goes, Meg. So far she hasn't actually said she's ready to come back, so I'll carry on as we are. These substitutes she's been sending are just paid by the day, as they turn up – or not, as the case may be. If the time comes to say goodbye to her, it might be easy to do it this way.'

She put her hands up to her face in shame. 'It's awful

talking about firing her. That's what was done to *me*!"

Jack didn't make the rejoinder that sprang to his lips – that Mrs Prior would find a new job more easily than Margaret Durley. Cleaning ladies are always in demand, but who wants a top executive of specialised qualification in a climate of financial frost?

He checked that train of thought. Any employer in his senses would want Margaret. She was pleasing to look at, had that unidentifiable air of being a somebody, was qualified by her intelligence and training to excel in her work. All it needed was an employer who had a vacancy for a woman with her abilities. And there must be such a one, somewhere. Specialised knowledge of travel, accommodation and entertainment must still be needed. No matter what company directors might say about cutting down, they were still going to swan about at the expense of the firm, if they could manage it somehow.

But Margaret's collapse of last night had scared Jack. He had never seen her so overset. Not even when he was carted off to hospital white as a ghost from internal bleeding – she'd been calm and collected then. But that was because there was action she could take. Now it was different.

Now she had to play a waiting game. It was new to her, destructive, demoralising. But everything would be different now that they shared the knowledge. He would help her. He would be her shoulder to cry on if she wanted to – but that wasn't likely to happen again.

Margaret went back to her office on Monday refreshed by a weekend much like any other she had spent at the house in Sussex, but with a difference: she and Jack had seemed closer than ever before. If there was any real meaning in the American word togetherness, that was what she and Jack had shared over those two days. He had been close at hand all through the usual socialising, ready to chip in if awkward topics arose. He even laid the groundwork for a little economising on their part. 'I've asked Margaret not to drive so much,' he remarked. 'She's very tired these days – gets home very late.' And when the servant problem came up, as it always did, he murmured: 'I'm getting a bit fed up with having a stream of strangers pottering about in the house – it's distracting.'

She had determined that from Monday on she would put all her energies into looking for a job. Her staff had now gone, having served out their notice or found something else. Lena too was supposed to have gone to her new post on a lower floor, but she found her waiting in the outer office as usual.

'Should you be here?' Margaret asked in surprise.

'I dare say not,' her secretary said, ruffling up, 'but they're going to have to come and drag me out if they want me. I'm not leaving you without a secretary.'

All at once Margaret understood how big a blow to her morale it would have been to have to call on help from the word processing pool. It demoted her by five or six grades to have to do that. And Lena, more in touch with what others thought, had realised it. It was her way of being a bulwark. Margaret should have a secretary, like all the other upper echelon executives, until she left.

'Thank you,' Margaret muttered, too touched to be able to manage any more.

'Think nothing of it,' Lena said with a wave of her capable hand.

But it caused ruffled feathers. Margaret got phone calls, first from the personnel office inquiring why she had detained Lena when she was needed elsewhere, and then from Lena's new boss who got very indignant. 'Good God, who do you think you are, ordering the staff around? Everybody knows you're on notice to quit. I'll see to it that ...'

'That what?' Margaret said, in genuine amusement.

'That I get the sack?'

'Oh ... well ... er ... But look here, I need that girl!'

'You'll have to take it up with her yourself,' Margaret replied. 'As you so brightly pointed out, I'm on notice to quit. I've no status any more. Nobody pays any attention to what *I* say.'

It ended with Twillan sending for Lena. Quite clearly he intended to tear her off a strip. Lena came back, pink of cheek and sparkling of eye. 'Huh! Little pip-squeak! I told him, you fire me if you want to. I don't care! I'll stay with Mrs Durley even if you do, so there.'

'And what did he say?'

'He ran his fingers through his hair and looked aghast. The he said he'd see what arrangements he could make. I take that to mean he's going to cover my absence with somebody from the pool.'

'You're a real Amazon, Lena,' Margaret said with admiration.

But when she thought it over she understood that Lena's courage came from confidence. She knew she could find a job by walking round the next corner in the City. If only I could do the same, thought Margaret.

To save embarrassment all round, she spent as much time as possible out of the building. That way, people didn't have to keep avoiding her eye in the corridors or the executive restaurant. It left Lena free to play some part in the work she was supposed to be doing.

Margaret was still on expenses. So restaurant and bar bills could be charged to Hebberwood. She took business friends and acquaintances out to lunch and afternoon tea and drinks, in hopes of getting a lead about an opening. She got it down to a fine art, introducing the subject: 'I don't want you to think I expect anything of you, but if you hear of a post that's in my line, will you remember me?' She gave them her card. And then it occurred to her that it was Hebberwood's

88

card, with the telephone number of her office, which wouldn't be hers in another few weeks. After the first three or four mistakes, she remembered to hesitate before handing over the card and to write her home number on the back.

On one of her job-hunting lunches, she ran into Charles Vernon. She heard his laugh, and turned her head – and there he was. He stared at her for a moment then raised his wine glass to her. She smiled and nodded, returning her attention to the guest whose help she was presently to seek.

'Who's your friend?' Malcolm inquired.

'Someone I used to see quite a lot, his name's Vernon.'

'Very silky,' said Malcolm, glancing at him with curiosity from behind the menu he was supposed to be studying. 'What does he do?'

'He's a director of Houg and Barnard –'

'The merchant bank? No wonder he looks silky. Satiny, I might almost say. So's the guy with him – very corridors-of-power, the pair of them.' The waiter came, thus distracting his attention from a topic Margaret would rather not pursue, and they were soon discussing Malcolm's yacht, which he intended to enter in the *Observer* Transatlantic.

Malcolm was in yacht-building. She knew very well that he would have no opening for her in his small, compact firm, nor did she want one. But he knew some very prestigious people, the kind who ordered boats from him at very high cost. Among these, perhaps, there was someone who needed someone like her. It was unlikely, it was clutching at straws, but she felt compelled to make the approach just the same.

Malcom's reddened nose and rather calloused hands were evidence of his devotion to sailing. Conversation with him consisted mainly in listening to incomprehensible accounts of how he luffed or battened or did some other necessary thing. Today his talk was all about a new knot he thought he had invented. Margaret heard him out, nodding now and again and watching while he produced a piece of cord from his pocket between the main course and the dessert, in order to demonstrate.

'It looks very complicated,' she remarked.

'Not a bit. The essence of a good knot is that it should be easy to do in all conditions. I've asked around among a lot of old salts but none of them know this one. If it's accepted, I'll have my name on it. What do you think of that!'

'You mean you'll be famous?'

He glanced at her, and caught the glint in her hazel eye. 'You're laughing at me. Oh, all right, I daresay I'm obsessed with the subject. Tell me about you, Margaret. Now I've moved to Norfolk I never see you any more.'

'You're not missing much,' she said. 'I'm not very good company these days, Malc. And the reason is . . .' She explained her situation. He listened in genuine horror, and looked sympathetic.

'Sure, sure, if any of my clients mention having something on the stocks, I'll let you know –'

Charles Vernon, making his way out of the restaurant behind his guest, paused in tall casualness beside them. 'Your game of cat's cradle fascinated me,' he declared as he looked down at Malcolm's cord. 'I couldn't go out without asking if it's a sponsored game, or what?'

'It's a ship's knot – Malcolm's invented it,' Margaret explained. 'You haven't met – Malcolm Howey, Charles Vernon.'

'Knots, really? You're in sailing? Oh, of course, now I come to look at you, I see you probably are.'

Malcolm, a simple soul, didn't understand that this was a put-down. He said equably, 'Yes, I build boats. If ever you want one, call on me. Any friend of Margaret's will get special treatment.'

90

'That's very kind of you.' The grey eyes lost their steely look. A slight smile dawned in them. 'You're buying a boat, Margaret?'

'Heavens, no. It's just a friendly get-together.'

'How nice.' His glance took in the exclusive restaurant with its panelled walls and shining silver. Something in his tone let her know he found that unconvincing, that if you were giving a friendly lunch to such as Malcolm, you didn't bring him here.

'Margaret was just asking me to keep an ear open for job possibilities,' Malcolm explained. 'I said I would, if I could remember.'

'Oh,' said Charles, and there was a momentary pause. 'It seems you're a good friend,' he added. 'Like me. Well, so long for now, my dear. Goodbye, Mr Howey.'

'Bye now,' Malcolm said.

As soon as Charles was out of earshot Margaret exploded. 'Why the *hell* did you tell him that?'

'What?'

'About the job.'

'But ... he's a pal of yours ... surely he knows?'

'No he doesn't – didn't.'

'But, Margaret, he'd be a lot more use to you than I am. Why on earth haven't you told him?'

'Because ... Oh, it all goes back into the past. Never mind.'

'Oh,' said Malcolm. 'I've put my foot in it. Oh, sorry, old girl. You know me – can read a wind like a book, but can't see a trap before I fall into it.'

She sighed. 'It doesn't matter. I suppose he'd have heard one way or the other, eventually.'

'Will he – I mean, what? What?'

'He'll do nothing.'

But she wasn't so sure. Charles hadn't given up easily, when she told him she intended to marry Jack.

During her relationship with Jack she had often been

91

left alone. Jack had never expected her to live like a nun, and took care never to ask if she found consolation during his absences. There had, in fact, been other men. When she looked back on them she could never understand why she had let it happen, because almost nothing about them was memorable.

Except for Charles Vernon.

She met him in, of all places, the Round House. It was while she was working for Paracelsus Travel. A group of tourists in London had no courier and needed to be taken to see a performance of a Bertolt Brecht play for which they had booked, their trip being a comprehensive examination of British theatre. Margaret, relatively interested in Brecht, offered to stand in. There she was, with a group of eight girl students and five men, translating from English into Spanish and trying to explain exactly what the Round House was and had been, when a kindly voice behind her offered: 'May I? Railways are one of my interests – I believe I know the Spanish for engine turntable.'

When she turned, this very handsome, fair-haired man was smiling at her. He seemed to be on his own. To tell the truth, he looked a little out of place there, in the audience of somewhat casual and younger people. She put his age at about forty.

True to his boast, he could converse in Spanish about the technicalities of the former rail shed. Not that the girls were content to leave all the talk to the men. They eagerly adopted him, so that he in his turn asked them all out to supper afterwards.

'Oh – surely – fourteen of us?' Margaret protested with consternation.

'Don't worry, I know a good restaurant where we can push the tables together. It isn't far.'

He led them out through Chalk Farm to what turned out to be a typical English fish restaurant, with waiters in striped waistcoats and bowlers. The Spaniards were entranced. Margaret thought they probably could never have had such a good time if their proper courier had turned up. She thanked Charles with genuine enthusiasm when at last she herded them to their minibus for the journey to their hotel.

She was astounded to get a phone call from him two days later. 'Who?' she inquired when he gave his name.

'*Es peligroso asomarse*,' said a laughing voice.

'Oh, our friend the train expert. How nice of you to call.' She paused. 'How did you know where to find me?'

'The name of the firm was on the minibus.'

It quite took her aback. He had looked so well-heeled, so top-drawer – she'd have said he wouldn't want to continue acquaintance with a girl who went around with a bunch of Spanish students in a minibus.

She was wrong, however. He let her know he very much wanted to see her again. As it happened, at the time Jack was in Cinecittá building a miniature Temple of Osiris for Carlo Ponti. She wouldn't have the opportunity to join him for some weeks yet. She was overworked, tired, and rather lonely. The worst of letting your friends know that you were serious about a man was that they tended to leave you to yourselves – and when Jack went away, it meant quite a bit of solitude.

'I wondered if you were doing anything this evening?' he inquired.

'I'm afraid I am. I have a meeting at the office, to bone up on some new regulations that have come in about health precautions.'

'But it won't go on for ever, I hope?'

'No, but it'll be fairly late –'

'I'm inviting you to supper,' he said. 'Supper is late for us Spaniards.'

'No, really, I can't . . .' She found she wished she was

wearing something more smart. She didn't want to go out to supper with him in a denim skirt and a shetland sweater.'

'Please come,' he said in a pleading tone. '*Es mi santo* – you wouldn't want me to celebrate my saint's day alone?'

'That would be dreadful.' She decided to tell this very well-dressed man her problem. 'I'm not really attired for going to supper anywhere.'

'What are you wearing?'

'Skirt and jumper.'

'There are lots of Spanish restaurants where a skirt and jumper would be perfectly all right.'

'Hm,' she said. 'But what would you be wearing, as it's your saint's day?'

'Oh, *traje de luce*, of course. No seriously, we could have a nice celebratory meal in a nice quiet place I know.'

'You seem to be a bit of an expert on restaurants.'

'As it happens, my firm finances one of the good food books. What about it – shall I pick you up? About eight? Half-past?'

'Better make it half-past.'

The meeting went on a little later than that. As the staff of Paracelsus came out, yawning, eyes popped wide at the sight of the Mercedes waiting by the kerb. Charles was wearing a pair of cord trousers and a checked blouson, which should have looked casual but somehow didn't because they were so terribly well cut. He handed her in and set off without delay. 'Are you very tired?' he asked with sympathy.

'I must say, I'm a bit beat,' she confessed. 'I hope I'm not going to fall asleep over your birthday supper. And by the way, I looked it up. This is not the day of St Charles.'

'Yes it is,' he countered in a tone of amused

94

admiration. 'He's better known as Diego, but he's Charles of Sezze, so there.'

That was typical of Charles. He always got his facts right, and he always knew what he was about.

The thought that he now knew she was out of a job made Margaret a little uneasy. She expected him to intervene – and then she would have to refuse his offers, and it would all be very awkward. The more so because anything Charles put her way would be very good indeed.

But she didn't dare let herself become indebted to him. She would be ready with some good tale when he called.

But he didn't call. And strange to say, it hurt her.

Chapter Six

Although Charles Vernon didn't ring, Malcolm did. It surprised her very much. He was usually so inept, and so forgetful about anything except boats. But perhaps the little scene over Charles had fixed her request in his mind.

'I dunno whether it's your kind of thing,' he said, 'but there's this guy who's just about to take delivery of a sloop, and he's into time-sharing.'

'Oh yes?' she said, her ears pricking up.

'I told him about you, and he said he was looking for someone to – you know – handle the inquiries and take people out to show them. It's pretty top-level stuff – he's got properties in Greece and Spain and France. What d'you think?'

'Well, I don't speak Greek, but –'

'I don't think the languages are so important. It's the being lovely to rich couples who're in the market for a luxury holiday home. Anyhow, have you got a pencil? I'll give you his number, and you ring his secretary for an appointment. He's expecting to hear from you.'

Margaret had never understood the word 'thrilled' before, but now she felt it described her feelings. Her whole psyche seemed to be in a flutter. She gave the number to Lena, and asked her to ring and arrange something – she had too much experience to ring herself and go through the usual put-offs and down-gradings of office switchboards.

Lena presented herself in person a few minutes later. 'Three-fifteen the day after tomorrow. They recognised your name the moment I gave it.'

'Did they really?'

'It's hopeful, is it? What is it? A big firm?'

'I've no idea as yet. It's this time-sharing thing, you know? A friend has spoken to someone on my behalf.'

'Mmm ... That's a growing business. You may be on to a good thing, Mrs Durley.'

On the Thursday she put on an outfit she knew was very becoming, a two piece in soft yellow crêpe. Strictly speaking, the cold early-summer weather didn't justify it, but she would take a coat. She lingered a moment over her fur coat but decided against it. That was a bit too lush even though it was only marmot, and anyway she'd never felt comfortable in it because she disapproved of killing animals for their hides. Instead she took out her camel hair; she would drape that casually over her shoulders and, if possible, take it off and leave it with the secretary.

'How do I look?' she inquired of her husband.

'First rate. By which I mean, not by any means second rate.'

'Mummy!' exclaimed Laurie, advancing upon her with hands outstretched and fingers still sticky with the muesli he loved to stir manually.

'No, darling, mustn't touch.' She crouched beside him, holding his hands away. She kissed him. 'Bye-bye for now. See you when I come home.'

'Be home before bed?'

'Yes, love, I promise.'

Jack went with her out to the car. 'Now be good, don't promise to go to bed with him even if he offers you twice your present salary.'

'I promise.'

He closed the car door after her, leaned in to kiss her

goodbye. 'My word, you smell so nice. It's a pity you have to go ...' He sighed.

'Now then, Love is of man's life a thing apart,' she scolded. 'So long.'

'So long, good luck.' He stood back, scooped up the toddler who had hurried out in hopes of grabbing his mother to delay her. He waved as she drove down their still-ungravelled entrance.

The hours until three-fifteen seemed to creep by. There was very little work for her now in the office. The Quebec meeting was over, nothing else had needed her attention except individual travelling arrangements for two of the company's elder statesmen. She used the time by calling a friend or two, making arrangements to meet. She talked to Rosie Chaney, who congratulated her on the forthcoming interview and wished her heartfelt luck. 'Let's meet so you can tell me about it,' she said. 'Will you know at once if you've got it?'

'I'm not sure. In any case, I'm booked for lunch tomorrow and then it's the weekend.'

'Shall we make it Monday, then? My shout this time.'

'No, Rosie, let me pay. I'm still on expenses.' She laughed. 'The time may come when I'll be glad of the chance to get a free lunch from you.' But she knew that wasn't going to be the case. She felt in her bones that this interview would yield the job she needed.

She had an appointment at lunchtime previously arranged, with Mrs Thorogood of *Business Travel Monthly*. She didn't expect to get a job offer from her and wouldn't have taken it if she had, because she didn't want to go into journalism, about which she knew very little. But Mrs Thorogood was another of those people who knew others with power and influence, and they were old acquaintances because of useful information Margaret had often supplied to the magazine.

'I'd heard about your dilemma,' the older woman

said as soon as they had ordered. 'To tell the truth, it wasn't entirely news to me because Bryan Seckwith had been approached to take over Hebberwood's travel arrangements.'

A couple of weeks ago Margaret would eagerly have asked, 'When was that?' and would have worked out how long Hebberwood had been contemplating the closure of her department without telling her. Now, that no longer mattered. The important thing was to find something else. She told Mrs Thorogood frankly what her circumstances were; for the first time she laid it all on the line, untroubled, because she had the feeling of security that came from the forthcoming interview.

'I understand, of course. You're in a narrow field, Margaret. Job opportunities aren't all that common, unless you were to go down a step or two and look for something in a travel firm.'

'Oh, I shouldn't want to do that,' she replied. 'I've got responsibilities, you know, Jane. I can't afford to take a big cut in salary.'

'Quite so. Well, good luck with the interview. In view of your need to make a good impression, I won't delay you or accept a liqueur with you.'

'Thanks, you're an angel – I don't want to turn up smelling of Grand Marnier.'

They laughed and rose. Margaret signed for the bill as she went out. They shook hands and parted. Margaret glanced at the Longines watch – she was too early, but it was hardly worth going back to the office. She set out with a swinging step in the cool June day to walk to Mayfair.

The offices of Lepham Properties were on a much smaller scale than the Hebberwood Tower but they were impressive. A beautiful old house in Albemarle Street was their headquarters. In the hall a commissionaire in a dark green uniform checked all visitors. She was sent up in a gilt lift to the top floor, where a black girl in what looked like a white cotton track suit welcomed her. In her Roland Klein suit, Margaret began to feel considerably over-dressed.

But as she followed the girl to John Sirker's office, she felt she fitted better into the elegant surroundings than her guide. The place had been lovingly restored and adapted. Thick grey carpet underfoot, Regency wallpaper, dove grey paintwork, touches of gold on the mouldings, lustres round the lights. It was soothing and charming – of course, to lull would-be clients into a false sense of security, she told herself with a grin.

The secretary left her for a moment to check that the boss was free. She returned at once to usher her in. The camelhair coat was left on a chair.

Sirker rose from his desk to welcome her. He was a big man, overweight, in a conventional business suit and dark tie. The only thing noticeable about him was the rings – he wore two on the wedding finger of his left hand and a heavy gold signet ring on the little finger on his right. Happily, he didn't wring Margaret's hand when he took it. He led her to a settee and asked her to sit, then sat beside her. The settee didn't sag – it was good reproduction Hepplewhite – but she thought she heard it groan a little.

'Now,' he began, 'what do you know about the time-sharing business?'

'Only what I've gleaned from advertisements in the newspapers and one or two information items on TV, I'm afraid.'

'You've never thought of going in for it yourself – as a holidaymaker, I mean?'

'Not yet, although I think it might have come. We have one child, a little boy, and it might make holidays a lot easier if we had a permanent base somewhere for holidays.'

100

'You have a son?' he asked, raising thick dark eyebrows.

'Yes, he's three.' She felt she must make her position clear at once, and gave a quick sketch of her household. She could feel Sirker's amusement but didn't let it sharpen her tone nor lengthen the explanation.

'I see. Very unconventional. Your husband shoulders all the household responsibilities?'

'Yes, I've no problems on that score.' She knew he was really asking if she was the kind who'd rush off if the pipes burst in a cold winter.

He leaned back in the corner of the settee. 'You say you have one child. Thinking of having another?'

'Not now. We were thinking about it until the closing down of my department at Hebberwood's, which caused us to talk it over and postpone it indefinitely.'

'I see.' He eyed her. 'Forgive me, Malcolm told me you were very bright, and I can see he was right, but he couldn't give me much more. Can I question you?'

'Of course.'

'You're – what age?'

She took that as an invitation to give him her curriculum vitae, which she did as succinctly as possible. He looked impressed, and was eyeing her with increasing appreciation.

'Right, that's very straightforward and helpful. Now let me tell you about this post. This isn't by any means a one-man business, but until now it's been up to me to handle our overseas visits to view the property. I'm finding it more and more demanding. My secretary has to deal with the travel arrangements for me and whoever I'm taking, and she does it, of course, but she's no expert. It's dawned on me it would be far more sensible to have someone doing all that, and meeting and greeting our clients before they go, also welcoming them back and easing them into the buying situation when they return.'

101

He paused. 'I've no clear idea of the kind of person I need. It's got to be someone who is good with people, who knows how to entertain, who has detailed knowledge of travel by air, and hotel accommodation. We do have apartments available to put up clients but it sometimes happens that they're already being used so that we have to find something else for them – and I'll confess to you we had an absolute disaster last month with a Texas businessman who was put into a dingy little hotel in Greece and complained of fleas.'

Margaret laughed, as she was expected to do. 'I think I can guarantee to send your customers to flea-free hotels.'

'Flea-free! That's good! I must remember that! Well, well, you have a good sense of humour, eh? That's necessary, too, because we have a lot of quite difficult people to handle.'

They were interrupted by the arrival of the secretary with a tray of tea. It was a reproduction Georgian service, not quite expert enough to trick Margaret's eye but no doubt impressive to foreigners. With the tea came Austrian biscuits, light as tulle. Margaret was invited to pour, which she did well aware that Sirker was watching her with minute attention.

She knew she looked good in her yellow crêpe behind the silver. She handed him his tea, offered the silver sugar bowl. She could have told him he was foolish to take three lumps, but knew better.

Over the tea he described the property overseas. From the sound of it, the man was a millionaire. She listened, asking questions when she thought it sensible. When they set their cups down at last, he smiled.

'Now you want to know how much you'd get, I suppose. Well, as you've gathered, I'm not selling apartments to filing clerks. I deal with people who've no worries about money. I like to ensure that my employees are unworried too.'

102

'I must say that sounds encouraging!'

He named a salary that was two thousand over what she was leaving at Hebberwood. She felt a flow of delight, and wondered if it showed in a flush of colour in her cheeks. Of course, there wouldn't be the company perks that she'd enjoyed with Hebberwood and perhaps it would come out about even. Time enough to weigh all that up later.

'That sounds very satisfactory, Mr Sirker,' she said.

'Call me John. Everybody does – even Sally, my secretary. We're very informal here.'

They rose. They shook hands. 'It's been nice meeting you, Margaret,' he said. 'I've a few other people to see, but you'll be hearing from me soon.'

'I look forward to that.' She hesitated.'Would it sound too eager to ask when? I wonder if you could give me some idea of when? I ask because of course I have other interviews to go to.'

'A few days, my dear, I assure you.'

'Thank you.'

Sally the girl in the track suit showed her to the lift again. 'Go well?' she inquired.

'As far as I could tell.'

'Hope you get it. We've had a bunch of zombies up to now.'

'How many?'

'Three others.'

'Are there many other applicants?'

'No, not many,' Sally said, remembering she shouldn't give away confidential information. She closed the lift door on Margaret. 'Good luck,' she said as the little gilt cage sank towards the ground floor.

Margaret was exultant. Everything was going to be all right! She found a taxi in Piccadilly without difficulty and was taken back to the City. One look at her face told Lena all she needed to know.

'You've got it?' she cried, grabbing her by the elbows.

'I think so. I'm pretty sure. Sirker's secretary told me they'd had poor applicants, and Sirker and I ended up on first name terms.'

Lena asked with a grin, 'Is he after something he shouldn't be?'

'I don't think so. He gives the impression of a man who's more interested in food and drink than women. No, it was a perfectly businesslike discussion.'

'What about the job, itself?'

'It sounds fascinating, Lena. I really think I'd enjoy it.'

'Super! Let's have a cuppa to celebrate.'

'I just had tea out of a silver-plated pot.'

'Well, have coffee then. I bought a cake, just in case.'

'Oh, Lena!' They hugged each other. It occurred to her that Lena was a very good friend, one she had under-rated until now.

They had coffee and pieces of cherry cheesecake, the remainder of which Lena would take home to be consumed by herself and her mother. Margaret couldn't help thinking she oughtn't to have censured Sirker for taking sugar in his tea if she was going to stuff herself with cheesecake – but it was a special occasion.

She rang Jack to tell him the good news. He replied at once: 'Of course. It's what I expected.'

'Oh, darling! You're biased.'

'Not a bit. I know you're first class because I see the way other folk look at you. Well, let's ring off now so I can hurry to my kitchen and set about preparing a celebratory dinner for my loved one.'

'Jack, nothing rich, please. I've just been scoffing cheesecake.'

'This chap offered you cheesecake as an inducement? He must be mad keen.'

'No, idiot, Lena provided it. But I've eaten a business lunch with Jane Thorogood and a great wedge of cake. Can we have salad and cold meat tonight?'

'What, no boeuf Strogonoff? No profiteroles?'

'Absolutely not.'

He laughed. 'I must say you're easy to please. Cold meat and salad it shall be.'

But he'd gone to the trouble of sculpting a little star from ice, to set among the round dishes of salad ingredients. 'That your star,' he told her. 'It's in the ascendant again.'

'But ice melts, Jack.'

'Yes, and flowers wither, and time passes – don't let's get metaphysical about it. If I'd made a cake with icing on it and you'd eaten that, you wouldn't say, Cake gets eaten.'

'Oh, you are a fool,' she said, shaking her head at him. 'And by the way, could you actually ice a cake?'

'I'm going to try my hand at it. I'm hoping to have got it down to a fine art by Laurie's birthday.'

'Jack ...'

'What?'

'If I get this job ... I think we've got to accept that I can't have another child for a while. I think quite a point was made about that by Mr Sirker.'

Jack munched marinated mushrooms and looked thoughtful. 'Well, we're not exactly in the sere and yellow yet, are we? We'll get to it by and by.'

'But I'll soon be thirty-five, Jack. I don't want to leave it too late.'

'Hey! Come on! You're getting all down. What is it, reaction?'

She blew out a breath. 'I suppose it is. I'm a lot more up and down than I used to be, aren't I?'

'Like a rocket,' He stretched out his hand and she took it. 'It's all going to be fine. You're not a loser, Margaret. Everything is going to be okay.'

On Monday morning she set off at her usual time for London. The postman was late. She came across him in

Bard Lane, and he waved at her. 'Want to take your letters?'

'Oh, thanks, Bob.' She took them through the window, sorted through, and saw one with a W1 postmark. She handed back the rest. 'There you are, I expect everything else is rate demands.'

'Too true,' the postman said, and walked on.

She hadn't time to open the letter then, but put it in her handbag. It was something to look forward to when she got to the office, something to show to colleagues in a certain amount of justified triumph.

Settled at her desk, she took out the letter and opened it.

She couldn't believe what she read.

'Dear Mrs Durley, Thank you for coming to see me last week. I was much impressed by your qualifications but for various reasons have decided to give the post to a later applicant. I wish you success in some other interview for appointment, Yours sincerely, John Sirker.'

Her exclamation brought Lena running.

'What's the matter?'

'I ... I ...' She held out the sheet of notepaper to the other woman, who took it in alarm. Margaret bent her head and put one hand in front of her face.

'The swine!' cried Lena. 'The rotten swine! He led you to think you'd got it!'

'I don't know ... I thought I had ...'

'Oh, Mrs Durley! I'm ever so sorry. Oh, lord!'

'I can't ... I ... Would you mind, Lena ...'

'Right,' Lena said promptly, and went out, closing the door with care behind her.

Margaret put her head on her arms on the desk, and shuddered with reaction. She felt deathly cold. Her heart was beating with a slow, hard motion.

'I'm going to have a heart attack,' she said to herself.

106

But then she knew it was nonsense. There was nothing wrong with her heart.

It was the blow to her self-image that had bowled her over. She was so certain John Sirker had intended to give her the job. She couldn't come to terms with the idea that although he clearly liked and admired her, someone else had been preferred.

She was inferior in some way to the successful applicant. Was she inferior? Had she been kidding herself all these years?

Perhaps this was something that was due to happen. A sword of Damocles hanging over her head all the time, waiting to fall and cut down her self-esteem.

But why did it have to involve her family too? If she was to be punished for her own arrogance, why did Jack and Laurie have to suffer? They had done nothing wrong.

Have I? she asked herself. She sat up and looked out of the window of her office. The view was of distant city blocks and the sky. Had other people in other offices done wrong in ignorance, as she had? Because she must have – otherwise why the punishment?

She had no idea how much later it was that Lena tapped and came in with the inevitable cup of coffee. She put sugar in as Margaret watched, and at her protest said: 'You need it. For shock. You're as white as a sheet.'

'I feel rotten, Lena.'

'No wonder. I could kill that man.'

'It's not his fault. He has to hire the person he thinks can best fill the post.'

'He needn't have been so matey with you all the same! You came back on Thursday with stars in your eyes – and you're not a fool, Mrs Durley. He let you think you had it.'

'I think I did, until someone better came along afterwards, Lena.'

'Better?' Lena said sceptically, and flounced out.

Margaret actually laughed. If only all prospective employers could see her through Lena's eyes, or Jack's ...

Jack ... She should ring him and tell him. But she couldn't bring herself to do it just yet. Later. Let him have at least part of the day in the innocent belief that their problems were all solved.

When she had drunk the sickly sweet black coffee she undoubtedly felt better. She dealt with some figure work then called in Lena to do some letters tidying up the closing down of business with one or two firms. She put through chits for payment to others. She made some calls.

Then lunchtime was upon her, and she had a date with Rosie at Brogan's. She was about to tell Lena to ring and cancel, then changed her mind. What would she do through lunchtime if she didn't lunch with Rosie?

Her friend was ahead of her in the tiny cocktail lounge of the restaurant. She waved a glass at her. 'I ordered myself a Campari, hope you don't mind,' she said.

'Of course not.' The cocktail waiter hovered, Margaret ordered Pernod. Rosie grimaced. 'I didn't know you drank that stuff. It always reminds me of liquorice all-sorts.'

Margaret held the same opinion. She'd no idea why she'd chosen it, unless it was that she knew it always made her light-headed very quickly – and she felt she needed something to lighten her mood.

Rosie was looking about the tiny cocktail lounge. 'That's Peter Shires,' she murmured, 'MP for some-where in Lancashire. And isn't that Dr Lukesey, who's on that TV show about getting fit?'

Margaret looked. It was so.

'Oh, I do like this place, Meg! It's nice of you to bring me here. It's just a bit beyond my usual run of entertaining, even though things are going well with the schools.'

'Summer season getting into swing?'

'Absolutely fully booked up. In fact, if I'd known we were going to have so many inquiries, I'd have taken on extra premises. Heaven knows there are enough small seaside hotels feeling the pinch just at present.'

Rosie looked as if she were doing well. She was wearing baggy pants with gathered ankles, a crocheted top in silver mesh, and a blouson of metallic sheen. Her hair was in a strange yet lovely shaggy halo that made its greying blondeness shimmer. The handbag dangling from her chair back was made of mere plastic, but it was posh plastic. She was the acme of contemporary intellectual chic, and Margaret felt herself dowdy by comparison.

They had just finished their drinks when the head waiter appeared with menus to summon them to their table. They found they were next to a well-known stage director and the lady of the moment. On the other side two professorial men were in earnest, low-voiced conversation. The two women took their seats, consulted the list of dishes, and ordered. Margaret chose a Chablis to go with the hors d'oeuvres and a Burgundy for the steaks.

'Two lots?' Rosie said. 'My word, we are celebrating! Well, don't keep me in suspense any more. When d'you start the new job? What's the man like?'

'I didn't get the job,' Margaret said.

Rosie dropped the spoon she'd been tinkering with. 'What?'

'I didn't get it.'

'But ... But ... You seemed so sure!'

'I did, didn't I? Serves me right.'

'Margaret!'

The waiter came with smoked salmon pâté. Margaret

stared at it as if it had come from Mars. The waiter placed hot toast in a gracefully folded napkin of blue checks. Rosie took a piece, began to butter it, then put it down.

'What the hell happened? Didn't you go for the interview?'

'Oh yes, I went.'

'And ... And ...'

'And was turned down.'

Rosie could think of nothing to say. In all her friendship with Margaret, which went back now fifteen years, she'd never known her to fail. Not at anything. At university she had gained a first class honours, she'd had the pick of all the men, she'd landed just the kind of job she wanted in the vac, she'd sailed into a job when she left university, she'd set her sights on Jack Durley and got him. When she wanted to get married, Jack had wanted it too. She'd wanted a son: she bore a male child. She'd wanted a not too expensive house in Sussex, a seeming impossibility. She and Jack had found it, had made it into almost a House Beautiful. She'd been courted for the job at Hebberwood, positively pursued by them with blandishments.

And now this. It was inconceivable. Rosie knew she wasn't helping Margaret by her continuing disbelief, yet she couldn't help it. 'Did you get on wrong footing with this guy? I mean, what happened? Oh.' She broke off. 'I suppose he made a pass at you.'

'No. He was heavily polite and very pleased with me. I came away convinced I'd got it.' She took the letter out of her Gucci bag and handed it to her friend.

With a glance for permission, Rosie read it. Then she whistled between her teeth. 'What a bastard.'

'Oh no. He has a perfect right to choose whoever he likes.'

'But I mean – this is only four lines.'

'I've discovered, Rosie – when you have to give

110

someone the push, the shorter the ceremony the more bearable.'

'Oh,' Rosie mourned, 'this is absolutely terrible. I don't know what to say.'

'Say nothing, eat. The toast is getting cold.'

With a dubious little shake of the head, Rosie obeyed. Although it seemed heartless, she was hungry. She never ate breakfast and Campari on an almost empty stomach gave an edge to the appetite. She crunched salmon-laden toast and felt a beast while Margaret pushed the pâté about on her plate. The wine had come. The waiter poured some into Margaret's glass and looked expectant, but she waved at him impatiently and Rosie's glass was filled, then Margaret's.

'That's right,' Rosie said, trying for a joke, 'let's get drunk.'

The staff at Brogan had instructions not to be in a hurry to remove plates when the accompanying wine was still to be drunk. So the bottle of Chablis had almost vanished when their pâté was cleared and the steak was brought. The Burgundy was already by the table, breathing. This time the waiter looked inquiringly at Margaret then poured it at once. Margaret took a deep drink; she adored Burgundy but seldom drank it because it made her sleepy. But who cared now if she took a nap at her desk this afternoon?

'What are you going to do now?' Rosie asked, after she'd watched her friend cut and eat at least a morsel of steak.

'Keep trying. What else can I do?' Margaret washed the steak down with Burgundy. 'Did you get any hopeful reactions from your rich kids?'

'Not too many. Most of them don't give a damn about Daddy's business interests. They've come to England not to learn the language but, most of them, to have a good time in a permissive society. The goings-on ...'

111

Normally she would have continued in this vein, passing on some bizarre stories of her pupils' behaviour. But this wasn't the time for sexy gossip. 'There's an Iranian boy whose family got out in a private plane with a load of gold. Pa is now in Monte Carlo throwing a lot of it away at the gaming tables, but he's investing in cargo handling equipment for the Middle Eastern countries. They want somebody to head up the office in London – but I have to tell you, they're not likely to hire a woman.'

'It doesn't sound like me, in any case, Rosie.' They ate and drank for a while in silence. 'Anything else?'

'There's a kid in our school in Bath who's something to do with ski-ing in Switzerland. I'm not sure of the ins and outs but I gather they're building some great leisure complex above the snow line. It's not built yet, Meg.'

'A leisure complex? Hotel, cabins?'

'That kind of thing, I think. But it won't be ready until late next year.'

'I see.'

'It's a prospect, dear. You could perhaps just get something to hold you until then, and then take it on.'

'If I got it.'

'Margaret! Of course you'd get –' She stopped. It was no longer an inevitable thing that Margaret would succeed. The idea shocked her.

'No, there's no of course about it. And by next year I'd be thirty-five – you'd be surprised how people take note of the age factor.'

'Oh, come on, Margaret –'

'No, it's true. A man of thirty-five heading into his forties is still going to be attractive. A woman of thirty-five is beginning to lose her looks, and if her looks are one of the factors in hiring her, they'd want a younger woman.'

'How can you talk like this? You're one of the best looking women I've ever known – the best looking in this room, for a fact!'

Margaret smiled. She didn't feel goodlooking. Her Jean Varon dress seemed to hang on her, her lips were dry, she felt there was perspiration shining on her forehead from the strange clammy sweat that seemed to seize her from time to time. All the accoutrements – the Gucci shoes and bag, the thin gold chain round her neck – they seemed to add nothing to her appearance except to say that she once had had the money to buy them.

They finished their steaks. Rosie, who seemed to burn up every calorie she consumed, decided to have dessert. The trolley was wheeled up. The display of rich foods seemed unreal to Margaret, as if they were props for the pie-throwing scene at a pantomime. Rosie lingered over pêches cardinales, brandied oranges, zabaglione, and various gateaux. As might have been expected, she ended up with a large portion of Sachertorte. To keep her company Margaret ordered a grapefruit sorbet, which melted in its cup while her companion devoured the torte.

While eating, Rosie tried to build up hopes of the ski-resort job. M. Alanou seemed a nice man; she'd met him three or four times when he came to visit Emile. She could talk to him about Margaret. Perhaps he would need someone to handle advance booking for the resort. Perhaps he would be looking for staff quite soon. At least it was worth inquiring into.

'But it would mean moving to Switzerland,' Margaret said when Rosie had talked herself to a standstill.

'Yes, I take that for granted.'

'I don't know that Jack would like that. He's travelled a lot in the past and come to the conclusion that he likes England best.'

'Oh, that's just chauvinism. He'd like Switzerland –'

'Do you think so? I love it as a place to holiday in, but it's awfully conservative. How do you think Jack would feel in a society like that?'

'Margaret, I know this idea of mine isn't ideal – but it's

something. I'll pursue it a bit so that if you get something better in the meantime we can just drop it.'

'It's awfully good of you, Rosie.'

Now it was time for coffee and liqueurs. Normally it would have been taken for granted that neither of them would want a liqueur, but today Margaret insisted. 'Please, Rosie. Let's have something to linger over. I've no reason to hurry back to the office. I've nothing to *do* there.'

Hearing the desperation behind the words, Rosie ordered cognac. Margaret chose Drambuie, and ordered a double.

'Darling, do you think you should?' Rosie asked with anxiety.

'Why not?'

'Well, grape and grain, you know –'

'You're having cognac –'

'But I haven't had as much wine as you, Meg. Are you sure you won't feel a bit *hors de combat*?'

'Does it matter? I'm not going anywhere or doing anything.'

'Don't talk like that. Listen, I'm going to tell you something I was keeping back. It may cheer you up or something.'

'What?' Margaret said, eyeing her a little vaguely.

'Charles rang me.'

Margaret blinked. 'Charles?'

'He said he'd seen you, with Malcolm Howey or someone, and heard you were out of a job.'

'Oh.' Margaret tried to make sense of that. 'What did you say?'

'I told him you were just on the move, from one job to another. Y'see, I thought this thing with Lepham Properties was a sure thing.'

'So did I, Rosie, so did I! Never count your chickens until they're old enough to run from the foxes,' Margaret rejoined, smiling a little at her own version of the proverb.

'That's what's important, Rose of all the world – to be smart enough to get away from the gnashing teeth.'

'Margaret, are you all right?'

'I'm fine. Just beginning to relax. I didn't think, when I started out to meet you, that I'd feel anything but terrible. *In vino sanitas* – that's a very well-known old Roman saying. Did you know I got the prize for Latin at school?'

'I believe you did. Listen, Megs, about Charles –'

'Good old Charles. He smiled down on poor Malc as if Malc were something that had crept out of a whelk-shell. D'you know, he still looks super? He must be getting on towards fifty, I s'pose, but he's got it all – still not a speck of grey in that hair of his, shoulders straight as a guardsman, and not a *nounce* of spare fat on him. Does half an hour a day in a gym – did you know that?'

'What I was thinking, dear, was this –' The wine waiter brough the liqueurs, set them before them with reverence. When he had gone Rosie resumed, 'I gathered that Charles is ready to rally round. Why else should he have rung me? It happens that I gave him a wrong steer, but look, Margaret, you can contact him –'

'No, no,' Margaret said, wagging her head. 'Can't contact Charles.'

'Why on earth not? Of course you'd avoid him normally, but this is different. You need him.'

'Can't contact Charles. Jack won't like it.' Margaret paused, to contemplate this last remark. 'Jack would ... not ... like it. There, that's better. Mustn't start slurring my words because I've had a drop of wine. Though, come to think of it, Rosalee, my darling, I drank most of that Burgundy. D'you know, I adore Burgundy? Never drink it generally. Makes me drop off to sleep. Puts on weight too. Dunno why. But then, if I'm not going to be in a job, doesn't matter if I turn into a plump housewife, does it?'

'Oh, come on, you're not going to be out of a job,

Margaret! Not if you ring Charles up and ask what he's got going.'

'Charlie is my darling ...' Margaret began to recite.

'Margaret, calm down –'

'I'm calm. Totally calm. Never felt calmer,' she shouted, quaffing her Drambuie. 'I hate this stuff, you know. Like drinking liquid toffee. So to counteract it I will drink my coffee.'

'Margaret, you're drunk.'

'Not-a-tall. Not-a-*tall*. I'm just slightly pissed,' she insisted loudly.

Heads were turning towards them in the restaurant. The professorial men at the next table looked pained. Drunken women, their glance said – nothing more offensive. All right for men to get drunk, but women, no.

'Poor old love,' Rosie said, reaching over and grabbing Margaret's hand. 'You're really in a state, aren't you? Come on, I'd better get you out of here before the management ejects us.'

'Haven't paid the bill, Rosie. Can't go without paying the bill. 'Sides, what's the hurry?' She gazed round the restaurant. 'Hey, what are you staring at? I'm talking to you!'

The professorial men quivered over their wafer-thin mints.

The head waiter appeared. 'Madam, can you get your friend out of here without further fuss? We aren't used to this kind of thing.'

'Neither is she,' Rosie said sharply, 'so don't be so snooty. Bring the bill, and then ask the doorman to call a taxi.'

'Certainly, madam.' His politeness was like ice. He withdrew, but attention was still directed towards their table by the other customers.

'You know what I think?' Margaret demanded.

'No, what, dear?'

'It's all part of a great design.' Margaret's voice was full of awe. 'Swings and roundabouts, yin and yang. Eh? Don't you think so?'

'I'm sure you're right. I just wish I knew what the point is. No, if you're going to have more coffee, let me pour it.' She took up the little pot and filled the demi-tasse. Margaret raised it with a hand that waved about in all directions. The coffee slopped out onto the Varon dress. She didn't appear to notice. Rosie felt a huge lump in her throat. How could this be happening? Margaret Durley, who had been so sure of herself, reduced to this helpless, maundering soul across the table.

The waiter scurried up with the bill. Rosie shoved her credit card at him. He hurried away and was back in no time. She shed currency notes on the little plate as a tip, pushed the credit card in her pocket, and went to Margaret's side of the table. 'Come on, my angel.'

'We going already? I thought we might have a party –'

'You've had all the party you need for today,' Rosie said. 'Come on.' She took one of Margaret's hands, pulled her to her feet, and put an arm around her. The waiter offered to take the other side. 'Don't you dare!' flashed Rosie.

He drew back as if she had hit him.

With Margaret heavy on her arm, she made her way to the door. A taxi was waiting, ticking loudly. This time she accepted the help of the doorman to get Margaret aboard. She gave the man some money then turned to the driver. 'She needs to go to Hebberwood Tower in Cheapside. Here.' She put a couple of notes into his hand. 'See she's okay, will you?'

'Right you are, miss.' He nodded in understanding and set off. Rosie stood under the canopy of Brogan's, watching it vanish. 'Damn!' she said. 'Damn, damn, damn!'

'Beg pardon, miss?' said the doorman.

117

'Nothing. Just a comment on the world in general, and women's place in it in particular.' She pulled the strap of her plastic handbag over her shoulder and set off at a smart walk towards her office.

No matter what Margaret might say, she was going to ring Charles Vernon.

Chapter Seven

The taxi driver became aware of tapping on the glass behind him. He slid it open, to hear his passenger say: 'I don't feel very well. Don't take me to my office, I'd rather go to my club.'

'I think that's very wise, miss,' he said, avuncular. Drunk ladies wouldn't be well received at a posh place like Hebberwood Tower. He took the address and decanted her outside the women's club, pausing to see if she could make it up the shallow steps to the entry. Then he drove off, shaking his head to himself.

Margaret smiled a hello at the receptionist on duty. This surprised the girl, who was new on the job. Margaret, however, took it for granted that it was Cynthia.

She went into the bar, feeling as if she were floating. 'Afternoon, Mrs Durley,' the barman said heartily. 'Haven't seen you for a while?'

'No, been busy. Gin and tonic, Harold.'

'One gin and tonic coming up.'

'Make it a double.' The wine had given her a thirst. She should really have asked for something long and cool, like a Pimms, but that took forever to concoct. She sat down at one of the little tables near the window and looked out onto the old paved courtyard with its tiny fountain in the shape of a boy holding aloft a conch shell. The sparkle of the water dazzled her.

Harold brought the drink. 'How are things, Mrs Durley?'

'Fine, Harold, fine. Cheers.' She took a large swallow. 'You might mix me another one to go down in search of this one.'

He frowned. Mrs Durley seldom had more than one drink, and then seldom anything as strong as a double gin. 'You sure?'

'Course I'm sure.' She glanced at the few women in the bar, most of them filling in time before going to some business appointment. In the corner was a club acquaintance whom she usually avoided like the plague, a known alcoholic who sponged on others for drinks and bored them with her problems. But today she needed anything that would blot out the emerging memory of the events in the restaurant. She seemed to remember creating a scene. Could it be true? Rather than think about it, she returned Judith Beardsley's smile and waved to her to join her.

They were still there when Harold closed the bar at four. Judith Beardsley said goodbye, having got three double whiskies out of Margaret, and walked carefully away to her next watering hole, of which she had many. Margaret, suddenly all at sea, looked up at Harold. 'You closing?'

'Only the bar screen, Mrs Durley. You sit there for a bit. Shall I ask the lounge waitress to bring you some coffee?'

'If you'd be so kin', Harold.'

'Sure thing, ma'am. 'He went away for his break, worried. He had four categories of 'ladies': the abstemious who spent very little in the bar, the dieters who asked him to give them tonic only when they asked for vodka or gin while entertaining guests, the ones who went on a spree once in a while when they had something to celebrate, and the alcos. It bothered him to find Mrs

Durley with an alco.

When the coffee came Margaret drank it, scalding her mouth. She knew from some obscure source that she needed to get it down, but not exactly why. After a while, feeling very wobbly, she went into the rest room and lay down on a chintz-covered chaise longue. She fell asleep almost at once.

When she woke she felt terrible. She got up very slowly and went into the ladies' powder room, to look at herself in the mirror. 'My God,' she said to herself, 'I look as green as a Marks and Sparks dress bag.' She glanced at her watch. It was six o'clock. What was she doing here? Why had she been asleep in the rest room? Clearly she had been drinking; her mouth tasted like a zinc sink and her stomach was queasy. But why? What on earth was she up to?

One thing was certain. She was in no condition to go back to the garage at Hebberwood Tower and claim her car. Still with no clear idea of what her actions had been so far today, she went to the reception desk. The unknown newcomer looked at her inquiringly.

'I ... er ... don't feel too good. I'd better have a room for the night.'

'Of course, Mrs –?'

'Durley, Margaret Durley.'

'You can have Room C on the second floor. Will you sign here?'

She did so.

'Been celebrating, eh?' the girl said.

'I ... er ... yes. I'll go up now.' She took the key. 'Have them send up some iced water and a pot of coffee, please.'

'Right away, Mrs Durley.'

In the bedroom she kicked off her shoes and lay down on the bed. The room swung about her. I'm drunk, she thought. Not as drunk as I was, but about a quarter seas over. Why did I do this to myself? I don't drink. Not like this.

A moment later she was rushing to the bathroom to be sick. She came back shuddering with reaction and self-disgust. Sick drunk! It had never happened to her before, not since one experience in her student days, when some idiots had taken her out for a pub crawl in her first term. The revulsion she had felt then had been her warning never to let it happen again. So why had she broken her rule?

The waitress came with the coffee and the iced water. She drank black coffee then water, black coffee then water, and by the end of the next hour felt she might live. She now had a head in which four tap dancers were outdoing Fred Astaire, but her stomach had calmed down and she wasn't dizzy.

Nearly seven o'clock. She must ring Jack to say she wouldn't be home. She could just say she didn't feel too good.

She picked up the bedside phone and asked the switchboard girl for the number. But the sound of her own voice scared her. It sounded weak, cracked. Jack would think she was dying.

'Never mind,' she said to the girl, and put the phone down. She'd wait a bit till she felt better, and then ring home.

She went downstairs. 'I'm going out for a breath of air,' she told the receptionist.

'Very good, Mrs Durley. Will you be wanting dinner when you come back?'

'God forbid!'

'Oh, that's all right then, only chef wanted to know how many meals to prepare.'

'Nothing for me, thanks. I might have a sandwich later.' But she hardly thought so. All she wanted was fresh air, solitude, and a return to normality.

The streets were almost silent when she went out. Traffic from the city towards the suburbs had almost ceased, and there were few night-time activities here. A few restaurants made a point of promoting their evening menus, but by seven o'clock most office staff had long since set off for home, and directors were either in lusher surroundings or at banquets in guildhalls. She walked up Ludgate Hill then through the turnings, across Queen Victoria Street, and down to the river at Painters Hall. Here everything was deserted. The blight of dockland had withered it, it was waiting to be brought back to new life. She walked along the river walk to the Mermaid, her head beginning to clear. The river was high. Occasionally a riverboat went by, the guide talking through his public address system, advising passengers to look to the right and see where Christopher Wren had lived so that he could watch St Paul's going up.

When she went through the underpass at Blackfriars there were two down-and-outs sitting against the tiled wall. One half-rose, holding out his hand to her. She hurried on, shivering. It wasn't that she was afraid of him; she was afraid of what he represented.

On the Embankment there were ragged men already bagging their benches for the night. The Silver Lady soup canteen would be along soon, to give them a little nourishment to see them through to next day's dawn. The sight distressed her. She crossed over to Carmelite Street and went past the School of Music. There was something on tonight; faint strains of madrigals floated out to her.

Suddenly she recalled the scene in the restaurant. Vague pictures formed and drifted away – the manager's face, disapproving, Rosie looking anxious.

Dear God! Had she really done that?

Of course not. It was something she'd dreamed during that sleep in the rest room. But what on earth had she been doing at her club? Why hadn't she gone back to the office? She'd had lunch with Rosie, that much she remembered clearly. She'd been going to tell Rosie her news.

Her news. Now she remembered.

She began walking very fast, to get away from the recollection. But it wouldn't be left behind. She'd had a letter this morning rejecting her application for the job with Lepham Properties.

It all came rushing back, overwhelming her. She stopped, leaned against the front of a closed shop. She felt very cold.

After some moments she got the better of it. She pulled herself erect in the deserted street and looked about. It was so lonely here, so forlorn. She needed to be where there were people, lights, activity.

She hurried through the serenity of the Temple to come out at the top of the Strand. But even there, though it had traffic running through it and pedestrians moving about, there was little gaiety. Perhaps the market in Covent Garden ...

She was on her way there when a figure sprang out at her from a doorway. In the failing light she was aware of an arm flashing out towards her. She gave a scream of alarm, and two people about to get into a car paused and looked round. Her attacker grabbed at her handbag. Foolishly, she hung on. He swung her back and forth to make her let go. Her shoulder hit the wall, her pearl earring came off and went rolling away on the pavement.

'Hi!' called the man at the car, and started towards her.

The mugger let go her bag, swore crudely at her, and ran off. Margaret sagged against the wall she had hit. The two men were hurrying towards her.

'Good gracious, what a thing!' said one. 'You all right, my love?'

124

'Yes ... thanks ... no harm done.'

'Get your handbag, did he?'

'No. I hung on.'

'Shouldn't have done that. Police say you should let it go. Still, all right this time. Help her, Johnny, she's all shook up.'

They got her to her feet, asked her where she was going and when she said she'd take a taxi to her club, they wouldn't hear of it. 'We're just going out,' said Johnny. 'We'll take you –'

'But it'll be out of your way –'

'Not a bit, what's it matter? Come on, my love, in you get. Dear dear, you've lost an earring. Look for it, Claude.'

'No, it doesn't matter. Please don't bother.'

'Hang on, it can't have gone far ...' Claude moved about the pavement and came back with it. 'There, all as good as new, eh?' He looked at her appreciatively. 'That's a super dress. Jean Muir?'

'No, it's Varon.'

'Oh, well, off we go.'

They saw her to the club entrance, right up the steps to the door. They looked at the place with amusement. 'Ladies' club, eh? Posh, isn't it?'

'Thank you very, very much,' she said, pressing Johnny's hand. 'You've been so kind.'

'That's us, isn't it, Claude. Well, goodnight, my love. Hot bath and two aspirins, eh? See you.'

They went, waving farewells. She turned into the foyer of the club. A figure started up from a chair. 'Margaret!'

It was her husband.

'Where have you been?' he exclaimed, seizing her by the shoulders. 'I've been going crazy worrying about you!'

'Jack! I was going to ring you, really I was! I wasn't

trying to keep anything from you –'

'Hey, hang on, hang on – I'm not accusing you. I was just worried, that's all.'

The receptionist was watching all this with interest. Jack couldn't have cared less, but Margaret felt herself stiffen under the scrutiny. 'Let's go up to my room,' she said. 'I engaged one because I didn't feel fit enough to drive home.'

'Good thinking,' Jack said, and putting his arm around her, went slowly up the stairs to the second floor. It exhausted her, that climb, although it consisted of only two flights of fifteen steps. She unlocked the door. They went in. She sank down on the side of one of the twin beds.

Now Jack was able to take a good look at her. 'What's happened to you?' he demanded. 'You look . . . battered.'

She glanced down at herself. There was dust and grit on her Jean Varon dress, a run in her tights, her hair was all over the place. One of her expensive shoes was badly scuffed along one side.

'It's nothing, some thug tried to get my handbag –'

'Margaret! Where and when was this?' He swooped on the bedside telephone.

'No, don't bother,' she said. 'I didn't get a look at him except to say he was young and white. It was in a turning off the Strand about ten minutes ago. Don't ring the police, Jack –'

'But we ought to. They may be able to pick him up by just telling a patrol to keep its eyes –'

'No, I can't,' she said, and heard the childishness in her tone. She took a grip on herself. 'I'm too tired, too much has happened today. I can't go through an interview with the police.'

'But they wouldn't be –'

'I don't care what they'd be. I just haven't the energy for it.'

126

For a long moment he stood with the receiver in his hand. The switchboard girl could be heard saying. 'Yes? Caller? Yes?'

He said into it, 'Sorry,' and replaced the receiver.

Then he came round the bed to her. He took off her shoes, took her handbag from her, took the pear clips from ears, smoothed back her rumpled hair, and then lifted her feet on to the bed. He put pillows behind her. It was like the opening moves in love-making, often made before, but this time there was only gentleness and nursemaid-like kindness in his touch.

He took the small armchair and pulled it close to the bed. He sat down. 'Now,' he said, 'tell me.'

'I meant to explain it all to you when I got back from the walk. I needed it to clear my head –'

He shook his head impatiently. 'Don't bother. I know you didn't get the Lepham job.'

She gasped. 'How could you know that?'

'Lena rang me. When you hadn't come back from lunch by about four o'clock she took it you'd gone home – and she didn't blame you if you had, she declared. When I said you hadn't turned up, she was a bit worried but said you might still be on your way. Calculating that if you'd set off about three, after lunching with Rosie, I thought you'd be home by four-thirty. When you didn't show, I rang to ask Lena to see if your car was still in the garage.'

'I should have got in touch with Lena,' she murmured. 'Only –'

'Never mind for the moment. I'll just finish my side of it.' He sighed. 'I got into a bit of a flurry, I don't mind admitting. By then it was six. I rang some of your friends. I rang Rosie, and she said you were taking the job failure very badly –'

'To put it mildly,' murmured Margaret.

'Well, precious, it dispelled one anxiety – at least I

127

didn't have to imagine you mangled under a bus. By what I think was a fine piece of reasoning I reckoned you'd go somewhere to get over the lunch thing, and rang the club. They said yes, you were here – that little twit on the reception desk doesn't seem old enough to know whether someone's suffering or not. But she did say you had been rather quiet, and had gone out on foot.' He paused. 'That nice old guy in the bar said you were in a bad way, and he'd noticed you walking towards the river. I was ... worried.'

She looked at him. It was true, he was pale under his tan and his freedom-fighter beard. 'You didn't think I'd decided to jump in?'

'Don't shrug it off like that, Meg. I know you. I know how hard you are on yourself. I thought you'd come to the conclusion you couldn't face all the diminution you've been undergoing.'

'The Incredible Shrinking Woman,' Margaret murmured.

'I don't see you like that. You're still the same lovely size and shape you ever were.'

'If only other people had your strange view of me ...' She lay back on the pillows, sighing. 'I made a complete fool of myself at Brogan's, I think.'

'You mean you got drunk. It's no big deal, Meg. Perhaps you should do it more often.'

'No,' she said with a shudder, 'I feel awful. I've still got a headache.'

He found the pitcher with the remains of the iced water. He poured some and brought it to her. He produced a new packet of aspirins from the pocket of his down jacket. He tipped out two, and gave them to her. She took them obediently.

'What's happened about Laurie?' she inquired, when they had gone down.

'I couldn't get a sitter. That took up a lot of damned

silly telephone calls. In the end I asked Patty Cooper-Watts to take him while I dashed up. He'll sleep through with their kids – I'll fetch him in the morning.'

'Poor Laurie, handed around like a parcel –'

'Nonsense, he loved it – a great adventure.'

'What did you tell Patty?'

'Just that you'd been taken rather poorly and I was going up to make sure all was well. Don't worry, I didn't tell her you'd tied on a snootful.'

'She's the last person I'd want to hear of it. She's so . . . perfect as a wife and mother.'

'Never mind about Patty Cooper-Watts. What about you? What do you want to do? Shall I drive you home?'

She looked at her watch. It was nine-ish. By the time they got home it would be ten-thirty-ish. In between those two points there was the drive, and her stomach was so uneasy she felt sure she'd be car sick. Never mind the headache which was still bumping against the inside of her forehead.

'I'd rather sleep here, I think,' she said. 'I feel a bit fragile.'

'That's how you look. Well, okay. Can I have your promise that you'll have at least a bite to eat before you settle down for the night? You need it, to help fight off the after-effects –'

'You're going?'

He was surprised. 'Well, I thought . . . This is a ladies' club.'

'But we do have married members.' She gestured at the other twin bed. 'Of course, intended only for the most chaste of married couples.'

'Hm,' said Jack. He seemed to be suppressing a grin. 'Well, all right, if you feel it would be a comfort to you, I'll sleep in the other bed.'

'I'll just ring down and book you in,' she said. He handed her the phone and she made the call. Then she asked for the kitchen. 'What would you like to eat?' she asked.

'What can they provide?'

'In the rooms, only soup, sandwiches, cake or biscuits.'

'Let's have a couple of rounds of sandwiches. I suppose it's too much to hope they'll have wholemeal bread?' Jack prided himself on his bread-making. He was to some extent a devotee of natural foods.

'Or we could go down to the dining room – dinner will be over but they serve things like omelettes and hamburgers up to ten o'clock.'

'Do you want to?'

She shook her head.

'Okay, let's have sandwiches and – you oughtn't to have coffee. Will they provide hot milk?'

'Oh yes.'

While they waited for the food, she bathed. She stretched out in the hot water thinking that this had been a day she would never forget, but would prefer to. She had made every mistake in the book – she, who prided herself on sensible decisions. She was really angry with herself for falling prey to a mugger. She had never thought of herself as the victim type before. But who knew what desperation had driven the young man who'd grabbed her bag? Desperation, yes. She knew about that now. Not until today had she experienced it. Now she understood.

When she came out of the bathroom the food had come. Jack was already eating: 'Sorry, love, but I'm famished – I missed dinner entirely.'

'Go ahead.' She watched him making short work of the sandwiches. She tried to drink the hot milk, but it had formed a skin over its surface and she found it nauseating. But with Jack's watchful eye upon her she swallowed some, and once the skin had stuck to the side

130

of the beaker it was easier.

She got into bed. Jack kicked off his shoes and leaned back in his chair. They switched on the radio and listened to the ten o'clock news. The usual account of disaster, terrorism, mayhem and economic downturns. She turned her head away on the pillows. By and by she began to feel drowsy. She let herself sink towards sleep.

A little later the radio was switched off. She heard the shower running. Then Jack tiptoed in, switched off the light. She heard him turn back the covers of the other bed.

'Jack,' she whispered.

'Yes?'

'Don't sleep there. Come in with me.'

He leaned over her. 'You want me to?'

'I mean ... Just hold me, Jack, that's all. Hold me.'

'Move over.' He slipped in beside her. She felt his naked body against hers. He put his arms about her and they fitted together like two cups in a crockery cupboard. She felt his wiry beard against the back of her neck. She snuggled against him.

In the early hours of the June morning they turned to each other and made love. Desperation had been done away with. She had plenty to live and strive for.

Chapter Eight

The time had inevitably come when the Durleys had to discuss their situation with Margaret's parents. To defend herself against the first outcry, Margaret had written to them, stating the case truthfully yet with optimism. She suggested she and Jack should visit the following weekend: they had avoided a meeting until now by first sending the presents they had brought back from Mombasa and then the holiday snaps. She posted the letter with a first class stamp and, as Jack had predicted, next day at about half-past nine Margaret's office phone rang.

'Darling!' cried her mother. 'How can such a thing have happened? What did you do to offend the directors?'

'Nothing, Mother. As I explained, it's an economy campaign – '

'But why should they pick on you? You must have done *something* – '

This was Stan Cooper-Watts' dictum. She bit back the reply about her mother knowing nothing about the present financial climate. Instead she said: 'I can't discuss it now, Mother. It's not convenient – I'm busy on something at the moment. We'll talk it all over at the weekend.'

Mrs Grant had to accept this. But she comforted herself by ringing Jack and telling him she thought it extraordinary, and crossquestioning him as to what Margaret had done to deserve dismissal.

'She hasn't done anything. It's not just her, it's the whole department, Mother-in-law. Nobody would demolish a whole department just because one person had blotted their copybook.'

That seemed so logical that Mrs Grant was silenced momentarily. She went off on a different tack. 'But they've been so inconsiderate! It's such short notice – '

'Actually, not,' Jack put in. 'She's been on three months' notice.'

There was a pause. 'And never told us?' she said in a choked voice.

Jack understood the hurt she was feeling. He said gently: 'Listen, love, it was because she dreaded the kind of hoo-ha you've just been making. Try to be cool about this. Nothing's to be gained by cross-questioning her about why it happened and how they dared. It's a fact of commercial life – things are bad and staff has to go. It's been a terrific blow to her – '

'Of course, I know that. And so unfair!'

'Yeah,' said Jack. Fair, unfair ... In the five years since his collapse, Jack had learned a new philosophy. He had come to accept that life was just to be lived, that was all. Making judgements about worthiness and justice got you nowhere. 'What Margaret needs now,' he said, 'is calm. Everything is hard enough for her out there in the business world. She doesn't want to be harangued – '

'As if I would do that, Jack! What an accusation!'

'I'm sorry. I say it because I got mad at her when I found out what had happened. She kept it from me for a while, because she couldn't bring herself to tell me.'

'Oh.' The last thing Mrs Grant wanted was to behave in any way like Jack Durley. She decided on dignified understanding. 'Of course the poor girl is entitled to handle her life the way she thinks fit. We'll talk it over when you come.'

'Okay. But, Mother-in-law – ?'

'Yes?'

'Keep it low key, eh? Support, not indignation.'

'I think I know how to be a help to my own daughter, Jack.' She broke the connection.

Jack groaned to himself. He'd offended her. He could only hope that her husband, a less abrasive character, would soothe her down. But he understood what a blow this was to both of them. Their clever, successful daughter, suddenly reduced to a mere member of the unemployed. It had to be *somebody's* fault.

'And probably mine,' he said to himself. Then he put it out of his mind and went back to the vacuum cleaner.

The weekend was as bad as they feared, and perhaps worse. Laurie never enjoyed visits with his grandparents – their garden was a lawn with neat edges and a border of bedding plants, and woe betide him if he so much as bent a leaf of grass. He therefore played mostly on the strip of ground in front of the garage, which got boring quite soon even with his own toys to keep him company. He therefore liked to clamber all over his father, and this made conversation difficult.

'Goodness me, can't you put the boy down?' Mr Grant inquired at one point with irritation. 'There's no discipline!'

Jack shrugged. If they had provided anything else for Laurie to do, there would have been no problem. He sought in his pockets, found a piece of string off a parcel, and persuaded the child to sit on the floor at his feet to experiment with it. The fact that he eventually tied his grandfather's chair to the leg of the television set wasn't well received.

After lunch it was easier; Jack put Laurie on the spare bed for his nap. Luckily he fell asleep at once. Jack went downstairs, hearing Mrs Grant talking to Margaret as they washed up. Give her her due, her tone was quiet and reasonable.

Mr Grant was waiting for Jack in the livingroom. He had his pipe going, which offended his son-in-law, though he made no remark. He himself had given up smoking on doctor's advice after the ulcer, and the smell of nicotine now made him queasy. But he wasn't here to make himself more unpopular with his in-laws.

It became apparent to him that Mrs Grant had left the way clear for her husband to have a man-to-man talk with Jack. 'Now look here, my boy,' said Arthur Grant, 'we've got to come to grips with this problem. We can't just sit about waiting for things to come right.'

'But Margaret isn't doing that. She's looking for a job. She explained to you about the head-hunting agencies, and having her friends on the alert – '

'I didn't mean that. I meant, what are you doing?'

'Me?'

'Dammit, you're the head of the family – '

'Am I?' Jack said, irritated. 'I thought Margaret and I were an equal partnership.'

'Oh, that's what you say. You know as well as I do that when it comes to the crunch, men always have to take the lead.'

'Only if they know which direction to start off in, Father-in-law. At the present moment, I've no idea.'

'Surely it's obvious?'

'Not to me.'

'Good God, man, you've got to get a job.'

Jack studied the older man. He'd always liked him better than Mrs Grant, who was inclined to be bossy and talkative. Arthur generally said less and seemed more tolerant of the way the world was going. This sudden outbreak of 'head-of-the-householdism' was surprising.

'At what, precisely?'

'Well, in the film industry, of course. I always understood from Margaret that you were a bit of a genius at special effects, and though I never quite understood the workings of it, certainly the films that had your stuff in it always seemed very convincing.'

'So you think I should go back to films?'

'It's the only thing to do.'

'Uh-huh. Have you noticed many films being made in Britain these days that demand skills like mine?'

'No, but there's television – '

'It's hellish hard to get into television. The trade unions are very tough. But I wouldn't want to, in any case. It's a rat race.'

'I don't see that it's a case of what you want or what you don't want. It's your duty. And if you don't want to go into television, you certainly must have contacts in the film world who could get you something.'

'Doing what?'

'You're being obstructive, Jack. There have been tremendously successful films in the past few years with all the special effects done by British technicians. All those space epics – '

'Mr Grant, my abilities don't lie in that direction. I was the guy who could produce a Turkish castle, or a medieval-city-seen-from-above – or even a pomegranate orchard for Sinbad. I don't know peanuts about space ships, and they wouldn't even give me an interview for that kind of work.'

His father-in-law brought his iron grey brows together and glared at him. 'It's my opinion you just don't want to try! You've grown to love this indolent life you lead!'

'Indolent?' Jack was about to expatiate on the work involved in keeping a large house and its grounds, caring for a lively three year old, and trying to do some creative shaping to a block of unresponsive wood. But he held his tongue. He knew it would sound womanish to Mr Grant, and he already understood how low the other man held him.

After a moment he said: 'What you're really saying is that I should get off my backside and get some kind of a job. Any kind of job, right?'

'We-ell ... ' The older man was a little shaken at the directness. 'Well, yes. It's just no right that you should let Margaret suffer like this.'

'It's not me "letting" her do anything. Margaret is a person in her own right, she decided a long time ago that she wanted to go all out for a career in the business world. That's still her aim. She doesn't want to be domesticated – and if that's what you have in mind, that I should go out to work while she stays at home, just try it on her. I think you'll find she's not in favour.'

'Oh, you've got her brainwashed – !'

'Me?' Jack was truly astounded. He sat staring at his father-in-law.

'You batten on her – '

'Now look here – '

'It's time you took on your responsibilities like a man! I don't understand you at all, shirking the basic requirements of your marriage!'

The raised voices had brought Margaret from the kitchen. 'What's going on?' she demanded.

'This is man's talk, Margaret. You leave this to me – '

'What have you been saying, Father?' She looked from one to the other, saw the flush of indignation in the older man's cheeks and Jack's startled, amazed expression. 'What have you been trying to do?'

'I've just been telling him what he ought to have known for himself. It's time you stopped letting him hoodwink you, with this rubbish about being a sculptor! Who on earth makes a living at sculpture – ?'

'Henry Moore?' Jack put in. 'Elizabeth Frink?'

137

'Jack,' Margaret warned. This was no time for comedy. She looked squarely at her indignant father. 'I know you meant well, Father, but I prefer to run my life for myself, thank you. I don't want Jack to give up what he's doing – ?'

'But he isn't doing anything! He's sponging on you – '

'So you think I'm a complete fool, is that it? No sense, no ability to see what's going on?'

'No, of course not – '

'I live with Jack, you know. I know how hard he works, even if you don't. That house of ours is no sinecure – '

'But Margaret,' wailed her mother from behind her, 'it's no sort of work for a *man*!'

There was a silence, and then Jack got up. He looked tall and fit and self-contained. 'That's it,' he said. 'That's what this is all about. Margaret and I have a marriage you can't understand so when something goes wrong outside it, your first instinct is to try to change that.'

'I certainly think it's up to you to – '

'Jack and I know what our obligations are, Father. We talked it all over at the outset, and I'd remind you that it was my idea, that I was the one who put it to Jack about opting out. I – '

'Oh, you can say that, but you can't tell me you would have wanted to reverse the normal way of things. Your mother and I didn't bring you up to be a hippie.'

'A hippie?' Jack gave a shout of laughter. 'My God, you don't even know what the word means. Margaret a hippie? Look at her.'

Mr and Mrs Grant did so. And certainly in her Vanderbilt jeans and loose silk shirt, with her hair tied back in a matching silk scarf, she seemed more like a Monaco holidaymaker than a hippie. Mr Grant looked confused and puffed hard on his pipe, while his wife sorted out her thoughts to start again.

'Look here, darling, you know we're anxious and we want to help. We talked it all over, your father and I, and there were certain things we felt had to be said. One of them was that Jack must pull his weight.'

'But he does, Mother. That's what you don't understand. He's running the house singlehanded and looking after the grounds. He's got Laurie to take care of. When I come home, there's always a good meal and –'

'Instead of skulking about doing woman's work, he ought to be out there earning your living for you!'

'Mother, Jack would earn a lot less than I do, even if he could get a job. Use your head.' Her tone was crisp and cool. She had stopped just short of saying, 'Don't be an idiot.'

Her mother looked at her with surprised dismay. She'd never heard that tone from her daughter before.

'We only want to do what is best for you, dear – '

'The best thing you can do is leave us alone to sort this out for ourselves. It's our problem, no one else can do anything with it.'

'But we have a right to put you wise – '

'If it were true that you knew what was wise, I'd be grateful for your help. But you're ... you're ...'

'You're saying we're just being interfering,' her father burst out.

Jack leaned down and touched him on the shoulder. 'I thought you and Mrs Grant were going to be calm and supportive?' The quiet words were not an accusation, but there was reproach in them.

'But if we see you making a mess of things – '

'We're not, Father. It's the world outside that's in a mess. Jack and I have a good life, a good marriage. It's not going to improve things if we turn it all upside down just because you and Mother think it's wrong. In fact, quite the reverse.'

A tense, unforgiving silence held them all.

'I think,' Jack said, 'that we should all back off. What about you and me going for a walk, Margaret? We haven't had any exercise today so far.'

'Good idea.'

He turned to his in-laws. 'Laurie will wake up in about a quarter of an hour. He likes a little drink of fruit juice when he wakes.'

'Of course, you'd be an expert on *that*!'

'You mean it would be better if I didn't know what suited my own son? Come on, Father-in-law, get yourself together.' He nodded at Margaret, and they went out.

Outdoors the formal little garden was standing up to a cool breeze, but the June sun was bright. They walked down the path and out through the gate, closing it carefully in case any venturesome dog should get in and lift his leg against one of Mr Grant's precious trees.

They walked for a time without speaking. Then Margaret took Jack's arm.

'Who was it said that the family is a battleground?'

'Sigmund, I think. It sounds like him.'

'Well, he was right. I apologise, Jack.'

'Hm ... I must say I'm surprised at how much they actually dislike me. I knew they thought I was a queer fish, but I never thought they saw me as a leech.'

'Is a leech a fish?'

'Zoology apart, what are we going to do?'

'About what?'

'About staying overnight as we intended. I don't think it's going to be very enjoyable, do you?'

She shook her head. They had left the outer rim of the cathedral city behind them and were now out among fields. They chose a lane beside ripening barley, with old chestnuts shading the hedgerow. By and by they came to a gate. They paused to lean on it and look at the landscape.

140

'Do I batten on you, Margaret?'

'Do you what?'

'Batten. Am I living off your immoral earnings, and kidding myself about the sculpting?'

She turned to lean her back on the gate while she studied him. She took her time about answering him.

'Jack, let's leave the sculpting out of it for the moment. Let's go back to the time we made our choice. You nearly died, remember?'

He made a non-commital movement of the head.

'Yes you did, you lost pints and pints of blood and there were all sorts of complications with pneumonia. Your specialist told me that you didn't have the temperament for intense competition. You'd been living against your grain from the time you went into the film industry. You were smoking sixty cigarettes a day and drinking too much. Right?'

'Yes, right, okay. We've established I was a wreck. Does that justify my living off what you earn?'

'But if you didn't, we'd have to pay someone to run the house for us, wouldn't we? We'd need a gardener too, for that expanse of ground would be a wilderness otherwise. Of course, on the other hand, we could let it go to rack and ruin and send Laurie to be minded from eight in the morning till seven in the evening – the only other alternative is that I give up work and stay at home while you earn our total income.'

'Well, perhaps I should do that.'

'At what? The film industry is just as much in trouble as everything else. And don't say TV because their advertising revenue has sunk alarmingly. They're not going to hire on any new special effects men, even if your kind of effects were what they wanted.'

'But I do have a degree in arts, Megs. Perhaps I could get a job teaching?'

'Oh, Jack! Do you think there aren't any unemployed

141

teachers? No newly qualified graduates looking for jobs?'

'You mean, who needs a thirty-eight-year-old seven stone weakling?'

She patted him on the arm. 'Don't downgrade yourself. But to go back to the main point, how much do you think you could earn if you got a job of any kind?'

'Dunno.' He was never good with figures, never had been even when gainfully employed. 'Six thousand? Eight?'

'That's a lot less than what I've been bringing in. You see? It makes no sense to throw everything overboard and start again with the oldfashioned style of partnership.'

He nodded, but sighed. 'All the same, your Pa made me feel a kind of effeminate gigolo.'

'They don't understand, Jack. They never have and they never will.'

'You're sure we're right and they're wrong?'

'Absolutely.'

She looked up at him with earnestness. She looked about seventeen. He took her in his arms and kissed her with a kind of passionate gratitude. She responded eagerly, but they broke apart as a car with picnickers nosed into the verge to settle for the thermos of tea and sandwiches.

They walked on briskly for a mile or so. Then he murmured: 'Well, what about tonight? Are we staying over or not?'

'I think we should beg off. No matter what I say to them, and what they promise, they're not going to be able to stay calm about this. It's better if we go home.'

'They'll say it's my fault, that I don't want them taking the blinkers off – '

'It doesn't matter what they say,' she burst out with sudden passion. 'Damn it, Jack Durley, you're my husband! I'm not going to let them behave like this to you!'

'Yeah,' he sighed. 'There you go. I wonder if I really am an effeminate gigolo?'

She began to laugh, and he joined in. When they had recovered she said: 'All right, you tell them where they get off. I don't care who does it so long as it's understood that I'm not going to retire to the kitchen just because my parents would prefer it, and you're not going to take a job as a scene-shifter or a floor-sweeper just to put your macho image right.'

They went back to Florinda, which was the name of the house. Mrs Grant had afternoon tea ready. Laurie was playing with the cake tins from the kitchen cupboard. Mr Grant was stooping over his lobelia and alyssum.

The little boy came charging into the hall to wrap himself round his father's leg. 'I built a tower with tins, Daddy! I built a big tower and it all fell down! Will you help me to build it again?'

'We'll have tea first, eh? How'd you like a piece of Grannie's cake?' He took Laurie's hand and went with him into the sittingroom.

There afternoon tea sparkled – lace-edged cloth, little forks for eating the strawberry gateau, silver tea service. The little boy was given milk and a piece of cake, though with many anxious glances from his grandmother towards her speckless carpet. Normally Jack would have done all he could to prevent the child from putting sticky fingers on the carpet or the furniture, but today he was feeling unforgiving towards his in-laws. Let Laurie put fingerprints on the washed Chinese flowers. The hell with them!

Mr Grant came in. They heard him washing his hands in the kitchen. When he joined them Margaret glanced at Jack. Accepting the lead, he said: 'Meg and I have had

143

a talk. We think it would be better if we went home after tea.'

'But... but...'

'We feel you won't be able to prevent yourselves saying more of the kind of thing we've heard already. And frankly, I'm not keen on standing for any more.'

Mr and Mrs Grant eyed him in blank amazement. It was clear they could think of nothing to say.

Jack went on: 'I'm not keen on being held up as an example of cringing opportunism. We've talked it over and we'd prefer to go home.'

'You can't do that!' wailed Mrs Grant. 'I've got a leg of pork – '

'Eat it in good health,' Jack said. 'But we'd rather give it a miss.'

'If you've talked my daughter into – '

'Okay, okay, let's get this clear, Mr Grant,' he interrupted in a hard voice. 'You say one more word like that to me, and I'll give you a bloody nose. Am I clear? Do you read me?' And as the older man went pale and shrank a little in his chair, he went on in a kinder tone: 'Ah, why can't you learn to *accept*? Why do you want everything to fit into your particular kind of pattern? Has it ever occurred to you to stop and wonder if you could be wrong?'

'What's so wrong about wanting what's best for our daughter?' Arthur Grant protested. 'You don't understand – '

'I think I do. I was a career man myself once, you know. I ran the race, I kept my eye on the winning post. There was a time when it was part of my outlook to get girls into bed with me, as many as possible – ah, yes, you blush to hear it but it's part of the success image. On looking back now, I think I must have been a right bastard. That's behind me, and so are other dumb ideas, such as that the only way to prove you're a man is to be out there in the market place battling for attention. The way we live suits Meg and me – '

'But it isn't going to work now, is it? I mean, face it, man – her job has folded – '

'I'll get another,' Margaret said, taking part at last. 'I will, you know. It isn't the end of the world that I've had to leave Hebberwood. Perhaps it'll all turn out for the best – when one door closes another door opens.'

Hearing at last these sweet old clichés, her parents began to relax. Shaking their heads, they sipped their tea. They tried to argue their visitors into sticking with the original arrangements but Jack was adamant. 'Sorry, Father-in-law, but you've blotted your copy-book with me. I think we need a bit of distance between us for a while.'

There was nothing to be done. Mr Grant, seeing he had made a hash of his intervention, fell silent. But as they loaded themselves and their overnight bag into the Metro, Mrs Grant burst into tears.

'Say what you like!' she exclaimed. 'The way you live isn't natural! And if you were any kind of a man at all, Jack Durley, you'd never have let things get to this state!'

'Goodbye, Mother-in-law. Goodbye, Father-in-law.' Jack let in the clutch and drove off. Laurie, aghast at seeing Grannie cry, twisted round in his straps in the back seat and wailed in sympathy. 'Dry up, Laurie,' said Jack in a loud voice, 'if you're not on my side, I don't know who the hell is!'

Chapter Nine

Margaret's leave-taking at Hebberwood Tower was an unhappy occasion. There was no presentation of any kind, as when she left Paracelsus, there was no little party at which she offered thanks for gifts from her friends, there were even very few cards wishing her well.

Those she'd considered as 'her' people were either in other jobs and couldn't take time off, or out of work and unwilling to spend money on fares. Jim Tares rang to wish her luck, and Patrick Hyde wrote a note to tell her he had enjoyed working with her even though it meant he'd given up a safe berth. That depressed her more than almost anything: she was aware that she had put him on the scrap heap, for at his age he would hardly find anything else.

She was called to the Salaries department and given an envelope containing details of her PAYE position. The Chairman of the Board offered her a second, which contained a cheque for such monies as were owing to her in view of her untaken holiday allowance plus the ex gratia payment. He offered her a drink, which she accepted. Her stomach almost rejected it but she swallowed it in the end. On her way out through his secretary's office, Constance jumped up. 'Oh, Mrs Durley, did he remember to ask for the keys and the papers for the car?'

'I'll leave them on my desk,' Margaret said.

At the end of the day she went down in the lift with the rest of the underlings, out of the front door instead of down to the underground garage. Jack was waiting for her outside. They had arranged to go out for a meal and to the movies to see a well-reviewed comedy.

In the middle of the film, Margaret found tears streaming down her face. She tried not to let them show, but in the end Jack turned his head. 'Come on,' he said. They drove home in their Renault, Margaret leaning against his shoulder, utterly silent. Their babysitter was surprised by their early arrival – very surprised indeed, since she was found in the master bedroom trying Margaret's cosmetics. Neither of them had the emotional energy to be angry with her. Jack paid her and drove her home without comment, although the girl kept trying to excuse herself.

Margaret sat by the dressing-table looking at the expensive array. Arpège, pure carnation from Hathaways, creams and lotions from Clinique, lipsticks from Charles of the Ritz and Galitzine . . . They would have to last her a long time because she didn't think she would be able to replace them until she had another job.

Tomorrow she would have to go into Brighton to 'sign on'. The mere thought chilled and diminished her. Then she would have to go to London and put herself on the Professional and Executive register. She was hardly likely to find the sort of job she wanted in Brighton. She had decided that, for the moment, it would help her to live more easily if no one in and around Ladhurst knew what had happened. She would take the London train each morning.

Jack had argued against this idea quite vigorously. He had given up self-importance a long time ago, when the specialists told him he was destroying himself with the need to be up-front in the film industry. Since then he had painstakingly taught himself to be honest with himself, so that now when Margaret insisted she didn't want anyone to know she was jobless, he thought it wrong.

But she argued so strongly that he began to understand that self-image was still terribly important to her. For so long now, she had been 'a success'. It was what she *was*, and how people saw her – Margaret Durley, successful careerwoman. It dawned on Jack that if she no longer saw that 'success' reflected in the eyes of others, it would diminish her. And just at the moment she didn't need to be made to feel any smaller. Finding herself out of a job was enough to bear. The loss of respect would be too much.

For once, he felt protective and almost indulgent towards his wife. Poor darling, he thought. If it means so much to her, I'll go along with it. After all, it's only another kind of play-acting. We do it all the time, pretending we believe everything our neighbours and friends tell us about themselves – that they're genuinely interested in art instead of in the prestige they see in it, that they have inside knowledge in politics or finance . . . We're all image-builders. If Margaret's self-image is so important to her, who am I to take it away from her? We'll play out her game.

It nearly came to grief the first morning when she was seen getting into a second class carriage by an acquaintance, a lawyer, who made the trip every day. But he, of course, travelled first class.

'Why, Mrs Durley! You're getting in at the wrong place,' he said, and shepherded her along the platform to a first class carriage.

She could do nothing else but accompany him. She felt her face flame into shameful colour but said nothing. Luckily, no guard came along to examine tickets.

But it was lesson one in deceiving the populace. She must travel later, when her business friends wouldn't be around. She didn't stop to wonder why she found it so necessary to maintain such a front.

Now Margaret could give all her time to job-hunting. Executive Selection Limited, prodded during her last week at Hebberwood, came up with several openings. She was amazed at the ineptitude of the selection. She had thought they would be more reliable than the other agencies she had dealt with. She had three interviews, at each of which she soon sensed that they thought her over-qualified. What they seemed to want was an elegant private secretary or personal assistant. The fourth firm wrote to her putting her off; on examining the form sent to them by ESL giving what they called 'her details' they considered that after all it would not be useful to see her and, wishing to save her time and trouble, they thought it best to cancel. That warned her she'd better not hope for much through ESL.

She planned her own campaign. She used her club as her base. The subscription, paid by Hebberwood, was valid until January 1st, but after that she wouldn't be able to afford it unless something very good came up. Meanwhile, there was no sense in not taking advantage of its facilities. Because it was a club for businesswomen, it had some businesslike addenda; a Ceefax machine, Telex facilities, a good bank of telephones, and an answering service available to members without extra charge. Moreover, as the heat of August came on, she was grateful for its changing room and shower; she got hot and sticky in the crowded train with its grimy windows and lack of air.

The financial situation began to worry her dreadfully. Money was running out much faster than she had anticipated. They had economised in every possible way, but certain things had to be retained. The Renault, for instance. Jack needed it to get anywhere. He ferried her into Ladhurst to catch the London train and brought her back each evening. On the morning trip he fitted in the shopping and delivered Laurie to his play-group. He had to use it again to bring Laurie home at midday – he himself could have walked it, but three miles was too far to expect a three-year-old to walk and carrying him on his shoulders was just a bit too much.

They had cut down the grocery bills considerably. Jack's vegetable garden supplied all their needs for fresh foods, and for the meat course they mostly had chicken or an omelette. Jack didn't mind any of this; what he ate wasn't important to him so long as it was fresh and well-presented, and he had ideas about leading them over to vegetarianism in the end. He had taken up yoga and meditation to help his recovery from the stress of his illness, and shared the view that pulses and legumes were better than red meat if one could just turn away from it. He knew that Margaret emphatically didn't share this idea: there was nothing she liked better than a good steak. But good steak is for those who can afford it.

As to wine, which they both enjoyed, they would eke out what they had in the cellar. When that was gone, Jack thought he might try his hand at wine-making. He knew from the experience of friends that it was a fiddly, time-consuming business, but he rather liked the idea. Closer to the good earth, somehow, than buying bottles in a shop.

So they had economised as far as they could. But bills kept coming in, and Margaret, doing sums with her digital calculator, began to be frightened. She tried to convey to her husband how bad it looked for the coming months, but he couldn't quite believe her. There was still money in the joint account when he wrote a cheque in the supermarket, wasn't there? They weren't on the breadline yet.

'You don't understand,' she protested. 'Wait till the heating bills start coming in when it gets colder. And the rates, Jack. And if rail fares go up again ...'

'Why do you get yourself in such a fret, love? Why can't you relax?'

'Because I can see our financial situation heading straight down the drain, that's why –'

'Look, Margaret, if I could only persuade you to do a few exercises, learn the relaxation technique –'

'Oh, Jack!' She flung down her pencil in frustration. 'I could learn to be relaxed as a jellyfish, but that wouldn't make any difference to the fact that not enough money is coming in – nothing like enough!'

'Well, it would mean you'd take it less to heart,' he suggested.

'You mean I could float around on Cloud Nine while we went bankrupt. What a great idea.'

He came behind her and began to massage the back of her neck with strong, hard fingers. 'You're all strung up taut like a nylon climbing rope. What good is it doing?'

'None, I suppose,' she said, surrendering herself to the pressure of his hands. 'All the same, Jack, something will have to be done.'

When she left Hebberwood Mr Twillan had given her an introduction to what he called a 'redundancy counselling service' where she could go without having to pay any fee, Hebberwood having guaranteed to pay the bill. Until now it had been a matter of pride with her not to contact them, because she was in control of her own life and would get a job for herself. But now as the bank balance sank, she knew she would have to ask for help. She didn't know what her next step should be.

She asked to see a woman counsellor and was given an appointment two days ahead. The offices were in an efficient modern block, the decor was Conranhire, the whole effect was unpretentious and workmanlike. She was greeted by a woman in her fifties, with rather heavy glasses and an ash-grey hair dye. But she had a good voice, calm and with warmth in it.

She questioned Margaret in an almost casual manner at first. She had already looked her up in some notes Hebberwood had supplied at her request, so they didn't have to waste time on basics. Margaret explained that she was sure she would eventually land a job of the kind she needed, but she had come to realise the interval might be longer than she'd at first supposed.

'Quite so. That's a good attitude. You relied on personal contacts at first, I suppose?'

'Yes, and it's possible something may turn up from those in the end. I'm now at the stage where I have a head-hunting firm looking for openings in the ordinary way, I'm on several agencies' books and of course I'm looking at *The Times*, and the *Financial Times*, and so on.'

'Good. You're basically on the right track. What about the government agencies?'

'Oh, I've done all the right things – reported here and there, and make the pilgrimage every two weeks ...' She grimaced. 'I hate it.'

'I know. But what can you do?' Mrs Larrabie sighed. 'Well, what do you want to talk about, other than those groundwork facts? Because you must have a problem, otherwise you wouldn't have taken the plunge and come to us.'

'I need advice on how to deal with our finances. I think we're going to get terribly into debt before long – and I can't bear the thought.'

The other woman surveyed her, and nodded. She could see the flush of embarrassment. It was a sign she knew well. Most people were made ashamed by their vanishing status.

'May we go into it in some detail? I'm not prying – I need to know how you stand before I can advise you.'

Margaret had been prepared for the request. She

brought out the documents needed to show their outgoings, a recent bank statement to show their balance, and a short list she had typed herself of their income.

Mrs Larrabie looked through it all in silence for a time, then asked one or two questions. Then they spent an hour going back and forth through the whole thing. As lunchtime approached, Margaret shuffled the papers together and looked hopefully at the other woman.

'The first thing you must do is see your building society and get the mortgage repayments reduced. It's absurd –'

'Reduced? Will they do that?'

'For a period, yes, of course. I was going to say, it's absurd for you to be taking money out of your small capital to pay monthly outgoings. Your mortgage is very high?'

'It certainly is. You see, we wanted to buy this almost derelict house with some land attached – it used to belong to some old horse-dealer and is called the Hostlers' House. Then there was the fact that I am the breadwinner of the family. Most building societies were a bit shy of that notion. In the end we were able to swing it but only with special conditions attached about repaying within a certain time. It's made the repayments very heavy.'

'If I were you I should go straight there this afternoon and ask to have a reduction, due to your present financial problems.' She touched her phone. 'Make the call from here, if you like. I'll leave you, if I may – I have a luncheon engagement.'

'Thank you. Before you go, is there any other recommendation?'

'I'd try to heat only one room in the house when the weather takes a chilly turn. Central heating is one of the most difficult expenses to meet. Use your car as little as

153

possible – your transport costs are high.'

'But we do need to use it. It's a long way to Ladhurst for the shops and the post office and so on.'

Mrs Larrabie smiled. 'Have you thought of using a bike?'

Margaret stared, frowned, and then began to laugh. 'My neighbours would stare if they saw me doing that! Then they'd know for sure that we're going broke.'

Mrs Larrabie paused with her hand on her doorknob. 'You mean you've kept all this a secret?'

Margaret nodded.

'Well . . . You know your own business best, but in my opinion that's a big mistake. Pride is a very expensive luxury, Mrs Durley.'

'But the people we know are so unsympathetic about this kind of thing . . .'

'I see . . . That's a pity . . . Well, forgive me, but I really must go now. If you want to talk to me again, just ring and make an appointment.'

'Thank you, Mrs Larrabie.'

The building society's branch was in Cheapside. She was told that the branch manager who had been so sympathetic to her application five years ago had been promoted to head office but that Mr Motley could see her at four.

She had lunch in a sandwich bar. She'd given up eating at the club because it proved impossible to get a cheap meal there: either you ate in the dining room where the prices were high, or you had a sandwich and a drink in the bar which always came to over a pound. For half that, she could get a coffee and an open sandwich in a cafe.

She then walked from Victoria to Cheapside. Gone were the days of casually summoned taxis, and even bus fares were grudged. She walked a lot these days, and it had made a change in her clothes. At first she had come to town in a good dress and the fine shoes her feet were accustomed to. But walking the streets of London had proved to her that royal shoemakers don't take much account of uneven pavements or cobbled forecourts. After much thought she'd begun to wear shoes with thicker soles and lower heels, and since those certainly didn't go with a designer dress she now wore what might be described as country casual clothes – still of good quality, still speckless in their appearance, but somehow they changed her image of herself. They made her feel provincial whereas she'd always been a city girl. She assured herself that when she got a job interview, she'd bring thin shoes and a good dress with her to the club, and change there first.

Mr Motley didn't live up to his name. He was sombrely clad in a dark suit and a navy tie. He invited her to be seated, listened gravely to her explanation of the different circumstances that now ruled, and pursed his lips.

'Dear me,' he said. 'Why didn't you come to us when you were first told of your dismissal?'

She flinched at the word, but knew better by now than to argue. 'I thought I would get another job at once.'

Mr Motley looked incredulous. 'In the present financial climate?'

'Listen, Mr Motley, I haven't come to discuss my past mistakes,' she said. Then she was sorry for the tartness in her tone and went on more quietly, 'I've taken advice this morning and been told the first thing I must do is reduce the amount of the mortgage repayments. Please believe me, I don't want to do this. But it's absolutely essential if we're going to be able to pay for food and fuel in the coming months.'

'Ahem ... Can you give me some details of your present income?'

She did so, with absolute frankness. He asked about

their insurance policies, she told him what he wanted to know. He was not the least bit friendly, as his predecessor had been. She thought afterwards that he felt a mistake had been made in ever granting the mortgage.

At his request, she filled in a form. It was an application for a reduction in the repayment sums. By now she was becoming immune to feelings of indignation when asked to supply details of her age, her marital status, number of dependants, and whatever else the form-writer thought fit to ask.

He glanced over it. 'Your husband ... he's here as a dependant?'

'That's right.'

'An invalid?'

'No, he's not ill.'

A long pause. 'Then why doesn't he work, Mrs Durley?'

'He does work. He keeps house and takes care of the grounds. The garden is enormous, he grows all our fruit and vegetables.'

'But he's not gainfully employed.'

'No.'

'Mrs Durley, don't you think that in the present case, that's ridiculous? If he were bringing in a salary as well, your circumstances would be much improved.'

'Really?' she flashed. 'If he got a job in Ladhurst as a shelf-filler in the supermarket – that would make a vast difference to our income?'

Mr Motley was perplexed. 'You mean he has no training?'

'He has a degree in art. If you can tell me where he can get a good paying job in some line of art, I'm sure he'd jump at it. Meanwhile it makes more sense to both of us for him to look after our son and run the place – if he went out to work we'd have to pay someone almost as much as he earned, to take his job on.'

'Ahem, ahem ... I suppose ... yes ... What you say has some truth in it.'

'Mr Motley, I came to ask for a reduction –'

'Of course. Well, leave it with me. I'll write to you in a day or so with the new terms. You do understand,' he said as he rose to show her out, 'that it can only be a temporary measure. The society must get its money back – it wouldn't be fair to our investors to subsidise mortgagees at their expense.'

'I understand that,' she replied in a stiff tone. Why did he make her feel as if she were asking for charity? It was a simple business transaction, that was all.

Just before he closed his door, Mr Motley fired his last shot. 'Surely,' he remarked, 'there must be *something* your husband could do? I'd think he'd want to, myself.'

'Thank you, Mr Motley,' she said, and walked out.

She went out into Cheapside, to vent her wrath on a Coco Cola tin that happened to lie in her path. She kicked it hard, so that it went under a bus and went pop. She wished she could do the same with the likes of Mr Motley, who considered that his role was to make judgements on her lifestyle.

If she had stopped to think about it, her lifestyle wasn't all that enviable at present. She was losing weight from skimpy midday meals and too much physical output, together with an unrelenting anxiety. It made her rather withdrawn and sometimes touchy when she was at home. Despite her own conviction that they were right not to change the way they lived, she found herself resenting Jack's routine. He worked hard, she didn't doubt that – he did the chores, he tended the garden, he serviced the car, he attended to all the things that needed mending, he kept Laurie amused. Yet somehow that all seemed more attractive than trudging around London, filling in time until an appointment, travelling home in a grubby train, and having nothing to report when she got there.

Even the weekends didn't bring much relief. She spent Saturday morning in the reading room at the library looking through the heavy newspapers and the business journals, hoping to see an advertisement that would mean just the right opening for her. The afternoon was given up to doing the accounts, juggling the money. Sunday, supposed to be the day of rest, found her incapable of resting. She went for walks with her husband and son, or kept up the usual social round, and was exhausted when the day was over from the sheer effort of keeping up appearances.

Even making love was no consolation any more. She was too tense, too conscious that there were more important things than sex. Jack said to her: 'You're no fun this way, Margaret.'

'I'm sorry. I'm going through what would be called a "difficult time", if I were an adolescent.'

'Crisis of identity, is that it? But in bed you ought to be the same woman, surely?'

'I do try, Jack.'

He groaned. 'That's what's wrong. You're trying too hard. I keep telling you, relax.'

'And I keep telling you, I can't!' she flared.

'Okay, okay, don't get your calculator in a coil. It's no big deal, If you don't want to, you don't want to.'

'Jack ... I'm sorry.'

'I know you are, and so am I. Better luck some other time, eh?'

She turned over in bed and closed her eyes and her ears to his disappointment. It is only needed this – to fail in this last stronghold of personal confidence. As she had said to Jack, she did try. But it was all joyless, a mere matter of duty.

She remembered once as a girl happening in on her

mother and one of her aunts in intimate gossip. Aunt Peggy was saying: 'Oh, no, he doesn't trouble me much over that.' Both women had blushed up to their hairline when the nine-year-old Margaret walked in. Later, when the girls at school began to discuss sex, she realised that what Aunt Peggy had meant was that her husband didn't make too many sexual demands upon her.

So now it became the same with Jack. 'He didn't trouble her much over that.' Although she understood his withdrawal from her, she didn't know whether to be grateful or unhappy.

It was the Durleys' turn that Sunday to have neighbours and friends in for brunch. This was a fortnightly affair among a wide circle, and there was a loose schedule of alternation. The Durleys had given one brunch during the period of Margaret's notice, but this was the first since she was one of the unemployed. It would have to be on a reduced scale, but reduced so as not to be noticeable to those who came. Jack, amiable as always when called on to play his part, came up with the idea of doing a vegetarian smorgasbord. Almost the last of their wine would have to be brought out, but they could also offer cider and apple juice. He had masses of vegetables from the garden, he made clever egg dishes, he bought several different cheeses in Sainsbury's. He baked bread in fancy shapes, and fruit tarts with the late raspberries and the early apples. He exerted himself to deck everything out in the cordon bleu manner. The result was a table to delight the eye, although they both knew that afterwards their guests would mutter to each other about the lack of meat on the menu.

Patty Cooper-Watts cooed over the food. 'I know your Jack is a devotee of contemplation and so forth,' she remarked. 'You've gone completely vegetarian, have you?'

'Not entirely. But it *is* a good idea,' Margaret replied.

159

'The diet is much lower in cholesterol.'

'Yes, dear.' Patty studied her. 'You don't look quite so good as usual. Have you been ordered on to a low cholesterol diet?'

'Oh no. No, it's just one of the things that seem good for themselves.'

'I see, dear.' As she drifted off with the laden plate, Patty murmured to Stan, 'I do believe Margaret's beginning to have high blood pressure or something. That would account for it, wouldn't it?'

'For what?'

'The way they seem to be cutting down on their activities.'

Among the guests were David and Caroline Keppler, fairly new acquaintances, sometimes glimpsed at the Cooper-Watt's. Caroline was very young, lissom and blonde, and also very bright. The Durley and the Kepplers had become acquainted through the chauffeuring to the station routine. David Keppler caught a train about the same time in the morning as Margaret, but travelled in the opposite direction, to Eastbourne.

Margaret had exchanged a few words with each almost every morning. Jack had got to know Caroline somewhat better, having once dealt with a fault in the ignition for her. That was as much as Margaret knew about them, but when issuing the usual general invitation to brunch, it had seemed only decent to invite the Kepplers too.

In a lull in the activities of hostess, Margaret found Caroline Keppler at her side. She offered wine to go with the stuffed peppers and rice she had chosen.

'Thank you, Margaret,' Caroline said, and let her fill her glass. It was a good wine, a hock from Rheinhessia with a very high reputation. Caroline nibbled a forkful of rice then murmured: 'Isn't this costing you a lot more than you can afford, though?'

160

Margaret turned her head with a start. Caroline gave her a smile of pure malice and wandered away to join a group of tennis enthusiasts.

For a long moment Margaret watched her. Just as she was looking away, Caroline's eye flickered towards her. The corners of her mouth twitched in a smile of cruel amusement.

She knew. It was the only explanation. She knew they were hard up.

But how could she know? And supposing she did know, why take so much trouble to tell her? And then the answer came to her in one of those sudden, inexplicable flashes of intuition. Jack had told Caroline. And he had told her in a moment of careless intimacy, after making love. She knew it as certainly as if Jack had told her. Fragments of half-remembered conversations, incidents she had chosen to ignore suddenly slotted into place. Caroline's frankly lecherous stare at Jack at one of the Cooper-Watts' lunch parties. Jack's hand casually resting on her shoulder while they talked at the station. His deep, sexy laugh ringing out across the station car park. And his lack of opposition to her keeping up the charade of going into London every day when she had expected him to lecture her on honesty and the values of friendship. Margaret had been so preoccupied with her own obsessions that she had misinterpreted his withdrawal from her. She had never thought that Caroline, or someone like her, was a possible threat. And now Caroline, because she was predatory and therefore annoyed with Margaret for retaining Jack's affection, had wanted to hurt her. The best way to hurt her was to give her this subtle moment of double humiliation.

She could feel the blush of distress rising in her face. She moved away from the buffet table and appeared to busy herself with taking a few used plates into the kitchen. There, she put the dishes in the sink and ran the

161

tap on them. In the demoniac way that such things happen, the water hit a spoon and was immediately deflected all over the wool print dress she was wearing. It brought with it flecks of mayonnaise and curry sauce. Spattered over the skirt, they ruined it.

'Oh!' she cried in vexation, and dabbed at the stains with a tea cloth. That of course only made them worse. Maurice Attins came in to ask if coffee was coming. She suddenly couldn't bear to be chatting with him or anyone else, and with a gesture towards her dress said: 'I must change. Coffee's in the Cona,' and fled.

Up in their bedroom she closed the door, sat down on the blue buttoned velvet chair, and bent her head. She told herself she wasn't going to cry. It was happening too often these days, this impulse to throw herself face downwards and burst into tears.

No wonder Jack had turned to someone else. What had he said? 'You're no fun any more.' It was only too true. Where had it all gone, her gaiety, her zest?

In a slow, painful movement she raised her head and looked at herself in the cheval mirror. She saw a slim figure – perhaps too slim – in a blue soft wool dress, exquisitely cut. Delicate shoes covered the slender feet. A diamond engagement ring sparkled with her gold band on her left hand, a heavy garnet gleamed on her right. Everything about her was in perfect taste. Her hair was softly caught back off her face by two small tortoise-shell combs and then allowed to drop forward in a smooth curve. But perhaps the style was too young for the face between the soft swathes of hair. Perhaps it would look better on a girl of Caroline's age.

Caroline was – what? – twenty-two. Twelve years her junior. But that wouldn't have mattered, wouldn't have mattered at all if Margaret had been in her normal state of mind. There would have been a light in her eyes, colour in her cheeks, no worry lines about her mouth.

She would have brought the good looks and experience of her thirty-four years to match the other woman's creamy seductiveness. And she would have been confident that she would win.

She wasn't confident any more. Too much had happened lately to show her that she wouldn't always win. She jumped up in sudden panic as the words, 'I'm turning into a loser!' shot through her mind.

She put her hands over her mouth as if she'd said the words aloud. She mustn't think like that, she mustn't. She had to keep on being a winner. If not, her whole life would come to pieces. She had built it on a foundation of success, a visible success that allowed her to shrug off criticism about herself, about Jack, about their marriage.

If she failed, criticism became valid. She was warping marriage, the role of male and female. She was perhaps even doing harm to Laurie. That was the kind of thing that would be said, and without financial success to validate their lifestyle, it would be difficult to brush off.

Caroline Keppler was a symptom, a symbol. If everything had been going well, Jack would never have thought of amusing himself outside their marriage. He wasn't promiscuous, although in his bachelor days he played the field. But she recognised that she had probably bored him with her continual anxieties, her lack of animation. She'd become a drag – that was the truth of it.

She must try to pull herself together. For a while now she'd acknowledged that it was going to be a long haul, this job-hunting campaign. She must, she really must, learn to switch off when she got home. Good or bad, the day had to be left behind her. She had to get back to being a wife to her husband.

'Oh, God,' she groaned to herself as she said it. Breadwinner, general manager, and lover, all rolled into one. Why did it have to be so hard? Why should she be asked to play such diverse a role? If she were a man, and worried to death over money matters, wouldn't there be a wife waiting with soothing words, slippers and a pipe, cool hands for the fevered brow? Being a woman made it all so much harder, and being married to a casual, handsome man like Jack made it desperately difficult.

She jumped up. Sitting mooning over it in self-pity wasn't going to help. She took off her dress and laid it over a chair back for later attention. As she was standing by the open wardrobe debating what to put on, Jack came in.

'I wondered where you'd disappeared to,' he remarked.

'I got ketchup on my dress or something.'

'Oh, that was it.' There was a faint anxiety in his tone. She heard it and knew he'd wondered if anything had happened to upset her. Perhaps Caroline had threatened to say something. Caroline, she rather thought, was probably selfish and demanding.

She turned from the wardrobe and put her arms lightly round Jack's neck. Her eyes looked up into his – hazel eyes darkened with hidden pain. 'What shall I put on, Jack?' she asked. 'I want to look nice.'

'You always look nice, precious.' He grinned, but with embarrassment as well as pleasure. He didn't quite know how to take her question. She seldom asked for fashion advice.

'I think I'm losing too much weight. I must try to drink more milk.'

'That'll be the day,' he said, for he knew she hated milk. 'Anyhow, you look good this way – like a greyhound in the slips.'

'A greyhound ... They race them, don't they. Good for a fast dash but no staying power.'

He really didn't know what had got into her but he was worried, he took hold of her and drew her close. She hadn't realised how cold she was until she felt the warmth of his body against hers. 'Come on,' he said, 'make yourself decent and we'll go down and look after our guests.'

'I suppose we must.'

'Mm?' He was rubbing his cheek against her hair. 'What's that? Well, we don't *have* to.'

If only she could melt into his arms now . . . Sweep him away in an embrace of irresistible sexuality . . . If only they could make love the way they used to, eager and savage and satisfying . . .

But it was impossible. There was too much hurt behind her feelings at present.

And besides, there were people downstairs who would be wondering what on earth had happened to their host and hostess.

The following morning Margaret looked back with a special interest as she went into the railway station. Caroline was parked some distance down the road from Jack. But she was leaning over her half-open driving door, waiting for him to come and speak to her. With a stifled sigh Margaret walked on into the booking hall. There was nothing she could do about it, nothing. The last thing she wanted was to turn into a nag. Once she started complaining that Jack was unfaithful, she would have sunk as low as she could go. She was never going to do that.

The Thursday was a day on which there should have been a meeting of the Ladhurst Festival committee. But there was no phone call on Tuesday and none on Wednesday.

'You'd better ring, Jack, and see if it's the usual time and place.'

'Oh, no,' said Jack. 'I want to get out there while it's still light and lift those begonias. If I don't, what d'you bet we get a sharp frost tonight?'

165

'All right, I'll ring,' she said. She wandered to the telephone with the address book in her hand and dialled. The call was taken by Sir Roger himself, sounding taken aback at hearing her voice.

'Well, Mrs Durley ... Kind of you to ring ... '

'I'm just checking for Jack. The meeting's on as usual, is it?'

'Ah, I see, naturally you expected Amy to be in touch.' Amy was the henpecked Lady Filmore, who did all his donkey work for him. 'I told her not to.'

'Not to,' Margaret repeated, puzzled.

'Yes, it seemed best.' A pause. 'My dear, I'll be blunt. You know me, always speak my mind. Eh?'

'I suppose you do,' she agreed, still puzzled.

'The committee can't carry excess weight. Every member must be able to contribute something other than just the time to sit and chat.'

'Jack understood that, Sir Roger. He's ready to – '

'I think you understood more than that, Mrs Durley. You're one for whom a wink is as good as a nod. Six months ago, your husband had a considerable value to us because he could convey our needs directly to you.'

'Well, he can still – '

'Convey? Surely, surely. But ... what good does that do us, my dear lady? If I'm rightly informed, you're not in a position to do anything about our needs.'

Another pause, this time on Margaret's side. Sir Roger said: 'I'm not making a mistake in this, I hope? At least – I don't mean I hope ... No, that was badly expressed ... '

'I understood what you meant, Sir Roger,' she said, regaining her voice. 'My importance to you has diminished, and therefore you don't need my husband's presence on the committee.'

'Not on the committee, no. Of course we'll need all the help we can get when we get to the launching pad. Jack's talents might stand us in good stead – he might do us some posters, for instance – '

'Or sell programmes at the choir concert?'

'Oh, now,' Sir Roger said, affronted. Then his calm superiority asserted itself. He was accustomed to be in a position of control, even in sticky situations like this. 'Our aim is to be of service to the community, isn't it? Every little helps – even selling programmes if that's all one can contribute.'

'You seem to have your intelligence system in good order, Sir Roger. But I think we could still have contributed a little more than programme-selling – '

'Of course, of course. It was you who used that example, not me. But one does hear things, Mrs Durley. And your circumstances have radically altered since we first invited Jack to be a committee member.'

'You want me to tell him not to come to the meeting?'

Sir Roger drew in his breath at the ice in her tone. Then he said, 'If he attends, that will be quite in order. But I think he'll feel somewhat *de trop*.'

'I'll convey that message.'

'No hard feelings, my dear.'

'That's what you think,' she said as she put the phone down. She went into the livingroom. Jack was delaying his gardening to enjoy a little Scott Joplin. She marched over to the record player and switched it off. Jack sat up, startled. 'Hey,' he protested.

'The Filmores know,' she said in a flat, abrupt manner. 'That's why they didn't remind you about the committee. They don't want you there.'

'What?' he said, aghast.

'Sir Roger's just told me as kindly as possible that we're no use to them any more.'

'You're kidding.'

'I'm not.'

He stared at her, and saw beyond a peradventure that

167

she was not. 'But how could they possibly know?' he gasped.

She met his eye and held the gaze. He frowned and looked away.

They both knew how it was possible. Caroline Keppler had been bitching about her.

And Margaret couldn't help hating Jack for it.

Chapter Ten

When Margaret woke next morning it was to the sound of her early morning tea-cup being put by her bedside and the murmur of Jack's voice as always: 'Seven-thirty, Margaret.'

She sat up at once, for it had always been her way to start the day quickly, not wasting time lounging about dreary-eyed while the energy flow kick-started. But as she was taking her first sip, it came to her there was something different about this morning. Something in her life had changed.

Then she remembered. Everyone knew she was unemployed. There was no longer the slightest need to keep up the pretence of travelling up to London every day.

She lay back on her pillows. No hurry. She looked at the clothes laid out last night. She wouldn't need them. Dark woollen suit, soft silk blouse in clover pink, Chelsea Cobbler shoes – none of that would be necessary.

When Jack came out of the shower in his towelling robe, he stared to find her sitting up in bed reading *A Gull on the Roof*, her bedside book. 'Shouldn't you be on the move?' he asked.

She shook her head.

'What's the matter? Not well?'

'I'm fine.' She laid the book on her knees and stretched luxuriously. 'Yes, fine.'

He gave her something between a stare and a frown. 'Then why aren't you in the bathroom getting washed?'

'Why should I?' she asked. She felt almost frivolous.

'Because you're going to miss your train if you don't get started.'

'What train?'

'The one that goes to London, bonehead. You remember it? It comes in at Ladhurst at nine-thirty and gets into London Bridge at ten-forty-five.'

'It can go without me today,' she said, and looked into her tea-cup. 'Any more tea?'

Too much taken aback to speak for a moment, he eventually managed to say: 'There's a nearly full pot downstairs.'

'Be an angel just this once and fetch me another cup, will you? I promise not to make a habit of it.'

'Of what? Having two cups, or not catching the train?'

As he took the cup, she gave him a brilliant smile. 'I've just realised, you see. I'm free. Free! I don't have to keep up a façade any more. I don't have to go struggling up to London and back every day. I don't have to stooge about filling in time between seeing people, looking in job agency windows, reporting to government offices. I don't have to sit at my club hiding behind the *Financial Times.*' She flung out her arms in a theatrical gesture. 'Free!' she declaimed. 'I can be as miserable as anybody else when I get a disappointment. I don't need to smile and smile until my face hurts. I don't have to pay the bill when I have coffee and cake with Lizzie Attins in Kardomah – I don't even have to bother about being just the same as usual to Lizzie Attins. God, the relief!'

The cup still in his hands, Jack sat down on the side of the bed. 'Jesus, you're right!'

'"If all the year were playing holiday",' she told him seriously, '"to sport would be as tedious as to work".'

'No doubt. That's Willie, I take it. But doesn't it go on

170

about "seldom come is wished-for come"?'

'Well, you have to be selective in your quotations. It's like statistics, you know – you can use them for anything if you know what to choose.' She felt quite light-headed. It was absurd, of course, because everything that had made her appear 'special' in her community was now in ruins around her. By and by the reaction would set in and she would be unhappy about it. But for now she really felt as she had described – as if shackles had been struck off her hands and feet. For the first time she realised that if her status was all her Ladhurst friends valued her for then they weren't really friends at all. Why had she ever cared so much about their opinions? Why had she found them so impressive? She was better off without them.

'Don't you have to sign on somewhere, or something?' Jack remarked.

'Not today. Tomorrow. Tomorrow I'll go up so as to be there as per instructions, like a good little girl. I may even go into the club and read the papers. But it occurs to me it would be a good deal cheaper to have *The Times* and *Financial Times* delivered and read them at home. The train fare is enormous – it's quite a saving not to have to pay it.' She gave him a little push. 'Come on, what about my celebratory second cup?'

'I'm on my way, ma'am.' He leapt up and hurried out.

She leaned back on her pillows and surveyed the sky through her windows. It was a bright, cool autumn day. Just the day for a long walk in the woods, scuffing shoes through the golden leaves, watching a squirrel rushing about laying up stores he wouldn't need for winter. She could go down to the river and play Pooh-sticks with Laurie. She could lie on a garden bed in the patio and get some late sun. She could read the latest Burgess novel. She could watch tea-time television with her little boy, catching up with that roll-call of characters who peopled

171

his world: The Wombles, the Flumps, Paddington, Roadrunner, Rhubarb ...

The door opened and the lad himself toddled in. 'Hello,' he said in a business-like tone. 'Daddy says you won't mind being bothered.'

Bothered! She felt a sudden surge of emotion – guilt, remorse, shame, god alone knew what else. She leaned out and took Laurie in her arms, then lifted him onto the bed beside her.

'No, I don't mind a bit,' she replied. 'What are you going to do today?'

'I'm going to teach Paddington to dig the garden.'

'To help Daddy? That's a good idea.'

'No, it's for my plot. I'm going to grow bulbs.'

'Bulbs? Oh yes. What kind?'

'Snowdrops. They're the ones with the little white helmets. Auntie Mary says they come up first.'

'So they do.' Auntie Mary was one of the girls who ran the play group. Margaret tried to remember whether or not this was one of Laurie's play group days. Yes, it was – so much for the plan to play Pooh-sticks. But after all, play group only lasted from ten till twelve. She could have him to herself after lunch, after he'd had his nap.

She was a little shaken to realise how little she knew of the day-to-day routine of the house. She didn't even know that he had a garden plot of his own.

'Can I help you teach Paddington?'

'Oh, *you* don't know how to dig,' Laurie told her. 'You never dig.'

'That's true, but I think I could help teach Paddington.'

'We-ell ... ' He gave it long consideration. 'You'd get your clothes all dirty.'

'That wouldn't matter, love.'

He frowned at her. 'But it always matters.'

'No, Laurie, not today, and not when Mummy's at home from now on.'

172

'Is it Saturday today?' he asked, fair head on one side. When she shook his head he said, 'Sunday?'

'Neither of those, but I'm going to be at home.'

'All day?' Eyes big, surprised and pleased.

'All day.'

'And tomorrow too?'

'Not tomorrow, not all day, but I don't have to hurry away and I'll be back soon.'

Jack appeared with the tea. Not only that, he'd brought a tray with hot toast and butter and marmalade, and a little vase with a late rosebud in it. 'Breakfast in bed, madam,' he observed. 'Fresh tea, and if you'd like something more substantial than toast, say the word.'

'Oh, Jack, it's lovely! Thank you!'

To her surprise, he coloured up. 'It's nothing,' he said. He leaned down to kiss her briefly on the temple. 'It's just to mark Freedom Day.'

Laurie demanded pieces of toast. She got marmalade all over the sheets. Normally she would have been disgusted by the mess she made but today it didn't matter. Nothing seemed to matter except being here with her husband and son, crunching toast and drinking tea and letting the world go by.

She went with Jack to deliver the little boy to play-school. It was on the other side of Ladhurst from the station so there was no need to go anywhere near it. Jack had a few things to buy in the supermarket. She accompanied him, taking the items from the shelf and dropping them into the basket he carried. It was extraordinary how different the shop was at this time on a weekday compared with the hectic Saturday shopping she was used to.

Everything seemed different. Even the light outside seemed different. The streets of Ladhurst were quiet, the old houses gleamed in the cool sunlight. When she got indoors, the Hostlers' House seemed different too – unfamiliar, almost. She was almost never here at

173

midmorning except on Saturday or Sunday, and seldom then, for there were always things to do or buy, visits to make or, if not, there were people here altering the contours of the house.

Her own home, yet she was almost a stranger in it. She shivered. It was scary. How high a price she'd been paying for her career! Yet even then, as she luxuriated in the peace of the house, she knew she would tire of it in the end. She'd had periods of domesticity before, when she was unmarried, intervals when she had holidays but didn't want to travel. Three days, four – that was enough. She needed the stimulus of challenge, business challenge. She needed to be pitting her wits, using her brains, surmounting problems. She wasn't the domestic type and she knew it.

But for now, it was soothing. She sat on the floor of the livingroom looking through the records, deciding what she would put on the stereo. Villa Lobos, perhaps: 'The Little Train of the Caipira' would just suit her mood.

She had just put the disc on the turntable when the phone rang. Jack was upstairs, busy with chores. She went to the hall and picked up the phone. Almost simultaneously, Jack picked up the bedroom extension.

'Well, hello you!' cried a light-hearted voice.

It was Caroline Keppler.

'Hello, Caroline,' Margaret said quickly so as to let Jack know she was on the line. 'How nice of you to call.'

There was a silence from Caroline. She heard the upstairs phone being gently replaced.

'Margaret,' Caroline said, neither as an exclamation or a question. It was more as if she were telling herself this unexpected voice belonged to Jack's wife. Then, recollecting herself, she went on: 'I wondered when I didn't see you at the station this morning as usual.'

'Oh, aren't you kind,' cooed Margaret. 'You weren't worried?'

174

'I ... er ... wondered if you had taken an earlier train, or something.'

'No, I didn't take the train at all – as you can tell.'

'I hope you're not under the weather.'

'No, I'm perfectly fit, thanks. It's good of you to want to know.'

'Are you ... er ... are you on holiday?'

'A fairly permanent holiday, Caroline,' Margaret said with a laugh. 'I daresay you know I'm very much at leisure for the moment. I'll be at home a good deal for the present.'

'Oh,' said Caroline.

Yes, my angel, you've spiked your own guns, Margaret told her in grim, unvoiced satisfaction. Now that everyone knows all about it, why the hell should I go up to London every day and leave the field clear for you with my husband?

'Well, as long as you're all right,' Caroline managed to say. 'I'd have been sorry to think your absence today meant you were sick.'

'I appreciate it, darling,' she responded. Her voice was light and good-humoured, but there was just enough steel in the way she said the word 'darling' to be a warning to the other girl.

'Well, see you soon, I hope.'

'It's not very likely,' Margaret said. 'We're having to cut down on rushing about, as I'm sure you appreciate.'

'Oh, I ... er ... Of course. What a shame.'

'Oh, it has its compensations. It means I can spend a lot more time with my husband.'

'Yes, there is that – '

'You must miss David when he's away all day every day,' Margaret went on remorselessly. 'The days must seem long.'

'Oh, I keep busy, you know. Tennis, golf, bridge ... And I like to nip up to London for the fashion shows.'

'It sounds lovely. I quite envy you, Caroline. Some time when you're driving up, perhaps I can cadge a lift?'

She heard the gasp of horror at the suggestion. Caroline said in a rush: 'Of course, dear. Any time. I must go now, there's someone at the door.'

'By-ee. Thanks for calling.' She put the phone down and gave it a pat. There, my young pussycat, that'll give you something to think about, she said to it.

A few minutes later, when she'd got the Villa Lobos playing, Jack came downstairs with the sticky sheets in his arms. He walked through to put them in the washing machine in the kitchen. Margaret strolled to the kitchen door.

'That was Caroline, as you gathered,' she reported.

'Yes, when I realised you were answering I replaced.'

'Uh-huh. She was just worried about not seeing me as usual. I explained to her that I'll be around most of the time for the foreseeable future.'

'Yes,' Jack said, and stared thoughtfully at the washing machine.

'Are we going to do the washing?'

'No, no. Not till we've got a full load. It would be wasteful otherwise.'

'So it would. Domestic economy. Are you going to work in the studio?'

'Thought I would. That African thing is coming along quite well.'

'I'll make some coffee,' she offered. 'We'll have it first, eh?'

'Good idea.' He was still thoughtful as he strolled out.

She made real coffee in the percolator, still celebrating this special day. She took home-baked oatmeal biscuits out of the cookie jar and carried it all into the sittingroom. 'The Little Train of the Caipira' had finished its journey and now it was time to turn over for the enchanting, exalting Aria for soprano and eight cellos.

176

She turned the record over, sat down and poured coffee, then leaned back in her armchair to enjoy both music and drink. 'I love this, don't you?' she murmured.

Jack crunched a biscuit. 'Now I think of it, it's ages since you sat down and listened to records.'

'Oh, there'll be time for that now. And I'll help you in the garden. And of course I want to play with Laurie. It took me aback this morning, how he seemed to think I would never do anything to get myself in a mess. He must think I'm made of porcelain, poor little lad. But it'll all be different.'

'Yes, a lot's going to be different ... '

Should she bring it out into the open? Say: 'I know about Caroline, Jack. And I don't mind, so long as it wasn't serious and it's over.' Should she deal with it and be over with it?

But to voice it made it definite, made it part of their experience. Jack would start apologising, explaining. She didn't want that. It had always been one of their tenets that so long as their love for each other remained as strong and permanent as ever, little side romances didn't matter. She knew, she *knew* that Caroline didn't matter. To talk about her would make her important.

The soprano was singing now: ' ... Una brisa amolecendo o coracao ... ' A breeze soothing the heart ... Hearts could be soothed, could be quietened although they had felt the pang of betrayal. There was nothing to fear now, Caroline was no threat any more.

She busied herself getting lunch while Jack worked. It felt strange to be sitting at the kitchen table scraping carrots, beating eggs, pitting plums. It was all in the oven when she went to fetch Laurie. He was astounded and delighted to see her in the car by herself. His face lit up, he rushed towards her. 'Mummy, Mummy – look, it's my Mummy!'

It was a good day. It almost made up for the fact that

she was out of a job and hard-up. She bathed Laurie, a thing she usually only did at the weekend. He, over-excited, soaked her to the skin. It didn't matter a bit. She tucked him up at last, and sat by him reading from *Paddington Bear* until his eyelids drooped.

Jack had a pleasant meal ready. He even had a half-bottle of brut champagne. 'I was saving this for the day you landed a job,' he explained, 'but somehow today seems worth a toast.'

'Oh, Jack ... ' She chuckled. He was so eager to have something to be happy about. All that had happened was that she had been found out. She ought to be ashamed. She saw now that she'd been behaving like an idiot. What did it matter if her neighbours knew about her downfall? It saved an expense of spirit – not to say money – to have it known. Again she wondered why she cared so much about their precious opinions. Jack was right. There was something to celebrate. She felt almost like she had come out of the closet. Against her will, perhaps – but she was her true self again, open and honest and ready to face life.

He poured the champagne. He held up his glass. 'What's the toast?'

'Freedom Day!'

They drank. After the meal they watched television for an hour, then switched off and talked. It was weeks – perhaps even months – since they'd talked in this aimless way. For the last hundred days or so she'd been obsessed with opportunities for work, money, their future. All that still had to be tackled, but this evening they didn't talk about that. They discussed the vegetable garden, what to do with their weekend now that they could please themselves entirely.

And at last they went up to bed, where yet another blessing was added to this strange day.

Next day she had to go to London but, having come to

her senses, was only going to stay as long as necessary to check in. Since she was here, however, she might as well drop in at her club and read the papers. The receptionist had a message for her. 'You didn't come in yesterday,' she said. 'I wondered whether to ring you at home?'

'Yes, will you do that in future, Betty?'

'Righto.' The girl handed over a telephone message slip. 'Pete Brenton called. Please ring him back.' The number was given.

Intrigued, she went to a phone booth. Pete Brenton was a man of about her own age whom she met frequently at business receptions and City banquets. Somehow he generally managed to get to her side, so she knew he liked her. He was in catering in a big way, a food buyer for airline catering.

'Hello, Margaret?' he said when he picked up his phone after the usual passage through switchboard and secretary. 'Nice to hear you. I spent quite a lot of time yesterday trying to run you down. That girl that used to work for you at Hebberwood finally told me to try your club.'

'I'm sorry I wasn't available, Pete. I stayed at home yesterday.' Wouldn't it just happen – the one day she didn't show up, someone wanted her.

'Can we meet? I've got something that might interest you.'

She almost begged: 'Tell me now, at once.' But she took a moment, kept her voice calm, and said instead: 'Well, I have a couple of things to do today but my afternoon is free ... ?'

'How about popping round to me for a drink? Four-ish?'

'Well, that would be nice, Pete. Thank you.'

'You know where I am?'

'Yes, of course.'

Four-ish. That meant kicking her heels most of the

179

afternoon. Why hadn't she said she was free for lunch? He might have taken her somewhere good, and it never did any harm to be seen in places like that. But ... she surveyed herself. She wasn't exactly clad for the 'in' places. Light tie-belted tweed suit, low-heeled shoes, high-necked thin sweater. She frowned a little. She'd even been a bit casual with her hair and make-up this morning. Because, of course, it hadn't seemed to matter as much. But she'd been wrong. She couldn't allow herself to slip into an attitude like that. When she came to town she must be ready to face the highest rank of the business world, just in case.

Once the routine chores were over she was at loose ends. She'd meant to go straight home on the train. She went to the Professional and Executive Recruitment Centre in Grosvenor Place just to check that they hadn't come up with anything for her; once again, the answer was, positions available but much further down the scale than she could afford to go.

She had lunch at a hamburger shop and went to look at an exhibition. By this time she'd seen almost all the free exhibitions in London but there was a photographic display in the National Portrait Gallery. She spent an agreeable hour there. Then she went back to her club to make herself as presentable as possible for the meeting with Pete Brenton.

She made herself recall all she could about Brenton. He'd only ever seen her in glossy surroundings so he'd expect her to be as well-groomed as ever. He himself was a man who went in for a fair amount of grooming – sleek, glossy, like a well-kept, well-fed hunter. If the truth were told, she hadn't greatly cared for him. She couldn't remember ever seeking his company. But, on the other hand, she remembered that he had sought hers – and that was what was important in the present circumstances. He liked her, he wanted to do her a good turn.

Of course, he wouldn't be doing himself any harm if he was finding the right candidate for the vacant post – doing favours for business acquaintances was part of the small change of the executive world. But he certainly wasn't going to recommend a woman who turned up looking like a country bumpkin.

There was absolutely nothing she could do about the low-heeled shoes. But her hair and her face could be improved. She got out her handbag hairbrush and set to work. By the time she had finished it was smooth and gleaming. She tweaked a tendril or two but was on the whole pleased. She did her face; she could have done better if she'd had the range of eye shadows on her dressing table but she made herself look fresh, alert, and trim. Now she looked at the suit.

It was no good, she looked impossibly country-lady. There was nothing executive about her. She spend two or three minutes putting on her pearl ear clips and taking them off again, and then it came to her. It was the high-necked sweater.

She took it off and put the suit jacket back on. Right – that was better. Now the effect was smart town-clothes. She would have liked a silk scarf to tie in the opening now laid bare, but it wasn't too low by any means. She re-did her hair, put on the ear-clips, had a last hard scrutiny, and was satisfied. She folded the sweater and put it in her handbag, a capacious one luckily; she was going to need that sweater going home, for the day was chill.

Pete's secretary showed her straight in when she presented herself. Pete sprang up from behind his desk. 'Margaret!' he cried, taking both her hands. 'It's been an age!'

'I suppose it has,' she agreed. 'Nice to see you again.'

'Come and sit down.' Still holding both her hands, he urged her to a conversation corner of the kind that was usual in the offices of glossy executives. The big armchairs were covered in Art Deco grey and black velvet. The coffee table gleamed in chrome and smoked glass. On it was the usual array of bottles in a Tiffany glass tray.

They sat. He asked what she would like and she chose Cinzano. He poured it, added ice and lemon from a little covered dish, and made himself a scotch and soda. 'Well,' he said, leaning back, 'here's to old acquaintance!'

'Likewise,' she said, and sipped. 'How's everything? This looks prosperous.' She indicated the cleverly decorated office.

'Oh yes, I had it re-done recently. Before that it was all High Tech. but that gets so boring. Do you like my lamps?' They were show-pieces, one on his desk and one on the low table, slender ladies in flowing draperies arched back in vaguely Oriental postures, holding aloft the round globes of clouded blue glass. She gave him the admiring smile for which he had paused and he burst out, 'Oh, you do look good! Simply marvellous. But then you always do.'

'We do our best, sir,' she said demurely.

'And how about you? How are things?'

'We-ell, difficult. Obviously you know I'm job-hunting. It's not a good time for it.'

'You can say that again! But look, as I said, I may have something for you.' He gave her an earnest glance and she looked attentive and appreciative. 'For the moment, no names, no pack drill, but I happen to know a very important bloke in an airline who's head-hunting.'

'An airline? Really? I thought I might have got a hint of that – I have some contacts in –'

'This is a new airline,' he went on at once. 'You know in my business I'm in close touch, and particularly with the Moslem area because of catering difficulties and halal and all that.'

'Yes, I understand. This job is with a Middle East line?'

'Right! They're interviewing –'

'But they're not likely to hire a woman?'

'You're so right!' he said, leaning forward to pat her hand in approval. 'Normally, you wouldn't have a hope. But this is a special post – handling female passenger problems, helping to design special waiting rooms for the women VIPs, seeing they have every facility, arranging hotel accommodation of a high order if there are airport delays, etcetera etcetera.'

She felt the beginning of a glow. This could be for her. 'But that's just my line, Pete!'

'Quite, quite. I told Ha–' He checked himself. 'I told my friend, I know just the girl. Now I don't want to make a meal of it, Margaret, but there's a short list. They've been putting out feelers for about two weeks.'

'How short?'

'I think there are four on it. But I can get you added on, no problem.'

'Oh, Pete – would you?'

'I certainly would. I only have to pick up a telephone and tell my friend to see you.'

'Tell him?'

'He owes me one.'

' ... I don't know what to say.'

He picked up his whisky and took a sip. 'There's only one thing.'

'What?' Her mind whirled with possibilities. Her religion – were they going to insist on a Moslem woman? Her age – was she too old? Too young?

Pete Brenton studied her with an inner amusement. Got you scared, have I, he said to himself. How enjoyable it was, to see the haughty Margaret Durley look unsure of herself. Too intelligent and too fastidious to bother about him – oh yes, he'd got the message she'd been sending out over the past few years when he'd tried to get close to her.

He had always wanted Margaret Durley. From the first moment he saw her, she had been his ideal of the kind of woman he wanted on his arm or in his bed. The final feather in his cap – to have a girl like Margaret tell him he was wonderful. But somehow she'd always stayed out of his reach, apparently impervious to his charms – which were considerable, he knew. Over a period of two and a half years, he had tried for Margaret Durley and had failed. What was worse, rumour had it that she wasn't unapproachable. He'd heard that she and Charles Vernon had had a hot thing going. If she could care for a stick like Vernon, why couldn't she care for a real red-blooded man like Pete Brenton?

When he heard she was job-hunting, he felt as if Fate had handed him opportunity on a plate garnished with watercress. He could guess what it was like to be 'redundant' – brought down, made to ask favours, your sense of security leaking away. Even the high and mighty Margaret Durley wouldn't be immune to anxiety and growing dismay. It was like finding a chink in the armour of Joan of Arc. Right, he told himself, now for the stake in the middle of the bonfire. I'm going to make you feel the heat, baby! You're going to burn for all the shrugging-off you handed me. Whatever happened, he would win. Whether she agreed or not she would feel humiliation. He smiled slyly as he spoke.

'I ... er ... I'm putting myself out a bit on this, you understand.'

'Yes, I see that, and I'm very grateful –'

'Yes. The point is, how grateful?'

She drew in a breath. He couldn't be serious. She looked at him. He *was* serious.

She hesitated. Play it daft, she thought. 'I don't understand.'

'Oh, come on, Margaret, we both know the score. And

you know I've always fancied you – always.'

'But ... Pete ...'

'It's all quite simple. I have a little *pied-à-terre* not far from here. Since it's Friday I can pack it in a bit early – everybody does. We can be there in ten minutes. Afterwards we can have a bite of dinner before you go back to Sussex –'

'Afterwards?'

'I've looked forward to it so much, Margaret, ever since I realised how this job would suit you and how pleased you'd be to hear of it.' He put down his glass and got up. 'You are pleased, aren't you?' He took her by the hands and pulled her to her feet. As he did so, the suit jacket parted a little so that he saw the curves of her bosom. He gave a grin of pleasure and slipped a hand inside the jacket.

Margaret jinked out from under the hot touch. 'Wait, Pete – you're going a bit too fast.' Her thoughts were racing. After all, what did it matter? Jack and Caroline – they could do it, and just for their own amusement. Margaret could gain access to a first class job by doing just what they had done. Why not? Why not?

Pete took her in his arms and drew her hard against him. That was when she knew she couldn't. The scent of his too strong eau de cologne, the glint of the heavy gold cuff-links, the grasping hand beginning to explore once again – he was a *stranger*. And one she didn't even like very much. To go with him would be nothing but prostitution.

She put her palms against the front of the fine worsted jacket and pushed. 'No, Pete. My husband –'

'What, him?' he snorted. 'Everybody knows he's a dead loss. Into yoga and the Maharishi –'

'No, he isn't –'

'Oh, come on, everybody knows he's cracked. Why you've put up with him so long, I can't imagine. Why

185

isn't he out there hustling for you, instead of leaving you to do it all? Forget him, Margaret.'

'I can't do that, Pete. I don't even want to. I've never –'

'Huh!' He was stung by those words. 'You've never, eh? What about Charles Vernon, then?'

'That was before I got married –'

'Oh, oh, what a tale! You and Jack were a thing, when you got going with Vernon –'

'I admit that, but I haven't been near Charles since I got married. It's different now, I've got a baby –'

'Good God, I'm not asking you to break up your marriage! Just a little fun now and then, that's all. And think what you're getting – besides me,' he added, trying for a lighter note.

'No, I can't, Pete. I'm not the sort.'

'Everybody's the sort, dearie, for a prize job like this –'

She shook her head. 'No,' she said, and picked up her handbag.

'You really mean it?'

'I'm afraid so.'

He was totally astonished. He got in her way to prevent her going to the door. 'What's your problem? I never had any difficulties before –'

'Lucky you. I hope your good luck continues. But it's not my way, I'm afraid.'

'Who the hell do you think you are, you stuck-up little bitch?'

She drew back. There was a terrible anger in his face. Perhaps it was true, what he said – he'd never had a turn-down before. His sexual pride was wounded. For a moment it looked as if he was going to grab her, but then his telephone rang.

He ignored it. 'You'd better think it over,' he said. 'You won't get many offers like this.'

'I certainly hope not.' His phone rang again. 'You'd better answer that, hadn't you?'

186

He leaned over, snatched up the phone, snapped, 'Not now,' and slammed it down. But she had reached the door while he did so. 'Wait!' he commanded.

She put her hand on the doorknob. He glared at her, his handsome face distorted with a grimace of fury. 'You're making a mistake,' he snarled. 'I can be a bad enemy.'

She hesitated. What he said was true. He only had to go around saying Margaret Durley had done this or that, and he'd be believed. Everyone in the business world liked a nice juicy piece of gossip, and generally to the detriment of somebody. Nor would it do any good if she retaliated in like kind. It seldom did a male executive any harm to have it said he was a woman chaser. Quite the reverse, in fact.

But she couldn't let herself be blackmailed into going to bed with him. The mere idea made her feel physically sick. She drew a deep breath and took one step back into his office from the door.

'Ah,' he said, 'thinking better of it!'

Into the smile of triumph that was beginning to dawn on his features, she threw her words.

'I wouldn't go to bed with you if you were the last man on earth,' she said, 'and I'd even go a long way not to have to see you around among the empty spaces. Good afternoon to you, Mr Brenton.'

When she got downstairs into the foyer of the building, she was trembling. She leaned against the wall for a moment and the uniformed commissionaire came over and said, 'All right, madam?'

'Yes, thanks.'

'Like a taxi?'

'Yes please.' When she had got in and given the address of her club, she was appalled at herself. She didn't take taxis any more. But she felt so odd that it was a good idea to get to her club and have a few minutes to

187

recover before she set out for London Bridge station.

A glance at her watch showed just before five o'clock. So early still? She'd thought hours went by in Pete Brenton's office. She ordered tea, and while she was waiting for it she went back over what had happened. After a few moments she found an old copy of the *Financial Times* and turned up a short feature that had interested her a couple of weeks ago. Yes, there it was. The new airline Pete had been talking about was All-Arabian. She went to a phone booth, dialled directory inquiries, and got their number. She rang, and asked the girl on the switchboard for the Personnel Officer. After a short delay she was put through.

'Personnel here, can I help you?' It was a man's voice with a slight accent.

'I understand you are looking for a woman executive to handle female passenger facilities?'

A pause. 'Where did you hear that, if I may ask?'

'A friend mentioned it. If it is true, I should be very glad to have more information, Mr –?'

'My name is Hamid. Thank you for your inquiry, madam, but the post you mention was filled from our own initiatives over a month ago.'

She drew in a long breath. 'Thank you very much. I'm sorry to have troubled you.'

'No trouble, madam.'

She put the phone down.

The bastard. Not only a quid pro quo, but a quid pro nothing. She put her forehead against the glass door of the phone booth and drew in several deep breaths. Pete Brenton, cheat and liar. If he had been there, she would have spat on him.

Later, sitting with the tea tray in front of her, she began to shiver. She was becoming very vulnerable. She had always had to fend off attentions from hopeful males, but this was the first time she had been in the role of easy victim. Brenton's anger had shown how much it was taken for granted that she'd fall in with his kind of suggestion.

She felt cold. And a little frightened.

Chapter Eleven

She rang Jack before starting for home, to explain the delay. She said quickly that she'd heard of a job opening and had gone after it, but it had come to nothing. That way, she knew he wouldn't pursue it.

'No sweat,' he said. 'Dinner's a casserole. Laurie will be waiting up to see you – he's completely confused, thinks today must be Monday because you went back to work.'

Laurie was sitting up importantly in sleeping suit and dressing-gown at the kitchen table. 'I can stay up now and again because I'm a big boy,' he explained. 'And Daddy says it isn't Monday. We had an argument.'

'Who won?' she laughed, picking him up to hug him.

'Daddy says you'll say who's right.' He had both arms tight round her neck. He whispered breathily in her ear, 'Say I'm right, Mummy! Me.'

'But I can't cheat. And besides, if today was Monday I'd be going to the office tomorrow – right?'

A long hesitation. 'Yes.'

'But I'm not.'

'Oh ...' Then a shout of delight. 'You aren't going away on the train?'

'No, Laurie. Not tomorrow or the next day or the next day.'

He leaned against her. 'That's good 'cos you can help with my bulbs. I digged them up to see if they were growing, and Daddy says I have to plant them all again. He says it would be cruel not to.' He sighed deeply. 'It's a *lot* of work.'

'But I thought Paddington was helping you?'

'He doesn't dig much,' Laurie said. 'He talks to me, you know, but he doesn't dig.'

'All right, Laurie, I'll help you plant the bulbs first thing in the morning.'

'It makes your hands dirty,' he warned.

'Doesn't matter. Besides, I can wear gloves.'

Laurie went into a shriek of laughter. 'Digging in gloves! Oh, Mummy, you are funny!' He waved his arm at his father. 'Mummy's going to wear gloves!'

'There you are,' Jack observed. 'The dispassionate view of your attitude to gardening.' He was grinning. 'Shall I take him up, or will you?'

'I will. And I'll wash up and be down in five minutes.'

'Right.'

During supper Jack studiously avoided asking about her day. As they rose to take their coffee into the living room he said: 'You seem kind of quiet.'

'Am I? It's just that, after our lovely day yesterday, London seemed so ... so ...'

'So much of a rat race?'

'I suppose so.'

'Then listen, Margaret I've had what I think is a marvellous idea. I've been bursting for you to come home so I could tell you. I think it could make all the difference to our finances!'

She almost stared at him. Jack – with a commercial idea? 'What is it, then?'

'It came to me after yesterday. I mean, it clearly was better for you not to have to go rushing up on that train –'

'If you're going to suggest I stay at home while you go out to work, I hope you've got something tremendously lucrative in mind for yourself –'

191

'No, listen, I'm suggesting we both stay at home.'

'Oh really? And do what?' she said, with obvious scepticism.

'Take paying guests.'

'What?'

'Paying guests.' While she was still speechless at the words, he went on with haste but with a sense of order that showed he'd given it a lot of thought. 'The spare room is a big room, it could take two. "Two sharing", as the advertisements say. Laurie's room is a good size too, but it would only take one. There's a bathroom for those rooms to share – we've our own, they wouldn't impinge on us. I haven't gone into how much we'd charge and of course it would depend on whether we cooked for them or they –'

'Where were you thinking we could put Laurie?'

'In the boxroom. Oh, I know,' he said, as she was about to object, 'it's small, and the window is tiny – but I could enlarge it –'

'But it's right at the far end of the house, Jack! It would be beyond these people we'd be taking in –'

'Yes, that's a big obstacle, I know, but otherwise it means changing ourselves round a lot. We *could* move out of our bedroom and use the spare room as ours, and that would mean we'd be next to Laurie in his new room, but the problem there is, we'd have to share the bathroom with the tenants because we'd lose our private bath. All the same, it's not insurmountable, because I could fit a bathroom in a corner of the spare room – I've though of it many a time, for the parents when they come, you know.'

'But how much would that cost, Jack?'

'Hm ... Dunno ... A fair bit.' Jack had never had to worry about cost when he worked for the film companies. If the director wanted a special little landscape, Jack would write down a list of materials and give it to the Costing Department. Either the Costing Department said yes and he went ahead, or it said no and he had to think of something else. But actual calculations had never come into his work.

'What would be involved in a new bathroom?'

'A fair bit, I'm afraid. Plumbing it in, linking to the drainage ... I could do a lot myself but the drainage bit needs an expert.'

'And planning permission.'

'Yes, I think so.'

'That rules it out, then. It would take forever.'

'Well, say we let our bedroom with private bath and put in a little cooking thing in a corner. I could easily screen it off. That would make it a bedsit.'

'We-ell ...'

'And Laurie's room would have to be just a bedroom. That means we'd have to offer meals, don't you think?'

'Jack, this sounds awfully complicated –'

'Yes, I know, but when you come to think of it, other people do it –'

'But not in houses like this.'

When they moves into the Hostlers' House, it had been in a very bad state. Yet it had thick flint walls and there was stabling. Jack had set to with a will. But because they had never foreseen having to please anyone but themselves, they had gone all out for space, for airiness. He had knocked down the interior walls and incorporated the stables so that the rooms were vast. They loved the look of it, had lived in it with the greatest pleasure. But if you wanted to let rooms, it made things very awkward. They had a few big rooms whereas they could now have done with a larger number of medium size rooms.

'I could put up partitions downstairs,' he was muttering now. 'Perhaps we could move downstairs and let the top as a separate flat –'

193

'But what would we do for a bath?'

'I could extend the cloakroom –'

'But that would cost quite a large sum, Jack. And once again, would we have to have permission?'

He sighed. 'Yes, I believe so.'

'Let's not think about anything that needs permission. We need something that's going to bring in some money soon, not in a year's time.'

'But you think it would work?'

'It's a good idea, darling.'

He flushed with pleasure. Her approval was like being made Businessman of the Year. They spent the rest of the evening discussing it, and drawing plans. They then spent most of the weekend walking about the house, making gestures to show how this could be done or that could be done.

By Monday morning they had come to the conclusion that, when it came right down to it, they could by altering their way of life completely make room for three paying guests. It seemed easier, from the point of view of providing facilities, if they offered meals as well.

'The point now is, how much would we make?' Margaret wondered.

'You see fantastic sums being asked for board and lodging.'

'But that's in town. We're a long way from anywhere. Ladhurst is our nearest village but there's nothing there, really. We'd have to set our sights a bit lower. And anyone who came here would have to have their own transport because the buses are hopeless.'

'But there's the teacher training college –'

'What're you hoping for, a lovely big Swedish gymnast?'

'Depends whether it's male or female.'

'I've no idea what we could charge. Let's get the local paper and have a browse.'

They unearthed old copies from the glory-hole and sat down on the floor to look through them. Jack groaned when he flattened out the 'Apartments' page. 'Good lord, is that all you can ask when you have strangers in your house disrupting everything?'

'It can't be right, Jack. They must charge extra for heating and lighting –'

'I expect so. I wonder how we could find out.'

'The thing to do is ring an agency and see what prices they expect to get.' She found the Yellow Pages book, looked up accommodation, picked a firm at random, and rang. Jack hovered in the background while she had a long conversation.

'The gist of it is,' she said when she put the receiver slowly back, 'we couldn't expect to get anyone staying permanently when there are so many more convenient places like Brighton and Lewes. We might make an occasional forty or fifty quid by offering 'weekend breaks in delightful country home" but he says most people would expect a farm or a manor house. I asked him how much he thought we might make in a year and he said, in a summer of good weather, perhaps three hundred.'

'Three hundred! That's not much for all we'd have to do.'

'No.'

'Perhaps if we did modifications –'

'We'd need capital and planning permission. We know how long it takes to get planning permission. And as for capital ...'

'We haven't enough?'

'We've scarcely any. If we'd started off with the idea of putting money into a savings account we would be all right but, mistakenly as we now see, we decided to invest it all in improving the house.'

Upstairs Laurie could be heard rousing from his

afternoon nap. A moment later he came toddling down the stairs.

'You wouldn't have liked it anyhow, would you, mate?' Jack inquired, boosting the little boy up on to his shoulder.

'Wouldn't have liked what, Daddy? What, Daddy?'

'Eel pie and sandy sauce, that's what!'

'No, I wouldn't like that – I'd hate that! Is it tea-time, Daddy?'

'Come on,' Jack said, and put an arm round Margaret to shepherd her into the kitchen. 'Let's have tea and cinnamon toast.'

'There's always hot chocolate sauce, Mis' Amelia,' murmured Margaret.

'What was that?'

'In some play I saw, once – everything went wrong in this girl's life and the black maid comforted her with "There's always hot chocolate sauce".'

'Humph,' Jack said. He put his son down on a chair at the kitchen table, provided orange juice and a biscuit, and switched on the toaster and the kettle. 'Seems it wasn't such a good idea after all,' he said somewhat defensively over his shoulder.

'It was a great idea, love,' she said, coming to put her arms round him from the back and rest her head on his shoulder blade. 'We just don't have the right kind of house for it.'

He wriggled to induce her to lean more comfortably. 'Seems to me I read of tycoons making their fortunes by buying property on credit and selling it at a profit. Why can't we do that, eh?'

'Because the bottom's fallen out of the property market, my angel.'

'You mean cruel fate has arranged it so we can't make easy money.'

196

'You can still make money, if you have some to start with and don't mind risking it. Neither apply in our case.'

Jack reached up to a fitted cupboard. He surveyed the contents. 'And now we haven't any cinnamon. Oh hell.'

'Darling, *pas devant*! It doesn't matter, we'll have plum jam instead.'

'There's always hot plum jam.'

'Yes, aren't we lucky?'

He half-turned and put one arm round her. He gave her a kiss on the nose. 'You're not bad,' he said. 'You don't mind a limited menu.'

'I'm having hot plum jam too,' Laurie remarked in a loud tone.

'Oh, so you shall, darling,' his mother said. 'In a minute.' Jack grinned and bent his head to give her a whole-hearted kiss.

The toast popped out of the toaster.

'Why are mechanical devices so insensitive?' Jack inquired of the world in general, and fetched the margarine.

Though their scheme had come to nothing, they weren't downcast. In fact, almost the opposite. The disappointment seemed to have brought them closer together. They had afternoon tea and then wrapping up well went out for a walk in the blustery late October afternoon. They swung Laurie between them as they walked, he crying out with delight at the swoops of movement. They saw a deer in the bracken, its coat almost the same shade as the rich golden brown of the crinkled fronds. It leapt away in startlement. The little boy was entranced.

'It's like Bambi! Bambi, Bambi, come back!' But he was soon diverted by seven magpies sitting in the trees. 'One for sowwow, two for joy,' he chanted, holding up

197

fingers. 'Three for a gill, four for a boy. And another one for a Daddy, and one for a Mummy, and one for Paddington.'

Margaret should have known it was too idyllic to last. The illusion was shattered by a letter in next morning's mail. It was from the building society, inquiring in formal terms but with visible anxiety if there was any hope of an improvement in their financial status 'so that the very large balance due on your mortgage may soon be reduced'. The financial manager went on to say that although at present there was no intention to 'alter the conditions of repayment recently arranged', they would like to hear soon that the original terms could be resumed and some attempt made to catch up with the debt incurred by remitting some of the repayment instalments. The letter ended by saying that a discussion in person might be helpful, and desired Margaret to ring Mr Motley at their Cheapside branch to arrange it.

With an inward groan she handed it across the breakfast table to her husband. He read it and frowned in perplexity. 'They know we'll pay them as soon as we can,' he said. 'What does it mean?'

'It means they're getting worried. I'd better arrange a meeting with Motley.'

'On with the Motley,' sang Jack, not really perturbed.

Margaret had no intention of going up to London specially to be lectured at by the building society's representative. She made an arrangement for her next intended day in town. Mr Motley was very clued up about her; he'd clearly been reading up their file.

'What exactly are your prospects, Mrs Durley?' he inquired after the first politenesses. 'Is anything in the offing, as regards employment?'

'I'm afraid not. I had a long talk with a man at the Professional and Executive Recruitment office and he said it would be a long haul. He of course has access to government statistics so he knows what he's talking about.' She smiled a little, hoping to take the toughness out of this report. 'There have been one or two openings, naturally, but a lot further down the salary scale than I'm hoping for.'

'Well, I see that point. But wouldn't it be a good idea to lower your sights a little?'

'It wouldn't help much. The jobs are all in London, and travelling expenses would eat up a lot of money, so that in the end I'd be taking a very big cut.'

'But you'd be better off to some extent. At present you're dipping into capital, I imagine.'

'We're just going on to an overdraft.'

'Oh, dear me.' Mr Motley looked grave. 'Mrs Durley – forgive me – it's not my place to offer advice on your domestic arrangements – but wouldn't it help if your husband got at least *something*?'

'We've been into all that! We've a three year old boy – either one of us has to be at home to look after him, or we have to pay someone. I think it would cost as much to hire a housekeeper as my husband would earn – or close to it. If we could get a housekeeper, even.'

Mr Motley nodded. Although he clearly didn't approve of the Durleys' attitude, he could see the logic of it. 'Then ... in a way ...'

'What?'

'Wouldn't you be better off living closer in to London?'

'I beg your pardon?'

'You seem to be very isolated where you are. A long journey into town for any possible job. No chance of getting anyone to mind the child unless they live in. A very expensive house to keep up and very heavy mortgage repayments. Doesn't it occur to you that you're not in the best position to be in the job market? Your hands seem to be tied in almost every way. Forgive me for pointing it out, Mrs Durley.'

199

He had shaken her so much she didn't reply. There was an awkward little silence. Then he went on: 'Well, we aren't heartless, of course. For the time being we'll go on with the arrangements in being. But I must really state with clarity that it can't continue for too long. You say, a long haul for a job that comes up to your needs and expectations. How long?'

'Mr Syams said, perhaps a year.'

Motley drew in a breath. 'I'm afraid the society wouldn't want to continue this arrangement for a year, Mrs Durley.'

'I see.' She got up, for the interview was clearly at an end. 'Thank you for being so frank, Mr Motley.'

'Not at all.' He escorted to his door, and detained her there with a curious look of sympathy. 'I do wish there was more I could do. I'd hate to think of *my* wife in ... Well ... Good luck, Mrs Durley.'

'Thank you, Mr Motley.'

She had a lunch date with Rosie Chaney, Rosie the hostess this time. It was a fulfilment of that laughing prediction Margaret had made, that the day might come when she'd be glad to have Rosie pay the lunch bill. They went to a good old steak house, and had their usual steak and salad and red wine. Rosie listened with sympathy while Margaret recounted what Motley had said.

'It means they're getting worried about their money,' she mused. 'I see their point, of course.'

'Yes, so do I, Rosie, but what can I do? Jobs don't grow on trees – not even jobs paying about half what I've been hoping for.'

'Haven't you had any interviews?'

'Three or four. Oh, wait till I tell you.' She described the meeting with Pete Brenton, watching Rosie's eyes widen first in disbelief and then in laughter.

'You mean this vain little prat thought you'd fall into his arms for his rotten job?'

'He certainly did, but what caps it all is, the job had been filled weeks ago.'

'No!'

'Yes!' She finished the tale, and Rosie threw herself back in her chair in indignation. 'I felt the same, Rosie – but now I come to think of it, I suppose it's just a version of the casting director's couch.'

'That doesn't make it bloody right!' Rosie exclaimed, so loudly that the diners at the next table looked up at her.

'Of course it doesn't. Especially when it's a swindle all through.'

'But if there really was a job, Meg ... If it was something genuine ... Would you do it?'

'Of course not. What a question.' She studied her friend, who was looking thoughtful. 'Would you?'

'Well, I'm self-employed so the question doesn't arise. But see here, Meg – men do it. Men use aggression, money, power ... I don't see that it's so terribly wrong to go in for a bit of barter.'

'What, you mean, half an hour's nookie for a job introduction?'

They went off into gales of guilty laughter. For a time they gave their attention to the food. Then, when the waiter had come and tempted Rosie into an affair with a piece of gateau, Rosie spoke again.

'All right, so you wouldn't go bed with a man for a thing like this. But you have got weapons you aren't using, Margaret.'

'I don't know what you mean.'

'Oh yes you do. You know damn well I'm talking about Charles Vernon.'

The waiter came with the trolley and cut a wedge of gateau. When it had been put before her and she had strong-mindedly refused cream, Rosie went on: 'You haven't been in touch with him.'

'No, and you know why.'

'I know you get scratchy whenever I mention him. I think you're being silly. Charles could probably solve your problem in two days flat.'

'Rosie, I can't.'

Charles was the only man Jack had ever had reason to be jealous of. There had been one or two others in Margaret's life, but Charles was the only one for whom she might have ended their relationship. He wasn't as much fun as Jack but in many ways she had more in common with him than with Jack. Their minds were on a wavelength of instant understanding. They could talk about finance, commerce, travel and the literature of foreign countries, experimental theatre, music ... Not to mention the fact that Charles Vernon had a strong physical attraction for her, with his fairness and his lean, almost soldierly, body.

She couldn't approach Charles for help. If Jack knew of it, he would instantly be edgy about it.

She shook her head at Rosie. 'I can't do it.'

'Why not? Charles wouldn't lead you to the casting-couch. You know he's not that kind.'

'I know that. I could go to him on terms of friendship alone. But ... but ...'

'But what? Jack wouldn't like it?'

'That's it.'

'Why does Jack have to know?'

'Rosie!'

'Oh, come on – don't be so highminded! Do you always tell Jack everything?'

'Well, I –'

'Did you tell him about this guy Brenton?'

'No, but that was because he'd've wanted to come up to town and punch his nose.'

'Hey,' Rosie said, pausing with a forkful of Black Forest gateau halfway to her mouth, 'tell him, will you?

202

And let me know the time and place so I can watch the slaughter.'

'It's all very well to joke, love, but what's the point of making trouble –'

'By telling something that's best kept quiet? I agree with you. So why don't you ring Charles and talk things over with him, without reporting it all to your husband?'

'I wouldn't feel right about it. I'd feel guilty.'

'You mean you can't have male friends? Your husband doesn't like it?'

'Oh, Rosie, I don't mean anything of the sort. Jack knows I've got dozens of male friends, whom I've been contacting.'

'And what have they done for you? Nothing!' Rosie pushed away the dessert plate. 'I think you must be crazy. You're in desperate need of a job, not only for yourself but for the good of your home and family. And there's Charles Vernon panting to help you –'

'What?' Margaret interjected. 'How do you know he's panting to help me?'

Rosie went rose-pink. 'Ah ... well ... if you must know, he's been ringing me regularly to hear how you're getting on.'

'*What?*'

'After that awful lunch we had at Brogan's, Margaret – remember? When you were so unlike yourself?'

'Don't remind me.' Margaret put a hand over eyes.

'I rang him. I was so *worried*! I harangued him about how you needed help and so forth and he said you would probably come out okay. He thinks a lot of you, Meg. I begged him to get in touch and steer something your way, but ... well ... he said you'd think he was interfering, and if any moves were to be made, they would have to be from your side.'

'He said that?'

'He's not being cold, love. He keeps saying you must

know he's your friend and you'll turn to your friends when the right time comes.'

'Oh, he's ...'

'He's a nice man. I think you're mad to turn your back on him so completely. I mean, haven't you any confidence in your own willpower? Do you really think you'll fall into bed with him if you meet for a business chat?'

'No, don't be silly, we were good friends as well as ... as well as ...'

'Lovers. Yes. You don't know how lucky you are, Margaret. I don't think many women can say that about their past affairs.'

Their coffee came. When it was poured, they sipped. Then Rosie said: 'He was on the phone to me at the weekend, asking if I'd heard anything more.' She paused. 'Hey, why don't I tell him about Pete Brenton? Him and his "I can be a bad enemy"! Let's get Charles to quietly ruin him!'

'Oh, Rosie, do be serious. I can't speak to Charles.'

'I don't see that. If you don't *tell* Jack, how can it worry him?'

'But that's deceit –'

'In what way? You're not doing anything bad. You're just contacting an old friend, as you've done with others. Do you give Jack a list of the men you've already contacted?'

'No, of course not –'

'There you are then.'

'But Charles is different.'

'Only if you make him so. *Charles* isn't going to make things "different". You're the one who's got all the hang-ups. As far as I can gather from what he says, he knows how things are, he's not got any ulterior motives. He just wants to rally round, as any other friend would – if you'd let him.'

204

Margaret shook her head. 'What you say sounds completely logical,' she agreed, 'but there's something wrong with it.'

'Hm ... It's up to you, of course. Perhaps you feel you don't want to be in a situation of ... sort of like being a beggar looking for a hand-out. Isn't that just pride? And the way I see it, Charles is too fond of you to hurt you by doing anything tactless. I mean, he's not going to write out a cheque or anything like that. But he knows a lot of people, Meggie. He could be a tremendous help.'

'I know, I know. Do you think I haven't thought of that a hundred times?'

'Well, think of it again, ducks, and take off the blinkers. Come on, I've a teacher of English-as-a-foreign-language waiting to be interviewed. I'll drop you off before I head that way. Where are you going?'

'Oh ... the club, if you don't mind, Rosie.'

'Right you are.'

When she got into the club the lounge was full of women and guests taking their after-lunch coffee. She went into the writing room, and drawing a piece of paper towards her, began doing the familiar sums again.

The interview with the building society branch manager had scared her. The implication had been: we can't subsidise you much longer. If she went after that post that Mr Syams had been so keen on last week? About half what she was hoping to earn, and on the north side of London – a terrible journey from Sussex, meaning a start two hours before the office opened if she were to be punctual. Perhaps she should ask to be sent for the interview. Perhaps she ought at least to talk to them.

But Mrs Larrabie of the redundancy counselling service had warned her not to go for interviews if the conditions were totally unrewarding. 'It only leads to rejections,' she'd said, 'and rejections are very bad for the self-confidence. But, on the other hand, when you go for something you really want, put your heart and soul into it.'

If only there would be such a chance! But as she went into her fifth month of unemployment, Margaret was beginning to see that chances of that kind were very rare.

Was Rosie right? Was she being too sensitive about Charles? From what she said, he wanted to help. Tactfully, he hadn't made the first move. Should she stop being fastidious, and call on his aid? As Rosie remarked, Jack didn't have to know.

She looked again at the frightening figure on the paper in front of her. By Christmas they would be almost totally broke, with an overdraft that would take years to pay off unless she got a very good job. And what then? What happened if the building society decided they weren't going to let the debt grow any more? Would the house be sold from under them?

At the thought, she screwed up the paper and put it in the wastepaper basket. Then she gathered up her Gucci handbag and her Italian leather gloves, and went to a phone booth.

She dialled the special number that meant the call would come through on a confidential line in Charles's outer office. His secretary, Mrs Stoppard, asked who was calling then checked to see if her boss was free. A moment later Margaret heard his phone being picked up.

'Hello? Charles?'

'Well,' Charles said, 'finally.'

Chapter Twelve

She said: 'I had lunch with Rosie and she was telling me you've been in fairly regular contact.'

'Yes. A roundabout way of hearing of someone you were once close to, but better than nothing.'

She heard the reproach in his voice. 'I'm sorry, Charles. You know how I feel.'

'Yes.'

Rosie, having got rid of her interviewee, had rung Charles out of a growing sense of alarm. 'She looks haunted,' she told him, her voice full of tears. 'She had a talk with her building society man and he's about ready to twirl his moustache and turn her out of house and home.'

'What's her bank doing for her?' Charles asked, seeing it from his own viewpoint.

'She never goes into figures with me, Charles. But I think they're pretty pushed. The way I remember it, they put all their money into that house. And though I don't know too much about it, I have a terrible feeling she stands to lose it.'

'It won't come to that, surely.' He made a sound of vexation. 'Why won't she come to me and talk it over?'

'It's the same old story. I tried talking sense to her but she ...' Rosie broke off and blurted: 'That's not the worst.' She then told the tale of Peter Brenton, a story Margaret would never have divulged to him.

'My God!' he said. 'Who is this man?'

'He runs some catering company, does big business with the Moslem airlines. That's all I know.'

'Hm.' His face grim, he made a note and buzzed for Mrs Stoppard. 'What does she plan to do next?' he asked Rosie.

'I don't know, I really don't. Starve quietly to death, I shouldn't wonder.'

'Oh, Rosie!'

'Do something, Charles. *She* won't.'

'No, I daren't interfere ...'

When Mrs Stoppard came in as he put back the receiver he told her what he knew of Peter Brenton. 'Find out what company he is with and what position he holds.'

'Yes, Mr Vernon. Do you wish me to get him on the line for you?'

'On no account.'

He sat with his hand hovering over the phone wondering whether to ring round in search of Margaret. Rosie's account of the interlude with Brenton had frightened him. He couldn't let things like that happen to Margaret. It would destroy her. She was ... fastidious.

He had just decided to dial Hebberwood's in hopes of information about her when Margaret's call was put through. Mrs Stoppard, announcing it, sounded delighted. It crossed his mind that she knew a lot more than she let on. With his heart beating like a schoolboy's, he picked up the receiver.

Now he said: 'I want to see you, Margaret.'

'Yes, all right.'

'I have a meeting in a few minutes which I absolutely can't dodge. But it will only last about an hour and it's Whitehall. I suggest we meet for tea at the Savoy.'

Tea at the Savoy! Of all situations of respectability! Margaret almost laughed as she said, 'Yes, that would be lovely.'

She walked down from St Pauls to the Savoy. She took some time to pretty herself up before going into the River Lounge, for although she had taken special care with her appearance because of the interview with Mr Motley, a morning's wear and tear had had some effect on it. She was wearing the precious mohair coat over a Calvin Klein dress. Her hair, washed last night, gleamed softly. She felt she didn't look too bad, and, being early, could stroll with nonchalance into the lounge.

But Charles was already there. He rose from an armchair to greet her. 'My dear, how wonderful to see you again at last!' He took her hands in his and held them for a moment, very tight. Then he released her, took her coat, and laid it over a chair. He sat down beside her but across the low glass table.

'You look just the same, Charles,' she marvelled.

'That doesn't seem likely. It's five years since we sat down with each other to talk.'

Their last conversation had been, in fact, a long and bitter argument. Margaret was saying they must end their liaison because she was going to marry Jack, and Charles was saying she was throwing herself away. He'd lost the argument. But he'd never lost the feeling that in the true balance of right and wrong, she really belonged to him. They were right for each other, he knew it. And five years had not changed his view.

'How have you been?' he asked.

'Quite well, thank you. Worried, of course.'

'Yes, you show the signs.' The Longines watch was too big for the fragile wrist, the cheekbones were too prominent below the hazel eyes. 'Why have you waited until now? Why let yourself become so worried?'

'You know all that.'

'But in the end better sense has prevailed.' The waiter came, inquired if they wished afternoon tea, and was nodded at and waved away. 'Well, tell me how things stand.'

She looked reluctant. 'I don't want to tell you a sob story, Charles –'

'Don't be silly. I want to know.'

'It's what you'd expect. Jobs of the kind I need are very, very scarce. Jack can't hope to find anything that would be any help. The house is a terrible expense, the building society is getting worried, and although the bank isn't saying anything I don't suppose they'll let the overdraft go on forever.'

'You want my help?'

She sighed but nodded.

'Tell me in what way.'

She looked down at her hands. 'If you were to hear of any post that might suit me . . .? As Rosie very truly says, you know a lot of people, and what's more you know the right kind of people.'

'I understand.'

If the truth were told, he had heard of at least two openings that might have suited her. But he had wanted to see her again, not to do good to her by stealth. He wanted her welfare, but not completely with altruism. Now he had what he wanted – they had resumed contact. And say what she liked, she had missed him. He could tell that by the eager way her eye ran over him, and by the attention she gave to his voice when he spoke.

Their tea was brought, and he watched her as she went through the old-fashioned ritual of pouring it for him. He leaned back in the cane armchair, the tea in his hands, and thought that for the moment he was entirely happy. He had the woman he loved across from him, in a gentle, quiet setting that suited her. He would help her and he would see her again. His life seemed brighter in all its possibilities.

He told her that if it were in his power, he would create

a post for her in his own organisation. But that wasn't possible.

'But now that I know how things stand, I'll put out a few feelers. It shouldn't be impossible to put something your way.'

'Oh, Charles.' It was a deep, deep sigh. There was gratitude in it, and relief, and a sense of homecoming, and the relaxation of tension. Things would be better now. Charles Vernon was coming to her aid.

It was he who remembered she had to travel home to Sussex. 'What train are you catching?'

'I said I'd get the two minutes past five from London Bridge.' She looked at wrist. 'I've missed that. The next one's five twenty-eight.'

'We'll do that nicely.' He put notes on the plate, shepherded her out, had the doorman whistle up a taxi and spirited her off to the station with no trouble at all. He parted from her at the barrier with a swift pressure of his hand on her shoulder. '*Courage, l'ami. le diable est mort!*' he quoted, and walked away quickly before she could attempt to say thank you.

Feeling unreasonably lighthearted, she rode home on the crowded train. Jack was waiting with the car. She kissed him and got in. 'Well, how did it go?' he queried as he nosed out of the forecourt.

'What?' She gave a guilty start.'

'The chat with I Pagliacci.'

'Oh.' She'd almost forgotten that, in the pleasure of renewing acquaintance with Charles. 'Oh, Mr Motley was very gloomy and seemed to be warning me that I had to turn up some money fairly soon.'

'Or else?'

'Yes.'

'Or else what? What would happen?'

'Let's not think about that, darling. I just have a feeling everything is going to improve from now on.'

211

He gave her a sceptical look, but wouldn't for the world argue her out of this mood of optimism.

Later in the evening she gave him an edited version of what she'd been told by Motley. 'But for the moment we don't have to worry,' she said. 'We still have some leeway. I've been thinking that I've got a few things I could sell –'

'Oh, Meggie, for God's sake –'

'Well, you know, those rugs I picked up in Jerusalem have gone up in value, and there's the jade you brought back for me when you did that terrible film in Hong Kong –'

'But they weren't collector's pieces, darling –'

'Those were presents from you ten years ago. I bet the price of even fairly nondescript jade has gone up in that time.'

'But why do you want to do it now, all of a sudden?'

'We just have to hang on, Jack,' she said fiercely. 'Just hang on! Into the New Year, perhaps – but if we can keep everything going until then, I have a feeling we'll surface again.'

He couldn't understand her mood. It seemed to be based on nothing except determination. But as always he bowed to her better knowledge of business matters and next morning helped her gather together the items she felt were of value and which they could well live without. The Sarouk rugs, the jade boxes, the silver tea caddies which had been a wedding present from her parents, the Alfera plate. They added some Victoriana which graced a little corner shelf unit in their living room, adding the right touch of 'period' to the modernised room. They spent the next day carefully packing it all into a big carton. Then on the Monday she telephoned around, finding out which of the salerooms had a convenient auction date.

She was asked to bring it all in for inspection the

following day, Tuesday. She needed to use the car but that would make it awkward for Jack, because Tuesday was one of Laurie's play-group days. They discussed this for a bit until Jack suddenly said, 'I tell you what! Let's all go up to London together!'

'What?'

'It's ages since I've been, and it'll make up to Laurie for missing play-group. What d'you say? I mean, you're going to use the petrol anyway, and it makes more sense to have three in the car than one.'

'Well, that's true –'

'We'll take Laurie to the Zoo –'

'The Zoo costs a lot these days, Jack –'

'Well, somewhere – the toy museum, how about that? And listen ...' He paused, looked embarrassed. 'I thought I might offer some of my sculpture to a dealer. There's a guy in Cork Street once made oncoming noises to me.'

'Oh, but that's marvellous! What a good idea!' She hugged him in delight. 'That would be marvellous, wouldn't it? If he took your stuff and you sold something? Right, that's the plan then. Tomorrow we drive up to London, deliver our goods here and there, take Laurie to the toy museum, and have a picnic in Hyde Park.'

It was extraordinary how much pleasure they got from it. It was almost a thrill to pile themselves into the Renault and be off in the early morning. 'I feel a real provincial,' Jack said with a grin. 'Do you realise the last time I came to town was to fetch you that time you weren't well?'

'And all you saw then was the inside of the club. What a shame, love.'

'Never mind. London, here we come!'

But the weather was against them. It came on a cold November rain, dampening their spirits while it made

213

the drive less pleasant. And motorways going into London on a weekday are no fun at the best of times. The valuer at Sotheby's looked relatively unimpressed by their offering, but he said that carpets were being regarded as an investment these days. The dealer in Cork Street studied Jack's sculptures with a jaundiced eye and said they were very derivative.

The only bright spot was the Bethnal Green Museum. The little boy clattered from exhibit to exhibit, chattering with interest, alight with pleasure. They bought him an old-fashioned monkey-on-a-stick as a souvenir. He even enjoyed the in-car picnic they had in a strange little closed down street near the old London Docks.

His parents were more subdued. They headed for home. Jack said: 'What the hell! I'm going to sell those pieces *somewhere*! I'll get one of those arty-crafty shops in Brighton Lanes to take them on spec – if I keep the asking price down low enough *somebody* ought to buy them.'

'Oh, now, Jack –'

'There are eleven pieces. If I say I'll take five quid apiece, that's fifty-five pounds.'

'But that's giving them away –'

'So what – It'd pay a couple of grocery bills.'

'But what about your show –'

'I think we've got to face the fact that I'm not going to show – not unless I pay for the gallery myself, Margaret.'

This had always been a possibility in their days of affluence – that he would collect enough work for a one-man show and that Margaret would finance the hire of a gallery. But those days were long gone. In a strange way, Jack was becoming more realistic as Margaret's hopes of former good times were rising.

She had arranged to meet Charles for lunch on her next official day in town. He took her to a small, beautiful little place in Hampstead. During the meal they didn't talk of business, but when he had chosen a liqueur he glanced up at her with a smile.

'Of course you're anxious to know if I've come up with anything. Not yet, I'm afraid. But it's only been a week.'

'I understand that, Charles. I'm not expecting you to perform miracles.'

Since he last saw her Charles had honourably murmured to friends in clubs that he was interested in helping a friend find a position. It was too soon to have much come-back, but the reactions had shown him this wasn't going to be as easy as it might have been even six months ago. There were an awful lot of men in the job market, with qualifications as good as Margaret's, to whom such conventional gentlemen would prefer to give first choice. They had nothing against women in business, they would assure you hastily. But when it came down to it, and you had to choose whom to interview, you'd naturally pick out the men ahead of the women. Women always had other things they could turn to – looking after their families, a part-time job, or something.

Charles had said nothing to this kind of chat. But he had understood it might take quite a long time to find something worth sending Margaret for interview. And, when it came right down to it, that didn't displease him. He had a terrible feeling that once she got a good job and pulled her household together again, he wouldn't see her any more. In the first place she'd be busy, and the second place she wouldn't need him, and in the third place there was this damned conscience of hers.

He was always careful never to mention Jack. He despised the man and knew that his contempt showed in his voice when he spoke of him. Moreover, while anxiety and desperation had led Margaret to resume her friendship with him, there was always the fear that her

215

strong sense of right and wrong would assert itself against even those forces. She might wake up one morning and say to herself: I mustn't see Charles again.

It was like tiptoeing through a minefield, thought he. But it was worth it. Just to be with her, to talk in a leisurely way about opera and South American folk music and the Venice Bienniale.

He made it a habit that they should meet every time she came to town. It wasn't always lunch. Sometimes they merely met for a drink, sometimes they had tea in hotels like the Cadogan and the Ritz, and then there were little receptions, gallery openings, exhibitions. He never delayed her homegoing – quite the reverse, he saw to it that she caught the train she had intended. And all the time she became more used to being with him, more accepting, more in tune.

He realised that he now wanted to marry her. His house in Highgate Village was small and beautiful, but empty. He wanted to have Margaret there to welcome him home.

Charles's first marriage had foundered on the rock of childlessness. His wife Angela had been unable to have children and after becoming totally neurotic about her failure to 'give him an heir', had become fairly promiscuous. 'My dear,' he said to her one morning, when she came in from some one-night stand, 'if you're trying to prove you can do with someone else what you can't do with me, don't bother. The medical facts are against you.'

She heard the contempt in his tone and flew at him. Then, subsiding in a sobbing heap, she cried: 'I want a divorce! I hate you! I can't bear to live with you!'

Nothing simpler. Their marriage ended as quickly as it could be arranged. But though he never showed it, Charles felt a real grief. It was while he was in the vulnerable state of après-divorce that he met Margaret.

Their affair had at first seemed to his level-headed view merely a way to learn to feel affection again.

But it became more important than that. He began to take it for granted she would be his wife. He never took seriously the idea that Jack would get her. Jack Durley was lightweight, 'unserious'.

Yet, in that strange way of women, she had preferred the lesser man – as he expressed it to himself. Well, she had had five years with him, and much good it had done her. She had a millstone of a mortgage round her neck, a little boy to provide for and grinding anxieties. When the moment was right, he would tell her how much he loved her and ask her to leave Jack. They would be married. For sure, Margaret would get custody of the little boy. Charles had never met Laurie but was sure he would adore him – and Charles would make him a good stepfather, would care for him as if he were his own, not even feeling less for him when, in God's good time, he and Margaret had a child of their own.

These schemes gathered in his head without his consciously thinking them through. All he knew was that, as the weeks went by, she seemed to belong to him. The highlight of his week was when he met her. He gave up too much of his time to her on that one day, but he didn't regret the re-organisation of his schedules, the pursed lips of Mrs Stoppard. Time and attention – those were his gifts to Margaret. And she, being a woman of business herself, knew how to value them.

Then came the day – almost unexpected to Charles, because of the dream-barrier he'd been erecting – that he heard of a job for her.

Brethwaite had nabbed him in the hall of the Stock Exchange one morning. 'Don't I remember you saying you need an opening for some gel of yours?'

'What?' Charles replied, taken aback.

'It was you, wasn't it, Vernon? Said you knew of a

217

super gel if anyone had a top-grade post? Property and travel and such – or have I got it wrong, was it some other fellah?'

'No, it was me.'

'Well, now look.' Brethwaite took his arm. 'Want to do a favour for a client of mine, d'you see? Needs someone – someone very bright, not too young, not too old, languages, money sense ... Does that sound like your lass?'

'Yes,' Charles said in a quiet voice, 'it does.'

'Let's go and have a drink and I'll tell you about it.'

Margaret got a phone call the following day. It was Mrs Stoppard. 'Mrs Durley? Mr Vernon would like you to ring him when it is convenient.'

'Oh? I ... Yes, thank you.'

Charles had to talk to her. He knew she wouldn't want to do it while Jack might overhear. She waited until Jack drove off to fetch the little boy from play-group then made the call.

'I've set up an interview for you,' he began at once. 'I think it is entirely right for you and all you have to do is turn up and satisfy the managing director.'

'What kind of job, Charles?'

'It's a firm with an office in, of all places, Richmond. Verdugo-Black and Company. Property all over the world – they're known to me, though the bank hasn't actually got any money in any of their schemes. Very sound and long-established.'

'Yes, I think I've seen the name ...'

'They are setting up a department to deal with banquets and conferences. They entertain stockbrokers, property magnates, bankers, you know the kind of people. Government ministers figure too – they gave a banquet to the French Minister of Commerce last month.'

'And that's the department I would head?'

218

'Yes, and it could grow. You understand, Margaret – the work couldn't be as great as at Hebberwood, you'd have a very small department. So the salary wouldn't be quite as good as you got before, but the perks are very substantial – Brethwaite hinted they could be in the region of a four thousand pound value so that means a car and so forth.'

'Oh, *Charles*!' she gasped. It was absolutely marvellous. Christmas was almost upon them – this would be the best Christmas present she could ever have. She pulled herself together and asked: 'How many on the short list?'

'There isn't a short list. This is by personal recommendation. All you have to do is turn up and the job is yours.'

'Charles!'

'Are you ready to write down the address and time?' He dictated to her. She thought his manner was very crisp and cool but told herself it was because he was in the middle of his business day and didn't want to waste time.

She couldn't know he felt the chill of death in his heart. More than once during the sleepless night he had told himself he didn't need to pass on the information. She would never know he had let this chance go by. That way, he could go on seeing her, building up his claim on her.

But he had a sense of honour, all the same. He had promised to help her. He couldn't change the terms of that 'help' without coming into the open and saying, 'Margaret, give up this anxiety about a job. Marry me and I'll make everything perfect for you.' It was too soon.

Honour demanded that he should pass on the news. And she would get the job, he was sure of that.

And thereafter she would always be grateful to him, so

that their relationship would never be the same. He would never be able to talk about love. It would put him on the same level as the despicable Pete Brenton, asking for some payment for favours conferred. She would start avoiding him, and he would lose her.

He was still arguing with himself when he instructed Mrs Stoppard to ring and ask her call back. He was even still in two minds when he heard her voice. He could make some excuse and wriggle out of telling her.

Yet he didn't. When she began to say thank you, he let her do so. He hardly heard her.

'Wish me luck,' she said at the end.

'Yes,' he said, cold with loss. 'I hope you get it.'

Chapter Thirteen

She was waiting with the front door open when Jack
drove in with the little boy.

'All our troubles are over!' she exclaimed, radiant.
'I've just had a phone call – a job interview fixed up for
the day after tomorrow and I'm the only applicant!'

'What? How come?' His delight, after the first
surprise, was as great as hers.

'It's by personal recommendation only. I gather it's a
brand new department and they've been getting friends
to keep their eye open. Oh, it sounds just what I wanted,
Jack! Banquets and conferences for an international
firm.'

He put an arm round her and with Laurie holding his
other hand, took her into the living room. There she told
him all about it, except by whose means she'd heard of it.
And Jack either didn't notice, or didn't think to ask.

'It's less money, I think, but it's likely to be a lot nearer
what I've been hoping for. Oh, darling, isn't it
marvellous! I shan't have to go up to town on that awful
train –'

'Yes,' he said slowly. 'It means you'll be out of the
house every day again, doesn't it?'

'Will you miss me, love?' She gave him a playful punch
in the shoulder.

He laughed and said nothing. Laurie was demanding
his lunch so they all went into the kitchen, where they

took most of their meals these days. Laurie had a lot to report about his morning's activity but while Margaret pretended to listen her mind was already ranging forward to the interview.

She must press her Varon dress and make sure her Kurt Geiger shoes were shining. She'd take the Asprey handbag – it was a little conservative but these international property magnates were often rather staid. Clear varnish for her nails just in case Mr Everton was the kind who thought coloured nails were like bloody claws. The camel hair coat ought to go to the cleaners and she'd just have time to get it done in Ladhurst, at Kwik Clean – although she'd have preferred to take it to the place in Davies Street. Kwik Clean was a lot cheaper, though ... But then it didn't matter any more! They didn't have to worry about pennies any longer.

The journey to Richmond was difficult by train. She drove there, glad really of the occupation it gave to her mind. If she'd been travelling by rail she'd have been fretting about every smudge she got from the carriage door or the seat arms. She had difficulty finding a parking place – Richmond proved to be busier than she'd expected.

The offices of Verdugo-Black were in a very beautiful tall Georgian house. The difference between this and Lepham Properties was that everything here was untouched, unharmed. She was met in the hall by a kindly old man who led her to the stairs and pointed to the door by which she should enter. The staircase was winding and graceful, with shallow steps suitable for ladies in hooped skirts or gentlemen the worse for wine. Inside the room to which she'd been directed, a young secretary sat at a walnut desk. 'Mrs Durley?' she said, rising. 'How nice to see you. Did you have trouble parking?'

'I'm afraid so. I'm not late?'

'Not at all. But Mr Everton is expecting you.'

She was shown in directly without any further ado. Everton rose from his desk to greet her. He was tall, thin, about fifty, and rather grave in manner. After shaking hands and remarking that it was a very cold day, he set a chair for her. She was to sit across his beautiful desk from him, in the manner of an oldfashioned interview – none of this congregating on settees for Mr Everton.

'Well, Mrs Durley, we are very grateful to Mr Brethwaite and Mr Vernon for directing out attention to you. Their recommendation is enough in itself but you'll understand I felt I ought to make inquiries at Hebberwood's – discreetly, of course.' He waited for her response.

'Of course. I quite understand.'

'They speak of you in the highest terms. We are very pleased with what we hear. So let me as an opening explain to you the kind of work for which we are hiring you, and you can tell me if you think it would suit you.'

It's a dream, thought Margaret. He's trying to make it all sound lovely so I won't *refuse*! She gathered herself together and looked attentive.

'We have property in all parts of the world, notably in America, South America, Australia and Africa. The emerging nations are very important with us. We entertain rather lavishly. I mean no slur on them when I say that their ministers – the emergent nation's ministers – are quick to take offence so everything must be on a very high level.'

'I quite understand.'

'The former Congo area uses French as its first language of international communication. I hope you are fluent in French, Mrs Durley?'

Margaret was replying before she realised that the last two sentences had actually been spoken in French. She replied in the same language. 'I believe I should have no problem in holding a conversation with anyone from a French-speaking region, although of course local accent might make the first two or three sentences unusual.'

'Excellent! Your German and Italian is as good?'

'I hope so.'

'And Spanish? Spanish is very important, naturally.'

'I speak it less well – but I can improve it quickly. I enjoy languages.'

He nodded in approval. 'Well, now, the tedious details about office work. We are setting up a department, quite new. Until now we have given the work to outside caterers and conference organisers on site, but we have had some terrible experiences – near disasters. As I say, some of these gentlemen are very touchy and their wives perhaps even more so.' He went on to speak of the number of staff she might need: 'Three or four at first, perhaps – could you find the right people?'

'Undoubtedly. I did that at Hebberwood.'

'So I gathered. Well, now, our need is urgent. Supposing you were offered the post, when could you start?'

'As soon as you wish.'

'Excellent. You'll want to know the salary terms and pension fund and so forth – we'll put it all in writing of course but let me give you a few basics.' He told her the salary and went on quickly to say that the perquisites made it much more attractive than would at first appear. 'It's money in hand, really. A large part of your living expenses will be met. A car, of course, and I think you will find the accommodation first class. The apartment is in a very pleasant area –'

The startled look on her face made him pause. 'Is something wrong? You don't object to an apartment? We can probably find you a house in due course –'

'But I've got a house, Mr Everton.'

He laughed at what he saw as her little joke. 'In

224

Sussex, I gather. Very beautiful country, Sussex. But hardly to the point now.'

Margaret was thinking fast. The job must be about to take her away from her home area. Where was it to be? The North? She didn't altogether mind moving to the North, but it depended which part.

'Whereabouts is the apartment?' she inquired.

'Buenos Aires, naturally,' Everton replied, raising his brows.

'*Buenos Aires?*'

There was a strange lull. Margaret felt hot, as if her breath were being drawn in through a furnace. Dimly she heard Mr Everton say, 'You didn't know that?'

It took her so long to answer that his lips were forming the question again before she said: 'I took it for granted your headquarters were here, in Richmond.'

'Oh, good gracious me, no! This is our British HQ but handsome though it is it hardly matches the activities of our corporation. Besides, we are an Argentine company. I thought you knew that, Mrs Durley.'

There was just the faintest touch of reproof in the last phrase. He meant she should have done her homework. And she should, and would have done if she had been in London, with the facilities of her club at her beck and call. But because she'd spent yesterday in Sussex, doing the chores to make herself look attractive, she hadn't bothered to make even the basic inquiries.

Rage at herself, and shame for her shortcomings, battled with the shock to make her brace herself for speech. 'I wasn't aware of that, Mr Everton. And I'm afraid I took if for granted I would be working in London.'

He shook his head. 'No, no, we don't wish to add to our liabilities in London. Everything costs too much here. Buenos Aires has many advantages for us besides being our natural base.'

'I see.'

'It surely can make no difference? You would find Buenos Aires very agreeable. There is a large English-speaking community, and of course there is an international set too. We have excellent theatre, ballet, opera – fine schools – I believe you have a little boy?'

'Yes.'

'If it occurs to you to be worried about things you may have read in newspapers about political activity – things of that kind – dismiss it from your mind. The apartment in which you would live is naturally fully secure – patrols at night, guards on the gates – and if you see that your maids and nanny are properly vetted there should be no problem.'

'I ... yes ... thank you, I understand about that. It's simply that I hadn't thought of going abroad.'

'But you've been abroad before, on business?'

'Not to be a resident. It's ... something I would have to discuss with my husband.'

There was a long pause. Then Mr Everton said: 'This is very disappointing, Mrs Durley. I hoped to settle this matter today.'

'I'm sorry. I'm afraid I couldn't give an answer without first talking it over.'

'Is that so? Well, naturally, I must abide by that wish.' He rose, sighing. 'Mrs Durley, after the first surprise is over, I'm sure you'll see that the opportunity I am offering is very worth the taking. Britain is finished, you know. For a career woman like yourself, the future lies in the New World. I urge you to think of that when you make your decision.'

'I will,' she said automatically. 'Thank you for being so understanding. If I had been better informed at the outset I wouldn't have made this difficulty.'

'I understand. Even the best of us fall short now and again. May I ask you to be in touch as soon as possible? I

226

have the draft letter ready to send out to you so that you can be on our roll of employees but of course I shall hold it until I hear from you. But it is urgent. We have a big gathering of Australian planning advisers in Melbourne in February and we really must get some of the groundwork laid.'

'I won't delay,' she assured him. 'Thank you for seeing me.'

'A great pleasure.' He stood with his door open watching her walk across the outer office and smiled again as she went out.

She went down to the narrow street outside and turned automatically along the pavement without knowing where she was going. By and by she found herself on a sloping, high embankment over the River Thames, with narrow lawns and gardens in terraces. Nothing grew in the flower beds. A cold wind blew from the brown waters. She came to a bench, sat down on it, leaned back, and closed her eyes.

Buenos Aires ...

The disappointment was so shattering she almost cried out aloud. It had all been so perfect – so right for her, using all her abilities. And Everton so keen to have her. To be used again, to be appreciated! And the money – all their problems solved, the mortgage arranged for so they weren't in debt, the overdraft paid off, freedom of movement with the second car ... Laurie's name left on the waiting list for that good infants' school, money to back Jack's exhibition ... The renewed respect of their neighbours ...

All that had to be washed out now. If she took the job, they would have to uproot themselves. Sell the lovely home, so much beloved because Jack had formed it for them out of a derelict shell, because Laurie had been conceived there and taken his first steps ...

One part of her mind was crying: 'No, no!' yet the

other part was thinking that they would get a good price for the place, they could invest it, have something as a cushion against the vagaries of commerce, especially if Verdugo-Black provided a rent-free apartment.

But ... South America! So far away, so totally unknown to them except by news that didn't make it seem attractive ...

How long she sat on the bench she didn't know. It was the cold that roused her. She was chilled to the marrow. Her thin leather gloves had been no protection – her hands were blue with cold, almost stiff. She got up like an old woman and went in search of her car. For the first few moments she couldn't recall to mind where she had left it.

When she reached it she fumbled for her keys. She was shuddering with cold and shock. She wasn't in a fit state to drive – she must have a hot drink, revive herself, get her body working again.

It was mid-lunchtime in Richmond. Everywhere was crowded and when she did espy a place with a space at a table she was told they didn't serve coffee only. Finally she had a cup in a sandwich bar, standing up. Her legs were trembling, she had to lean on the narrow counter. She was staring at a blank wall covered in pink plastic. The shade was nauseating; she felt sick. But she forced the coffee down, hot and strong and sweet, with plenty of the sandwich bar's little wrapped cubes emptied into it.

As she drove home at last she tried to think of a way to break the news to Jack. She should have rung him before she set out, prepared him for it. But she hadn't known what to say, and she still didn't.

Her son saw her arrive. He raced into the kitchen shouting, 'Daddy, Daddy, Mummy's home!'

Jack swung the door open as she approached it. He began to say: 'Well?' in a bright, welcoming voice, but checked when he saw her face. He moved back a little.

228

She walked into the big hall and swung to face him.

'The job's in Buenos Aires,' she blurted.

'*Buenos Aires?*' he exclaimed, in an exact repetition of her own reaction.

She nodded.

'Oh, my God, that's the end of *that*!' He shushed his son, who was dragging at him demanding to speak. 'How terrible – are you very upset, love?'

'No, wait, Jack,' she said quickly. 'Don't just dismiss it like that. It's a marvellous job – there's an apartment in a good area and servants and a nanny thrown in – and it's a good tax situation there, I'm certain – and –'

'What?' Jack broke in. And then, his voice rising almost to a shout, 'You're not suggesting we take this stupid job?'

'Why not? Britain's finished – the future lies with the New World –'

'In a pig's ear it does! I'm not taking my son to a dictatorship to be brought up like a little grandee! Good God, Margaret, what are you thinking of?'

'I'm thinking about our financial situation!' she flared. 'I'm thinking about bankruptcy! I'm thinking about another six months of hunting for something and ending up with a job a lot below this in prospects –'

'Prospects? Is that all that matters? You don't mind where the hell you go as long as there are "prospects"? Christ, Margaret, why have we been giving donations to Amnesty International all these years, if it isn't as a sign we don't approve of dictatorships?'

'Listen, Jack, we're not political. It's not our business how other countries manage their affairs –'

'The hell it isn't! Since when have you thought that? What happened to your principles?'

'We can't afford principles! We have to be sensible –'

'Oh, yes, go on! You'll be telling me next that you only obeyed orders!'

At that taunt from the history of the Nazis, fury

grabbed at her. 'How dare you!' she screamed. 'How dare you say that to me!' She threw herself at him, fists flailing. 'You and your highmindedness, and your relaxation classes – what does it solve, what does it help? *You* don't have to worry and contrive and beg for help.'

All her pent-up anxiety, the misery and guilt of not telling him about Charles, the shame of continual rejection – she gathered it together and hurled it at him as her fists hit at his unrelenting figure. 'Futile, footling fool! Pottering about, having great ideas! Sell your sculpture for fifty pounds, go on! Make a big contribution towards solving our troubles! Tell all our friends how you lived by your principles while your wife and son starved! Simpleton! You're a joke!'

She became aware that Jack had captured her arms. He wrapped himself round her so that she was engulfed, forced into inactivity. She heard from a distance his voice: 'Margaret! Margaret! Stop it! We mustn't do this to each other! Sweetheart, don't! You're frightening Laurie.'

Gradually the red mist receded. She heard her son wailing. She felt his hands dragging at her skirt. She staggered. Jack held her close. She heard him saying: 'It's all right, son, Mummy's all right. Be good, stop crying.'

She felt herself being lowered to the settle in the hall. Jack's arms let her go. She realised he was picking Laurie up. Laurie screamed and struggled. 'My Mummy! Mummy, Mummy!'

She held out her arms. Laurie dragged himself from Jack and scrambled up on her knee. He put both arms round her, hugging her like a vice, weeping with deep, racking sobs. 'Mummy, don't be upset! Mummy, don't, don't ...'

She held him close. Tears streamed down her face. She rocked him, murmuring against his silky hair: 'It's all right, darling, don't cry. Everything's all right. Sh ... now, shh ...'

It took a long time for his weeping to subside. Even then, his body was racked by shuddering breaths. She sat with him in her arms until she gathered enough strength to get up and take him into the kitchen, where she wiped the tear stains from his pale little face.

'Want a biscuit?' she asked.

He shook his head, gazing at her in fright, holding on to her dress.

'All right then.' She sat down by the kitchen table, while he sank down cross-legged on the floor at her side.

Jack had disappeared while she comforted Laurie. She was glad. She didn't want to face him yet. For perhaps fifteen minutes she sat unmoving, breathing deeply, staring unseeing out of the big picture window.

At the end of that time she got up. She went into the hall, Laurie pattering after her. She picked up her handbag. Jack appeared as if by magic. 'Where are you going?'

'For a drive. I've some thinking to do.'

'About what?'

'About us. And this job.'

'Margaret, if you take this job you go on your own.'

'Oh yes? Perhaps that might be as well.'

'You think so? Laurie stays with me.'

'We'll see about that.' She gave a little curt laugh. 'And what would you live on, pray tell?'

'I'd sell this place. I'd manage. Just Laurie and me – we don't have big ideas about how to live.'

'I wonder if you have any ideas? Sensible ones, I mean.' She walked to the door.

The little boy caught up with her. 'I go too,' he stated.

She hesitated. But why not? 'All right.' They went out. He clambered quickly in the front. She said, 'No, Laurie, in the back,' but he refused. He clung to the back of the seat. He was determined not to be parted from her. She gave in, got into the driving seat, and drove away.

At first she just kept the car in motion, aimlessly.

There was no sound except the engine.

Then Laurie said: 'Daddy was very naughty, wasn't he? You hit him because he was naughty.'

Her head jerked round to him. She said: 'No, darling, Daddy wasn't naughty.'

'But you smacked him.'

Red surged into her cheeks. Yes, she had done that. She said: 'It was Mummy's fault.' and then, in extenuation, 'I was upset.'

'Upset?'

She searched for the word he would understand. 'I was in a tantrum.'

He frowned. 'Do Mummies have tantrums?'

'Yes, unfortunately, Laurie.'

'But you won't again,' he urged.

'No, I won't, darling.'

He nodded in satisfaction. That having been settled he returned to silence.

But he had jerked Margaret back to awareness of reality. Instead of reacting to the needs of the car like an automaton, she began to think.

She had known Jack wouldn't want her to take the job. Part of her own reaction to the news had been the certainty that Jack would never go to Argentina. But did that mean she had to give it up altogether?

They might be able to afford two homes. Jack could stay in Sussex and she could fly home – how often? Once a month? Surely it would be possible to manage a flight once a month.

Laurie interrupted this flow by saying, 'Are we going to see a Bambi?'

She hadn't given it any thought. She glanced about her, recognised the road they were on. 'How would you like to go and look at the sea?' she said.

'The sea! The sea! And boats! Motor boats!' Laurie said, suddenly filled with enthusiasm.

She shook her head at herself. How could she leave Jack and Laurie and only see them once a month? She couldn't bear it. And it would be bad for the child – she remembered how he had reacted to the scene she had just enacted, and how he had refused to let her out of his sight after it. What would he say if she disappeared for a month at a time?

No, she would have to persuade Jack to come with her. It was only sense. He would get used to the political situation. After all, not everyone in the country was a rabid Fascist or a Marxist guerrilla. It was idiotic to suppose so. They would make new friends, of their own kind – and there would be an English school for Laurie, no problem. They would come home for vacations – probably the vacation allowance would be large, six weeks at least and probably more.

Her parents ... Well, they would miss her, but she didn't see much of them even now. After the quarrel between Jack and her father it had taken a long time for normal relations to be resumed but at least her mother called – and it was just as easy to speak on the phone across the Atlantic. More expensive, of course, but expense wouldn't matter.

And she needn't make it a job for the rest of her life. She could put out feelers after a year or two and find something nearer home. Why, of course, that was the way to put it to Jack – a couple of years abroad – more like an extended holiday than anything else. They could let the Hostlers' House. Two-year lease – just about right for some foreign diplomat to take it during his tour of duty in England.

Simplicity itself. Why hadn't she tried that approach?

Because she had known very well that his reaction would be the same.

Jack simply didn't want to go. He had reasons that he considered paramount. And of course, it would be a terrible wrench, and an upset for Laurie no matter how you looked at it. Most of the children he'd be meeting would be foreign-speaking. Naturally he'd learn Spanish quickly – children were natural linguists. But the first few weeks of strangeness and disorientation ...

Still, he'd get over it. He was resilient. And she needed the job, she *needed* it.

But the fact was that if she transported them all to a foreign country where Jack would hate it and even Laurie might have his unhappy times, she would be doing it for her own sake. No one else in the family wanted it. Jack didn't, and if her little boy could have a vote he would vote against it. He loved his life just as it was. And change was bad for children.

They reached Brighton. She found a parking space without difficulty for there were few about on this cold afternoon in late November. Already it was tending towards dusk. She let the little boy stand on the seat to gaze out at the grey sea, but soon that wasn't enough.

'Let's go down and throw a stone,' he pleaded. 'Like this –' He made vigorous throwing motions.

'It's too cold, Laurie –'

'Oh, just for a minute, throw a stone, Mummy!'

In the end she gave in. 'But only for a tiny minute,' she warned. He rushed away from her, a bright little elf in his scarlet jersey and dungarees.

She helped him find a suitable stone and he threw it. It sank with hardly a splash. She moved about finding him one or two more.

I must take care not to ruin my shoes, she told herself, I can't afford to get them messed up.

Then she straightened. I can't afford to get them messed up. The choice was already made, at some subconscious level while she'd been arguing the pros and cons with herself.

She couldn't afford to scuff her shoes because she

couldn't afford to replace them. It meant she wasn't taking the job with Verdugo-Black. Perhaps she had always known she wouldn't, from the moment she heard its locale.

She fetched Laurie from the water's edge and took him to the car. Darkness was really coming on now. 'Are you hungry?' she asked, for it was about his supper time.

'Did you bring a picnic?' he asked.

'No. But we could have a hamburger.'

His delight was so great that he hugged her, and she felt the easy tears spring to her eyes again. God, what had happened to her that she kept on finding herself on the verge of an outburst of tears?

They went to a McDonald's and had hamburgers and french fries and a milk-shake for Laurie. She herself had coffee. It was all terribly 'un-wholefood' and she knew her husband would have been outraged.

On the way home Laurie fell deeply asleep. At the house she picked him up and carried him in as Jack opened the door to her.

'He'd better just go straight to bed,' she said.

'He missed supper.'

'We had hamburgers.'

'Ye Gods. He'll have a nightmare.'

'If he does,' she said, 'it won't be because of the hamburger.'

'No,' he agreed with a grim smile. He made as if to take the child but she shook her head and carried him upstairs.

There she undressed him and gently sponged away the surface dirt without waking him. She put him into his sleeping suit. When she covered him up he gave a great sigh, turned over, and slept on as deeply as ever. Reaction to the scene that had frightened him, together with the day's outing, had exhausted him.

She changed her dress and freshened up before going

downstairs. Jack looked out of the kitchen at her and said: 'If you had hamburgers you won't want to eat, I suppose? No? Well, I'm just making myself a sandwich. There'll be coffee in a minute.'

She came to join him in the big, warm kitchen. 'I'll ring Verdugo-Black at some suitable time tomorrow and say I can't take the post,' she said.

He nodded.

'I ... I'm sorry for the things I said,' she faltered.

'All right.'

She looked at him. 'Aren't you going to apologise too?'

He shrugged. 'I apologise.'

'Thank you.'

He put his sandwich on a plate and the plate on a tray and carried it into the living room. He switched on the television set for the early evening news on BBC 2. He went back into the kitchen for the coffee pot. She followed him out and they sat in silence while the news was read and Jack ate his sandwich.

He got up and switched off the set. 'Nothing else until nine,' he informed her.

'Jack, there's something I have to tell you.' It had been nagging at her all the way home. She had flared up at him because of her suppressed guilt about seeing Charles Vernon. She would tell him, and everything would be cleared up. Jack would be angry, but after all ... She had only seen Charles in public places a little over half a dozen times, and his first effort at helping her had ended in this fiasco.

'Don't let's talk any more about the job –'

'It isn't about the job, Jack. It's more personal –'

'No, don't tell me about it –'

'But it's important, Jack –'

'No!' He threw himself back into his chair.

She was silent, stunned by his vehemence.

236

'When you and I got married,' he said, 'we agreed, didn't we, that we were two distinct personalities, with a right to privacy. I don't want you unburdening yourself onto me, Margaret. I just don't want it.'

She stared at her husband. She knew him so well. He was defending himself against something that would force him to be equally honest.

She heard him saying, when she told him about the new job: 'It means you'll be out of the house every day, doesn't it?'

She, poor fool, had thought that he was saying he'd miss her. But all at once she knew he'd been thinking it would make things easier for him.

Caroline Keppler, of course. She shouldn't have underestimated that young woman's persistence, nor her need for something to amuse herself through her long days alone at home. The Kepplers had their housework done by an expensive house-care service, and their garden by two cheerful old men who arrived twice a week, and their cooking by a daily cook formerly a sous-chef at the Savoy. Caroline had absolutely nothing to do all day. Jack was her occupation.

Margaret had imagined she had scotched the whole thing once she began to stay at home more often. But how very easy it was to arrange to meet. Jack liked to go for free-range eggs to a smallholding about four miles off. The woman there adored Laurie: what easier than to leave him there for an hour or so? And when Jack went to the main library every fortnight to change his books, he didn't like to take the little boy in with him because it was dull for him; so he left him with Caradoc Evans, who ran the Crafte Shoppe. But who could tell how long he actually spent in the library?

She understood that if she told Jack something about some man, he would feel he had to reciprocate. She thought to herself: our marriage has had enough shocks for the present. I mustn't take any more risks.

She remained silent as Jack had bidden her. By and by he put on a record of Duke Ellington, with the volume turned down. The insistent beat filled the room. Blues singers understand about being unhappy, she thought; the blues are the voice of the weary heart.

She lay unsleeping for a long time that night, and Jack was awake too. She wanted to shake his shoulder and ask: 'How many have there been?' For there was no reason to imagine Caroline was the only one. For three years since the birth of Laurie she had been out of the house every weekday and it had never occurred to her to think that he was unfaithful. But while she was away being Somebody Important in the City, who could tell what Jack had been doing?

He was a very attractive man, with an easy smile and his amiable manner and his deep, rich voice. He was, as the approving term had it, sexy. The dark good looks behind the guerrilla fighter's moustache, the rather lanky, upright figure ... she had seen the interest in the eyes of many a woman as they went into a restaurant.

The bedroom was cold since they had turned down the central heating to save fuel. Normally she would have hugged close to Jack for warmth. But tonight she lay chilled and wakeful until at last the wheeling stars out in the black sky bore her consciousness away and she slept.

It had been arranged with Charles that she would see him as usual on Friday. He had taken it so much for granted she would get the job that it hadn't occurred to him she would want to be in touch before that. She went to London and paid her duty call on the Professional and Executive Recruitment Service. Then she walked to Charles's club. He was giving her lunch there; his thinking had been that they had very good vintage champagne there, and she would want to drink a toast.

When he went to fetch her from the ladies' hall, it was

238

immediately clear that everything had gone terribly wrong. 'What happened?' he said, taking her by the elbow.

'The post was in Argentina.'

'Dear God!' It was a gasp of dismay. 'Margaret, I had no *idea* – '

'Of course not. I never thought that.'

It might have passed through her mind. Charles wouldn't have been unhappy to see her settled in Buenos Aires with Jack still in Sussex. He could easily invent reasons for going to Argentina. But the fact truly was that he had thought the job was based in Richmond.

He began to conduct her out of the club's hall. 'Where are we going?' she inquired.

'Well, you don't want a celebratory lunch *here*.'

Head drooping, she nodded.

The club's porter called a taxi. Charles put her into it and gave the driver an address. Margaret didn't ask their destination and said nothing when they drew up outside the Highgate house. He conducted her indoors and took her coat. She sank back into the deep Chesterfield, bathing in the luxury of the warmth, the profusion of flowers and plants, the elegance of fine things that surrounded her.

He brought her a brandy. She sipped it. He sat beside her and said: 'There will be other openings, darling. Don't be sad about this.'

'I'll get over it. It's just ... just ... '

'I know. The disappointment has upset you. I understand.'

'Yes, I know you do,' she said with sudden vehemence. 'Jack doesn't! I don't seem to be able to ... ' She faltered into silence. She set down her glass with a trembling hand.

Suddenly she was in Charles's arms and he was kissing her with a fierceness that almost hurt her. But she was

239

returning his kisses, holding him hard with her arms, straining against him in passionate gratitude for his love. They pressed themselves into the corner of the great deep sofa, arms wound about each other, harshly seeking the assuagement of a long thirst.

Presently he released her. He pulled her to her feet. With his arms about her shoulder he led her, unspeaking, to the pretty staircase. They didn't speak at all as they went into his bedroom.

Until the climax of their love-making, in fact, they said not a word. And then Margaret was gasping, 'Yes, yes, yes!'

But whether it was to Charles's demands or her own need for fulfilment, she couldn't tell.

Chapter Fourteen

They saw each other as often as they could until the interminable end-of-year holiday that takes in both Christmas and New Year. Immediately after that Charles had to go on a business trip taking in Singapore, Hong Kong, Taiwan and Indonesia.

'I can't get out of it,' he explained. 'If I back out, they'll send my assistant as number one, and he'll agree to idiocies that will take us months to unravel.' His assistant was a splendid young man, business school graduate, scion of an old banking family and a whizz with figures – but soft as butter when it came to negotiation.

Margaret understood. She assured him she'd survive the absence, although she knew she would find it hard. When he said he'd write to her care of her club, she shook her head. 'It's not necessary,' she said. 'We know we're thinking of each other.'

'Yes.' He held her hand. 'I wish I could fix something up for you,' he mourned. 'But times are really hard. The one or two openings that I've heard a whisper of, they want a man. I'm sorry, my love, but it's true – men are getting first choice when it comes to upper echelon posts.'

'It's all right.'

'There isn't even anything coming up in the future –'

'Rosie has this contact through her school, a family

that's putting a lot of money into a ski resort and leisure centre – they will be wanted somebody – '

Charles frowned and she paused. 'I know about them,' he said. 'Banque du Lac have money in that. The Swiss are insisting on Swiss nationals being employed – they have their little problems there too, Margaret.'

Because it was their last meeting before his departure, she didn't let it show what a shock his words had been. She'd been keeping that hope in front of her – if all else failed, by next summer perhaps she'd have got this Swiss job. But now ...

The money from the sale of their rugs and bric-à-brac had come through. It helped a little. But during the long holiday, when there was no point in going up to town because all the offices were closed, she occupied herself going over and over their accounts. She had a next year's calendar on which she marked all their forthcoming bills. Rates in March-April, heating bills, petrol costs ...

She kept her conclusion to herself until after New Year. She and Jack hadn't exactly been avoiding each other – that would have been impossible when they were both at home and trying to make Christmas fun for Laurie – but they certainly hadn't had much to say to each other. Nor were there many Christmas visitors. Almost all their Ladhurst friends had fallen away and even Margaret's parents had gone to Majorca for the sun.

But on the 2nd January after the evening meal, she brought her file of bills and liabilities out, and put it on the low table by the side of her chair.

'I want to tell you something, Jack,' she began. 'A business thing.' She said this quickly so that if he feared a disclosure of something personal he would have his mind set at rest.

'Go ahead.' He was watching her, worried by her grave manner.

'We're going to have to sell the house.'

A long silence. Then he said, 'I've been expecting it.'

That at least was a relief. She'd thought he'd make an outcry against it. But he seemed to take it almost in his stride.

She had been coming to this conclusion for the last ten days, and was accustomed to it by now. It had first come into her head while she thought she might just possibly be taking the Buenos Aires job, then as their financial situation in all its starkness came home to her, she had made herself see it as a necessity.

She went through the figures for him. He listened, nodding, but from time to time she sensed his thoughts were elsewhere.

He was thinking about Caroline Keppler. It couldn't be that Margaret was embracing the idea of selling up just to get him away from Caroline? No, Margaret wasn't that sort.

'Where are we going to go?' he inquired.

'We've got to go into London – not right into the centre, we can't afford Belgravia or Kensington but we've got to be within easy travelling distance. And it's got to be a place that's a lot cheaper to run.'

'We've got to have a garden,' he put in. 'I understand we've gone past the point where we can afford all the ground we have here, but Laurie's used to a garden – we can't coop him up in a flat.'

'We'll have to see,' she said. 'Prices are the main thing. I'd like to sell and buy so that we end up with a bit of money in hand.' Her voice wavered. 'I can't go on like this, with absolutely nothing in the bank. It scares me.'

To her surprise he came to her and sat on the arm of her chair. 'Poor old Meggie,' he said. 'It's really rotten for you, isn't it? And it'll be a blow, giving up this place.'

'For you too. You built it up yourself, after all.'

'Yes, I'll miss it.' He sighed. 'But to tell the truth I've

243

been on the verge of suggesting a move, myself. It's a terrible lot of work keeping it going, you know – I was beginning to worry about the cost of tar wash for the orchard and things like that.' He paused. 'I suppose we couldn't sell off a piece of the land – for building?'

'We couldn't get planning permission for building, Jack. And who wants to buy an old orchard or a single paddock at the far end of an unmade road? No, it's best to sell out and go in for something a lot less grand. But the way I look at it is, we ought to be able to come out a little ahead, clear up the overdraft, get rid of the mortgage – the last point is the biggest one. We can't go on any more shelling out money, even at their reduced rate – we simply must bring down our outgoings to something we can manage, because I begin to think I shan't get a suitable job within the foreseeable future.'

'Margaret!'

'It's true. There's not a whisper of anything, and one chance I thought might turn up trumps around June has just vanished. The fact is, Jack ... '

'What?'

'I'm going to have to take what I can get. It's no good dreaming of walking into the executive suite any more. I'm going to have to earn enough to pay off whatever mortgage we take on for the new place and just keep our heads above water that way.'

He put a hand on her shoulder and pressed it. They sat in silence. They were closer in that moment than they had been since the day she came home and lashed out at him because of the Buenos Aires job.

They put the house on the market and when she was next in London she rang a few estate agents from the club. Lists of London houses were sent to them. Having seen Richmond, she had thought it would be rather nice to move there – the Royal Park so close at hand, and the houses so pretty, and the river nearby. But the prices were quite beyond them. She decided on Wimbledon, or Edgware, or one of the other outer suburbs. She was determined to be on easy travel routes to the centre of London, where jobs would be possible.

It fell to Jack to show the first would-be buyer round the Hostlers' House. 'My God,' he said when he collected her from the station that evening, 'I almost got it sold from over my head! He was terrifically keen, love. I don't think there's the slightest problem about selling.'

'Thank God for that.' She leaned back in the passenger seat, exhausted. 'I had a long session with Mr Motley. I could tell he's very relieved we've made the decision to sell. I think he was on the verge of telling us they would have to foreclose otherwise.'

When Charles returned from the Far East at the end of January, he found her pre-occupied. He listened in silence to her news. She nerved herself for his reaction – she expected him to say, 'Don't sell up, I'll give you the money to see you through.' And if he did that, she would have to refuse, because she couldn't accept money from him.

But Charles already knew that. He had tried to give her, as a Christmas present, a charge account at Harrods. She had adamantly refused to accept it. In the end he gave her a record token, grinning wryly as he bought it. But she couldn't accept anything from Charles. It would be too belittling to Jack – as if she were saying silently to him: You see, other men can provide, even if you can't!

It wasn't in her nature to hurt Jack. She thought back with undying shame to the things she had called him when they had that awful fight. She valued their marriage, not only because of their son but because they had meant much to each other over a long time. She had married Jack, knowing what he was. If the financial circumstances had changed, that wasn't his fault. He mustn't be punished for something he hadn't done.

It was bad enough that she was being unfaithful to him. She didn't justify herself by saying, well, he's going to bed with Caroline. That was totally different. She knew Caroline meant very little to him.

Whereas she had fallen in love with Charles. It was not the same as their first liaison six years ago. Then she had liked him, and fancied him, and thought him tremendously attractive. Now he was the safe harbour to which she could return when the storms were too much for her. His stability and good sense, his immediate understanding of her fears – these were the things that made him essential to her. He gave her what Jack could not, a resting place, a sweet refuge from her cares.

For his part Charles understood her only too well. Her pride was his greatest enemy, for it prevented her from permitting his intervention. He picked his way carefully around any mention of her immediate monetary problems. If she insisted on selling up her home, he couldn't stop her, nor would he insult her by trying to buy it off.

In fact, in some secret recess of his mind, he was glad that she had come to this huge decision. Let her see what it was like to live in the less rural situation of outer London. Let her discover the disadvantages of neighbours close at hand, complaining about her son's ball coming over the fence. Let her go through the drudgery of an everyday job without the prestige of high executive status. Perhaps it would teach her that her marriage was costing her too much. And when she learned that lesson – then Charles's chance would come.

The prospective buyer whom Jack had shown round proved to be a hard bargainer. He told the estate agent he thought the house was over-priced for the accommodation it offered. 'I'm afraid he wants you to bring the price down a bit,' said Mr Bendigo, the estate agent. 'Of course we understood you'd accept less, as is usual . . . '

'But how much less?' Margaret asked with apprehension.

'We-ell . . . he wants you to come down by ten thousand.'

'Ten thousand!'

'It's a lot, I know, but what he says has a lot of justice. There are only three bedrooms, after all – and the grounds are so big it means having to have a gardener, but there's nowhere to accommodate the usual gardener-and-housekeeper. No spare bedroom for them, no flat, no gardener's cottage.'

'Good God, it's not a stately home we're offering,' Jack burst out. 'It's – '

'A very nice house. Yes, I know what you mean, Mr Durley. But the fact is . . . you see, you reconstructed the old place to suit your individual needs. That makes it difficult for anyone wanting to buy. It's a long way from anywhere, quite difficult to keep up, but only room for a small family, really. You see?'

'You didn't say this when we first talked about it,' Margaret accused.

'No, we-ell, you see, these things come up best when clients hear them from would-be buyers.'

She shook her head. 'We can't accept a price as low as that, Mr Bendigo. We have to buy something in London with what we get for the Hostlers' House.'

'We-ell,' said Mr Bendigo. It was his favourite word, capable of expressing doubt, agreement, or interest. 'We needn't worry too much about losing this purchaser. There'll be others.'

She saw that he was waiting for them to learn sense, the hard way. She accepted they would have to lower their asking price, but she really couldn't let it go too far below their target price. The cost of a house in London was frightening to her. To get something in a district she

247

liked, they would have to pay almost as much as they'd get for the Hostlers' House.

But as the days went by she began to see they really weren't going to do as well out of the sale as she'd hoped. The drawbacks pointed out by Bendigo were real. What they were offering was a pretty but unmanageable house. They would have to take quite a lot less than they had hoped.

Which in its turn meant they would have to be content with something less prestigious in London. Margaret took the car and went prospecting, looking at maps and visiting empty houses. Everything she saw that was within their budget began to seem poky and dreary. She got very discouraged, but tried not to show it. Jack meanwhile had his hard times. Prospective buyers were shown round the house and annoyed him by making silly criticisms. 'That guy this afternoon,' he would report with ire, 'said he didn't like factory-made tiles arranged in rows over the sink. I told him in no uncertain terms they'd been designed and made for us at a local pottery – you should have seen his face!'

'Jack ... It's no good antagonising buyers ... '

'He wasn't going to buy. He and his wife only came to make a day out. They asked me to make them a cup of tea! I told them I hadn't time and shoved them out.'

So it went on. The object of the sale had been to pay off their debts and give them a new start but as the weeks passed it began to be clear they would scarcely manage it. Margaret had at last found a little house with some character where she thought they might make a new beginning – in Kingston, a little semi-detached Victorian cottage not far from Bushey Park. Its asking price was lower than its position merited because it had been lived in by an elderly lady who had let it get into a bad state. Jack, having been taken to see it, was full of enthusiasm: 'I can do a lot with that, Meg! It means camping out for a bit in one room while I get it sorted out, but bit by bit I can make something of it! And of course the garden's a decent size – not up to what we're leaving, but I can get a few things in for the summer so we can have fresh vegetables.'

'And Bushey Park quite near for Laurie – '

'Yes, great, I can take him there every day.'

They made an offer, the usual dickering went on, and they settled at last for a price they were sure to reach when they themselves sold up. They had three offers now for their own house, none of them as high as they'd hoped but it became imperative to accept one if they weren't going to be crippled by a bridging loan. The solicitors got to work, contracts were drawn up, and the day came when the deed was done: their joint signatures on the documents meant they were leaving the Hostlers' House. They would be in their new home by Easter.

Margaret thought back with incredulity to last Easter. They had gone to Mombasa for a holiday. Mombasa! It seemed impossible that they had ever been able to afford such a thing. She tried to recall the spirit of confident optimism in which she had returned home from that holiday, ready to take up her work again and hoping to lay a plan before her board of directors for a new department which she would head.

She had lost all that now. Her confidence had been badly shaken by the events of the last year. Her job was gone, her marriage had changed from an easy partnership of affection to a mere domestic fact. But perhaps once they had left Sussex everything would improve. She and Jack had been closer again these last weeks, during the turmoil of selling and buying the houses. She had not seen Charles, and she was sure Jack had not seen Caroline. She couldn't tell how she was sure – it just seemed so.

She left all the business of packing up and selling off

what they didn't need to her husband. It was now absolutely imperative that she got a job. The building society had been very co-operative throughout all the financial arrangements for the new house but now they expected her to make mortgage repayments like everyone else – much lower payments than hitherto but they absolutely must be met. To meet them she must have a job. She must take what she could get.

During the house-hunting she had had three job interviews set up for her by the Professional and Executive Recruitment Centre. She'd admitted that from now on she wouldn't be expecting top echelon offers, so they had been able to arrange for her to see three prospective employers. At each of the interviews she felt she'd done well, impressed the recruiting officer or interview board. Yet she didn't succeed with any of them.

It was the third interview that gave her the clue. She was being surveyed by the firm's staff officer, a young middle-aged man with rather too much weight round his middle but kindly eyes under sandy brows. She'd thought he looked a little surprised when she was shown in, but couldn't think why – he knew of course that she was a woman applicant so it couldn't be that.

They talked through her qualifications, he sketched the work she might be doing if she got the post. He asked if there were any questions she wanted to ask and, as always, she spoke up well, with intelligence and confidence. He replied to her questions briefly, watching her with slightly perplexed eyes. When the interview was heading towards its close, he sat back in his chair and picked up her curriculum vitae.

'You seem a bit over-qualified for this job,' he murmured on an inflection of inquiry.

She smiled. 'That's a good thing, surely?'

'Er ... I wonder? You're accustomed to command, I take it.'

'Well ... yes.'

'You see, Mrs Durley, if you got this job, you'd have to take orders, not give them. I mean, you wouldn't be head of a department nor even assistant head. Do you think ... I mean, would you adapt?'

'Of course, Mr Lord. Being in business is a constant process of adaptation.'

He nodded, but not as if he were convinced. 'Thank you then, Mrs Durley, you'll hear from us one way or the other in a day or two.'

She left the office sure that he liked her, that he was impressed by her ability. Yet the letter that came was a turn-down. After she had got over her disappointment, she sat down in the livingroom of their new cottage, and tried to think what had gone wrong.

Over-qualified? She looked through her summary of jobs and the reference from Hebberwood Breweries. Was it this that caused prospective employers to shy away from her? Did they think she'd be unable to accept direction, that she would be uppish, unco-operative? Naturally a head of department didn't want a woman on his staff who knew more than he did. She should have thought of that.

Next day she went to see the employment officer at the P&E centre. 'Is there anything else you think I could apply for?' she inquired.

'Not just at the moment, I'm afraid.'

'Mr Syams, the next time something comes up, would you be so kind as not to send out all the information about me that you have there?'

'I beg your pardon?'

'I think I've failed in those three chances you set up for me because I scared them off. I walk in as a former head of department when all they want is a general intelligent staff member. Don't you see? The man who's going to have to give me orders doesn't like it. He feels – '

'Mrs Durley, it's up to us to do the best we can for you.

It wouldn't be right to play down your experience – '

'Please! I need a job, Mr Syams! I can't spoil my own chances by showing up like Wonder Woman when they want the quiet version with the horn-rimmed glasses.'

Syams laughed. He'd got very fond of Mrs Durley in the months since she first came to the Recruitment Centre. 'I see what you mean. Hm ... It means you'll have to re-write your curriculum vitae to suit your new persona.'

'I've already done it,' she said. She brought an envelope out of her handbag.

'But your reference from Hebberwood – ?'

'I'll arrange that,' she said. 'I'll speak to Mr Twillan. I'll get him to do a watered down version.'

There wasn't time for that. Next day she got a phone call from Syams to say a travel firm urgently needed a Bookings and Foreign Correspondence Executive due to the sudden death of a previous employee. 'They don't mind male or female although the chap who died was – well – a man. He had a heart attack. Do you want to go for it? It's urgent – bookings are flowing in from the public and it's a fairly small firm so they have to fill the post.'

She asked about the salary and conditions. It sounded reasonable. She would only be getting about half what she'd had from Hebberwood and the only perk seemed to be the possibility of free or cheap travel abroad. But it was all to do with work she'd already learned very well. 'I'll go for it, Mr Syams. Thank you.'

This time she didn't, as before, put on one of her best dresses and top it with the camel hair coat. Nor did she don shoes from Rayne and gloves from Rive Gauche. She chose a dark wool suit and a plain silk blouse, and carried a handbag from a chain store. She looked smart and attractive but not elegant. It was just the effect she'd intended.

252

Her husband frowned at her as she set off for the bus to Kingston Station. 'Not very glam?' he queried.

'No, I've decided glamour is for film stars.'

'You sure?'

'Yes, love. I've made a plan. I really hope to get this job.'

'Good luck.'

'Thank you.'

The travel firm had its headquarters in Ebury Street, an easy walk from Victoria which she reached by train after a change at Clapham Junction. She was asked to wait. She was almost sure the previous applicant was still being interviewed. She found she was nervous. That was new – normally interviews didn't worry her. It was because this time she was playing a part. She had to give the impression she knew enough to do this job, but not enough so that she would frighten her employer.

The managing director was conducting the interviews. He had a partner with him, an older man who said little. The managing director was Oliver Armitage, a man with something of a name for expertise about Roman and Hellenic antiquities. The firm specialised in taking groups to areas of special interest in Europe and South America; Margaret knew of them from her prior experience in the travel business.

'Mrs Durley,' he welcomed her. 'Do sit down. I've read your application with interest. You worked for Hebberwood's travel department?'

'That is so.'

'What was your work?'

'I arranged travel and accommodation for the directors, heads of departments, publicity men, specialists – that kind of thing. And their wives and families, of course.'

'I see. You were with them – how long?'

She let him take her through it. She played down her

personal involvement with the top brass of Hebber-wood. She didn't let it become known that she had had a big staff under her. The one thing she used as a factor was her languages, which she knew would be of paramount importance in a firm like this. Armitage glanced with satisfaction at the quiet man at his right as the interview ended. 'Well, I think that's all I want to ask. What about you, James?'

The other man conducted a cross-questioning about customs requirements and the law concerning foreigners in various European countries. He caught her out once, when he asked her about petrol allowances in Yugo-slavia. She smiled in apology: 'I'm sorry, I haven't any actual experience in arranging travel to Yugoslavia – but I'd certainly learn all that.'

'I'm sure you would,' he agreed. 'Is there anything you'd like to ask us?'

She asked the expected questions, about salary and holiday allowance and pension rights. When it was time to leave, Armitage inquired: 'Ah ... If we should wish you to start immediately, Mrs Durley, could you do so?'

'Certainly.' She hid her eagerness.

'That's very helpful. We may be in touch fairly soon. We only have to take up your reference.'

'Oh yes.'

'No problem about that?' he said quickly, catching something in her voice.

'Not at all. I was going to say, if it's urgent, you could ring them.'

'Thank you, we have a couple of other applicants to see. Good morning, Mrs Durley, thank you for giving us the chance to see you.'

She went out, convinced she'd got the job. All she had to do was to prevent Mr Twillan from spoiling everything by telling the truth about her. She hurried to the nearest telephone box and rang Hebberwood's. She laid out a line of coins in front of her in case she should be held up by the switchboard but to her relief was put through almost at once.

'Mrs Durley!' Twillan exclaimed in pleasure as he came on. 'It's such a long time since I heard from you! How's the world been treating you?'

'Not too well, Mr Twillan, and that's why I'm ringing you.'

'Indeed? My, my, I'm sorry to hear that. You know there have been a great many changes here, too, since you left – '

'Mr Twillan, excuse me, I'm in a phone box and my money may run out if I don't tell you quickly why I'm ringing. May I?'

'Oh – of course – '

'I've just been for a job interview, Mr Twillan. I think I got the job but I had to keep it from them that I'd been head of a department in Hebberwood's.'

'I beg your pardon?'

'I'm going after a lesser post, you see. I . . . It's difficult to explain. There's nothing doing up at the top of the ladder, Mr Twillan, so I've had to come down several rungs.'

'But – my dear Mrs Durley – that would be a waste, surely?'

'Mr Twillan, it's almost a year since I left Hebberwood's and I haven't been able to land a single job. And it's very important that I get this one.' She drew a deep breath. 'I *need* this job, Mr Twillan.'

She heard him clear his throat in embarrassment. 'Well . . . I understand . . . of course times are hard . . . '

'Mercury Travel will be ringing you. A Mr Armitage, I think. I've just come from the interview and they liked me, I could tell. But they only want a medium-grade executive, you understand, someone to handle bookings and foreign correspondence. They aren't in the market for a high-powered lady.' She hesitated. 'Is this clear to you, Mr Twillan?'

'I ... er ... I think so. What do you want me to say to them?'

'If they inquire, say I worked *in* the old T&A department. Don't let them know I ran it. They'll ask why I was given the push and of course you'll say, which is true, that the department was disbanded. If they ask what I was being paid, I ... I ... I'd like you to say you can't remember for sure without looking it up. I think they'll tell you not to bother because they're in a bit of a bind – they desperately need to get someone in the office to deal with this stuff that's piling up.' She paused. She knew she was giving him orders, but there wasn't time to pussyfoot – his other phone might ring at any moment and it would be Mercury Travel taking up her references. 'If you could play down my role with Hebberwood's I'd be very grateful, Mr Twillan.'

'Mrs Durley, I don't think I should be asked to tell any lies – '

'No, no – I'm not asking that.' She felt something like a sob rising in her throat. '*Please*, Mr Twillan. Help me.'

There was a little silence. Then he said, gently, 'Of course. Though it does seem strange, being asked to make less of you than you deserve.'

'It's what I need, really it is. I'm tired of being awfully clever and efficient but unemployed. I'll be eternally grateful to you.'

'Leave it to me, my dear.'

The pips sounded. 'I must go,' Margaret said.

'Very well. Good luck, Margaret.'

She went home, afraid to be hopeful but nevertheless feeling it in her bones that Mercury would be in touch. Sure enough, soon after breakfast next morning, when she was helping Jack paint the hall, their elderly telephone rang. Hastily wiping her hands on a turpentine rag, she picked up the instrument they had inherited from the previous occupant. It was the man Armitage had referred to as James.

'Mrs Durley? James O'Dowd here. Mrs Durley, if you could be ready to start work next Monday, the job at Mercury Travel is yours.'

'Oh!' Although the major part of her brain had been expecting it, some lesser part had been warning against disappointment. Now she stood speechless.

'Mrs Durley? Mrs Durley? Are you there?'

'Yes, I am, Mr O'Dowd.'

'Can we expect you at nine o'clock Monday morning?'

'Yes, of course. Thank you.'

'No thanks required. We were very impressed with you. You'll bring your insurance cards and so forth?'

'Yes, I will.'

'Ask for Elizabeth Sojorr. She'll show you your desk and so forth. We'll give you the first hour or so to settle in and then we'll see you at coffee time to put you in the picture. All right?'

'Yes, thank you, Mr O'Dowd.'

'Fine. See you Monday. Letter follows, as they say.'

She put the phone down, ran into the hall, and threw her arms round Jack. 'I've got it!' she cried. 'I've got it!'

'The job?' He swung her round. 'Eureka! Great!'

'Mummy, Mummy – what is it?' shouted Laurie, running in from the back garden at the whoops of delight.

'Mummy's got a job, darling!' She scooped him up and swung him. 'A job, angel! Everything's going to be all right now!'

'It's good, isn't it?' the little boy shouted in delight, not really understanding. 'Ooh! Can we have fruit yoghurt?'

'Yes, darling, fruit yoghurt, and crisps.'

'Crisps too?' He began to dance about the hall. Order was only restored by the necessity to stop him before he kicked the paint tin over.

Chapter Fifteen

Mr Motley of the building society was extremely relieved and glad to hear of Margaret's job. He had been keeping their mortgage in being by a kind of personal juggling which could easily have ended in disaster, but now that there was an employer's name to enter in the new documents he set about having them prepared with alacrity.

'I'm so glad,' he told her as he shook hands when she was about to go. 'Not only so that we can have all this cleared up –' he gestured at his desk – 'but for your sake too. It's been a long haul for you.'

She nodded. 'I haven't enjoyed it much. But I suppose I've learned a lot ...'

'Well, good luck in the new home.'

'Thanks, Mr Motley. You've been very kind.'

'Not at all, not at all.' He sighed after she'd gone. He wouldn't see her again, probably. Not unless things took a turn for the worse again, and he wouldn't wish that on her. She was a nice girl. He wished he'd met her years ago, before she was married ... He pulled his thoughts together with a jerk. Woolgathering ... that would never do.

Charles was neither relieved nor particularly glad to hear about the job. He regarded it as part of Margaret's necessary education. He hadn't seen her so often since the New Year but he hadn't let that worry him too much because when she was in a state of nervous tension over house-hunting and job-hunting, they didn't have so much fun together. Now a period of comparative tranquillity lay ahead, during which she would have to acclimatise herself to that poky little house and that potty little firm.

Charles had taken the trouble to drive past the new house. To his eyes it had the appearance of an artisan's dwelling, and not in very good repair at that. As to Mercury Travel, he'd asked the invaluable Mrs Stoppard to make inquiries about them. They were stable, well-regarded, but hardly high-powered. A few months' drudging for them would make Margaret appreciate what he could offer her in its place.

It was true, the offices at Mercury Travel were not luxurious. They were in a narrow four storey house in Ebury Street, with the reception office and director's suite on the ground floor. Up a narrow steep staircase on the first floor was the planning department, above that the bookings department, and on the fourth the accounts shared the floor with a mini-computer and a small kitchen where tea and coffee could be prepared. There was of course no staff canteen; it was taken for granted that employees would go out to lunch or, under pressure of work, snatch a sandwich at the desk.

What Margaret found hardest to bear was the noise. She had always been accustomed to having an office to herself since almost her very first days as a business-woman. Now she shared an open-plan area with eight other staff, and the telephones never seemed to stop ringing. The rattle of electric typewriters, the chatter of telephone conversation, the rattle and clang of filing drawers being opened and closed, the chatter of the computer from the top floor ...

Another hardship, though she didn't let it show, was having to do her own typing. She had always been

259

accustomed to dictating correspondence; now she had to do her own, for only the directors had a secretary and the rest of the correspondence was dealt with either through form letters put out by the computer or by personal letters typed individually. Margaret reminded herself that having to type was no hardship. But for the first few weeks she found it very tiring because she was unaccustomed to it.

Overtime was taken for granted. It was paid for, but she would have preferred to get home rather than stay cooped up in the office dealing with telephone queries in other time zones. She had often stayed late at Hebberwood's, but that had been different; she could saunter down to the garage then and drive home to the uncrowded countryside. Now she had to travel by rail to Kingston, and the trains after about seven in the evening were a little scary, apt to be empty and threatening.

She and Jack had debated whether she should drive to work in the Renault. But it meant finding somewhere to park when she got to Victoria, and that was a difficult undertaking. Besides, if she went into one of the big commercial car parks, the cost was quite high. And, finally, Jack could make good use of the car to transport the various raw materials he needed for house improvements.

Before they moved into the cottage he had done a quick job on the livingroom. Now he was at work on the kitchen. He had dismantled all the equipment except the plumbing, so that they had to cook their meals on an electric hot plate in the livingroom for the present. It was all terribly inconvenient and not the least bit relaxing to come home to, but he was making a good job of the kitchen with relatively inexpensive materials. Gone were the days when they surveyed a wall and said: 'What that needs is ceramic tiles,' then went out to order them. Now Jack used cheaper ingredients, yet his craftsman's hands wrought them into something very pleasing.

But when he had finished the kitchen there was the bathroom to do, and then the diningroom, and then the upstairs rooms ...

'It sounds like the Forth Bridge,' Charles laughed when she told him. 'He'll just get to the top of the house and finish when it's time to start redecorating below.'

She shook her head. 'Your standards of decoration are higher than ours, these days,' she reminded him.

'Margaret, I don't know how you bear it! It all sounds so ... second rate!'

'There's an old saying about cutting your coat according to your cloth ...'

'But you needn't be restricted to such narrow cloth, my love –'

She turned away, shrugging off his words. She thought once again he was on the verge of offering her money, and wanted to avoid it.

But he had had something different in mind. He'd wanted to tell her he was serious about her, that she could share his life with him if only she would make the break. Instinct told him to hold his tongue. The moment wasn't yet right.

They were in his house in Highgate, early in the evening of a fine July day. Margaret had been in her new job for two months, long enough for the novelty to have worn off. She was supposed to be working late, as far as Jack was aware. Charles had given her champagne and smoked salmon sandwiches, then they had gone to bed together in the lovely high-ceilinged room where the westering sun touched the moulded cornices with gold. He leaned up on an elbow and studied her.

'You've changed,' he told her. 'I like the way you wear your hair now.'

'Easier to handle,' she murmured. She ran her hands through it. It was rumpled after their love-struggle, her brow still had the touch of sweat under the hairline.

'I love you, Margaret.'

'I love you too, Charles.'

'Do you really? Or do you say it because you feel you ought to?'

'I love you, Charles. I didn't think I'd get so serious about you.' She sighed. 'I don't know why I let it happen.'

'Because you needed me. That was it, wasn't it?'

'I suppose so.'

'I could do so much more for you if you'd let me, darling –'

'No, don't talk like that.' She pulled herself up, glanced at her wrist. 'I must go, Charles.'

'No, not yet, it's barely seven –'

'I must. I said I'd be home by eight.'

'A few minutes either way won't make much difference –'

'Yes, I must, Laurie will be waiting to say goodnight.' At four years old now, he was allowed to stay up till she came home.

Charles said no more. Against that argument, he had nothing to offer. He went into the small dressing room while she dressed and freshened her make-up in his bedroom and then, unasked, he drove her in his Porsche to Kingston. The journey took almost no time at all on the by-pass. He set her down at a bus-stop so that she could finish the journey as if she had come home in the usual routine.

'Goodbye, darling. Shall I see you Tuesday?'

'Let me ring you and let you know,' she said. She never liked to be tied down too far in advance; he knew it, and didn't press. 'Goodbye, Charles.'

'Goodbye for the present, my love.'

He stayed parked until he saw her board the bus. She waved to him as she was carried away. She looked back and saw the powerful car move into the traffic stream and vanish from sight. She sighed. It was hateful having to part from him like that, but what could she do?

At the sound of the garden gate opening, the front door opened too, and Jack was in the hall. At his side was Laurie, with a large piece of sticking plaster on the side of his head.

'Darling!' she cried, and ran up the tiled path. 'What happened?'

'A boy hit me, Mummy,' he told her importantly.

'Hit you?' She picked him up and looked over his head at her husband.

'Not to worry,' he said. 'He's all right.'

'Oh, is he? With a square foot of Elastoplast on his head?'

He shook his head at her warningly, and she fell silent. Laurie in his sleeping suit clung to her, but was clearly drowsy. She took him upstairs and put him to bed. He held her hand for a moment or two then settled down under the sheets.

She ran downstairs. Her shoes hammered on the uncarpeted treads. 'Now,' she burst out as she came into the livingroom, 'what happened?'

'It was at play school,' he told her. 'I got there as usual to collect him at twelve, and there he was with the bandage on. Seems some kid took offence and hit him with a wooden train.'

'Hit him? Jack, what are you talking about? Laurie doesn't get into fights!'

'This kid is easy to provoke, apparently. It wasn't a fight, exactly. He's a bit of a difficult character, this one – name's Bobbie Withers, seems he's got problems. He's had a go at some of the other kids.'

'Jack!'

He shrugged, and went to the sideboard. 'Want a drink?'

'Have we got anything?'

'I could whip up a gin and tonic.'

She nodded, and as he prepared it said: 'I hope you told them they must get rid of this Bobbie Withers.'

'Well ... I was a bit annoyed, as you can imagine. But all they said was that children are aggressive and Laurie must get used to it.'

She stared at him. 'What? Get used to having his head cut open?'

'It's not as bad as that, love. He's got a slight cut and a bruise. They'd called a doctor who said he was okay, didn't need stitches or anything like that.'

'Called a doctor!' She was aghast. 'He's not going back there!'

He brought her drink, and sat down opposite with his own. 'Listen, Meg, I think we've got to come to terms with it. We're not living in posh little Ladhurst any more, with the cocktail set. Life is a bit more real and earnest hereabouts –'

'But not to the extent that Laurie's going to have to learn self-defence! He's not going back to that play school!' She took a gulp of gin and tonic to assuage her wrath.

'I wonder ... There's nobody for him to play with around here. The neighbours on both sides are elderly, and the nearest family – the MacIlvrays, you met them on Saturday – their youngest is eight. That's too big an age gap.'

'We'll find another play group –'

'They mostly close down for August anyway.'

'Right, we'll find another for September. But I'm not having him at a group where one of the other children is likely to attack him for no reason.'

'All right, all right, calm down. No great harm's been done.'

'How can you take it so easily?' she flared. 'He might

264

have been badly hurt –'

'He might fall and break a leg in the park, if you want to start getting anxious about everything,' Jack said. 'He's got to learn to live with life as it is. Don't get in a state about it.'

Laurie seemed none the worse for his battle. The sticking plaster was taken off two days later and the following day he'd forgotten about it. When he asked why he wasn't going to play school, Jack told him it had closed until the autumn, which satisfied him.

Margaret found it less easy to dismiss. Apart from scratches and grazed knees, and small childish ailments, Laurie had never had anything go wrong with him. To think that he could be hurt in the safety of a play school was unsettling. What would it be like when he had to go to infant school? Gone were all the hopes of a private school for him; he would have to take the rough and tumble of state school.

Something of this came out in conversation with Charles when she saw him again. It was the opening he'd been waiting for.

'Margaret,' he said, 'I could give that boy a marvellous start in life if you'd let me. There'd be no anxiety about little neighbourhood toughs – we could send him to a good private school like Hill House.'

The name of the school held her attention for a fraction of a second – the idea of Laurie's attending it flashed like a neon sign and then went off. She heard the rest of the sentence echoing in her mind. 'We?' she queried.

'You and I. You must know I want to marry you, Margaret. This isn't a casual affair we're having.'

They were in his car, parked at a spot where they had a view of Epsom Downs. This evening there had been time only for Charles to meet her and bring her partway home, because he had had a late business conference.

But they were so at ease with each other that it contented them just to sit and talk, arms lying lightly along each other's shoulders.

'But ... what about Jack?' she faltered.

'What about him? He's a grown man. He's had five or six years lolling about at your expense. It's time he went out and earned a living for himself ...'

'No, you don't understand,' she said. She sighed inwardly. Why did everyone find it so difficult to understand? 'He hasn't lolled about at my expense. He's worked hard – he's run the house, brought up Laurie, tried to be a sculptor. He's –'

'He's had it easy,' Charles interrupted. 'Stop making excuses for him. He let you shoulder all the burdens –'

'But that was the way we wanted it! And in any case, he had burdens to carry. It's no fun, you know, bucking convention. He's done it well, hardly ever lost his cool when people were snide –'

'Is that what I'm being?' Charles asked, hurt.

'No, I didn't mean that. Darling, you know I didn't! But it's no good trying to justify leaving him by belittling him. Jack's his own man, even if you don't understand or approve of him.'

'Well, since he's his own man, he'd survive the break-up of your marriage –'

'But then you're talking about taking Laurie away from him –'

'Naturally! The child usually goes to the mother, and heaven knows we could give him a far better life than Jack ever could. Unless he pulled his finger out and got a job, I don't even know what they'd live on. Of *course* Laurie would come to us.'

'But ... I couldn't do that to Jack,' she broke out. 'I haven't the *right*.'

He turned in the driving seat to face her. He frowned. 'I don't see what you mean. Of course you've the right.

You're the child's mother – you want what's best for him.'

'But you see ... Laurie is almost more Jack's child than mine. It was Jack who looked after him when I went back to work. It was Jack who walked the floor with him when he was teething. It was Jack who saw him take his first step –'

'Yes, and he robbed you of all that!'

She shook her head with a vehemence that was almost fierce. 'Why do you say things like that? I chose it that way. I'm not saying I always enjoyed the way things worked out, that I didn't sometimes envy those moments I'd missed. But the fact remains that it was Jack who cared for Laurie, and if you want to hear the truth, it's to Jack that Laurie turns when things go wrong. Jack has first claim.'

'But in a court of law –'

'I'm not talking about a court of law! I'm talking about what's right! I could never take Laurie away from Jack, never, never!'

Charles saw that he'd made a mistake, that he must go no further with the thought tonight. He must let the subject drop, but not until he'd put himself into the right again.

'I wouldn't want to hurt Jack,' he agreed, with a little unhappy shrug. 'I've nothing against him, Margaret, you know that. Except, of course, that he makes your life difficult –' As she was about to break in he went on quickly: 'Not intentionally, I agree. But you deserve someone better, someone who could share your burdens more equally. It's because I care so much that I see the weight you carry in your marriage. Forgive me for trying to interfere, Margaret. Put it down to a deep concern for you.'

'Of course, darling,' she said, and melted into his arms in gratitude and love.

When she got home she was only a little later than she would have been at the end of a normal working day. The house was full of a very appetising smell. Jack called from the kitchen, 'Two minutes to wash your hands and then dinner's served.'

'Right.' She ran upstairs, threw down her handbag, changed her shoes, washed her hands, and was back in time to sit down at the kitchen table with Laurie as Jack turned from the oven with a big platter. 'Chicken and chips for three, courtesy of Colonel Sanders!' he announced, and plumped it on the table.

She stared at it. Not only was there chicken and chips, but coleslaw and sauce and sweet corn. The whole array must have cost five pounds.

'Jack!' she cried in alarm. It was a large part of a week's housekeeping.

'Gorgeous, isn't it? You see, I took Laurie into town to see a railway exhibition at Central Hall. It was great, wasn't it, Laurie?'

'It was soo-oper,' sighed the little boy. 'They all went round and under tunnels –'

'And we got so immersed we stayed longer than I intended – incidentally, thought I might see you at Victoria on our way home. I almost rang your office to say we could meet up and come home together –'

She coloured up like fire, but Jack was so engrossed in putting large pieces of chicken on plates that he didn't notice. 'Anyhow,' he went on, pushing his son's eager hand away from the container of coleslaw, 'when I realised the time I thought I wouldn't have time to do all the salad ingredients I'd planned for tonight. So I just popped into the fried chicken shop and got us a surprise party!'

'It's a party!' squealed Laurie. 'And we got fruit yoghurt to eat for pudding.'

'Jack,' Margaret began, 'this must have cost –'

'Oh yes, it cost a lot, but it's only once, you know, and I thought –'

'You thought what? That it didn't matter if we couldn't afford meat again until next week?'

He looked up at her suddenly. All at once her disapproval, her annoyance, came home to him. 'Well, there's no need to look like that about it,' he said. 'I haven't stolen anything or hit a policeman –'

'Can I have my coleslaw now, Daddy?'

'You can't have any coleslaw, Laurie,' Margaret said. 'It'll make you sick –'

'Daddy said I could! You promised!' Laurie wailed, turning tear-filled eyes on his father.

'Yes, all right, Mummy didn't know I'd promised. Here you are.' He put about a saltspoonful on the little boy's plate. It wasn't going to do a healthy little boy any harm, but that wasn't the point, she felt.

'Eat up your supper, Laurie,' she said. 'It's nearly bed time.'

'Yes, Mummy.' Subdued, but glad to have won his point about the coleslaw, Laurie ate. He didn't notice that his parents said very little during the meal. He was busy with memories of his adventurous afternoon, which had included a journey by rail to London, a long session with marvellous train sets that looked almost real, and an ice-cream from a kiosk just outside the hall.

He went up to bed obediently, had his bath, and was tucked in by his mother. He was by then too sleepy to notice she seemed quiet.

When she came down again Jack was looking at the evening paper to see if there was anything worth watching on television. 'Well, say it,' he remarked as she sat down. 'I'm a wasteful spendthrift and should have my head examined.'

'Well, it wasn't very sensible, was it?'

'You don't want to hear my side of it?'

269

'I heard it. You were short of time when you came home so you splurged a fiver on quick food. Quite apart from the fact that we've always agreed we won't give Laurie things like that –?'

'Ooh! And who fed Laurie hamburger and milk shake at Brighton one day –'

'Jesus! Are we going to go back over ancient history? Besides, you know that was a day when I was upset –'

'Right, so it's okay when you get emotional but not okay when –'

'Don't let's have a row about it, Jack. I don't want a row. I'm tired and all I want is a bit of peace and quiet –'

'And you think I'm fresh as a daisy, do you? I've had a long day too and I was rather looking forward to a bit of peace and quiet – but no, in you come and take off about the cost of the meal without any kind of hello or how are you.' He was on his feet staring down at her. 'The trouble with you, Margaret, is that you've got a mind like a calculator!'

He walked out. She heard him go upstairs into the spare room and slam the door. After a bit she could hear him moving about. She picked up the discarded paper, looked at it, and put it down. She went into the kitchen and did the washing up. She felt aggrieved and hard done by.

Yet as the evening wore on and her husband didn't reappear, she began to feel guilty. She had lashed out at him because of the conversation she'd had with Charles – Charles had said that Jack was unthinking, selfish, and she'd spoken to him as if it were true.

But after all, who was going to have to economise to cover for the expense of tonight? Who did the catering? She had no right to flare up like that unless she was going to sit down and plan menus.

And moreover, to overspend so as to give them all a treat was such a small thing, compared to her own misdoings. While Jack had been taking their little boy to see model trains, she had been with her lover. Who was really to blame here? Why should she visit on Jack her own feelings of guilt?

She sighed and smiled and shook her head. It was a storm in a tea-cup after all. She'd apologise to him at bedtime.

But when she went up to bed, Jack was still working in the spare room. She tapped on the door and called, 'I'm off to bed.' He replied curtly, 'Goodnight.' She echoed the word and went into their bedroom. She meant to stay awake until he came in but she was too tired. It was the first time they'd had a row without saying sorry before the sun went down.

When she got up next morning Jack was still asleep. She tiptoed about getting washed and dressed, and as she passed the spare room door curiosity made her open it and glance in.

Jack had got out his charcoal and sketching block. There were outlines with numerals written beside them. They made no sense to her, but she felt a little surge of resentment. He was thinking of taking up his sculpture again. With so much still to do in the house and garden, he was going to waste his time on chipping at blocks of wood or stone – expensive wood and stone, too! She went downstairs to make her coffee and toast. Her little boy woke soon after and she heard Jack go in to him. Her irritation with him hadn't abated. She picked up her belongings, called, 'I'm off!' and left the house for work. The fact that she hadn't looked in on Laurie would tell her husband how displeased she was. She was punishing them all, herself included.

The uneasy atmosphere at home didn't abate. Jack seemed unusually cool with her, as if he felt she ought to make the first move towards an apology. Well, she'd wanted to do that, at the very outset. But now he was compounding his extravagance by wasting his time on his carving. He went up to the spare room every evening, leaving her to the company of the television set or the record player when she was home. As a result, she accepted Charles's invitations when she might not have done.

'What's wrong, Margaret?' Charles asked. 'I can tell you're on edge. Is it the job?'

'Oh, no, I've worked my way into that. I've got used to working in an uproar. No, the job's all right.'

'Then it's at home?'

'I haven't admitted anything *is* wrong.'

'You don't have to. I can tell. I can sense your moods, my dear.'

She leaned against him. His lovely house breathed peace and contentment around them. The french windows were open on the evening-shaded garden, allowing the scent of stocks and honeysuckle to drift in. They had eaten pheasant and drunk Burgundy, for August was with them now.

'Sometimes I wish ...'

'What, darling?'

She shook her head. She'd been about to say, sometimes I wish I'd married you six years ago. If she had, this house would have been hers. She could have come home in the evenings from her office to this haven, with servants to wait on her. There would have been none of the endless chores that awaited her now, evenings and weekends – no stripping down of paintwork, so sizing of walls, no digging up of ancient privet hedges, no pursuit of silverfish behind flaking plaster ...

And Charles would have been there. Charles, eager only to see that she was happy. Caring, loving, offering total security and ease, sharing her love of opera and ballet and languages ...

What did she really have in common with Jack? There had been a strong physical attraction which had lasted many years, but that seemed to be dying now. She and Jack hadn't slept together for weeks. There had been a delight in his quirky character, but now she found him tiresome – or at least, he wasn't as cheerful and amusing as he used to be.

Neither are you, whispered a voice within her. She shivered and crushed the thought.

'Have you thought any more of what I said to you three weeks ago?' Charles asked in a quiet voice.

'About ...?'

'A divorce.'

She shook her head.

'Why don't you think about it, Margaret? Really face it? The only thing that's keeping you and Jack together is the boy, and if you're honest you know I could do much better by him than Jack.'

'But he *is* Jack's son –'

'That doesn't mean you must stay tied to him for ever, sweetheart. You owe something to yourself, you know. You don't have to put Jack first all the time.'

'But I don't –'

'Well, have it your way for the moment. But think about what I'm saying, Margaret. We could have a marvellous life. You like this house, and if you wanted I'd keep it on, but we could buy something in the country too – Berkshire, perhaps. Laurie would love it. He might like to take up riding, he's about the right age. We'd find him a good day school nearby, there are plenty, I'm sure. You could drive in with me each day if you wanted to, although –'

'Wait, wait! It's all castles in the air, darling –'

'It needn't be! We could have a wonderful life, you and I and Laurie! It's in my mind so often, my dear! When I see you here, even for these short visits, I think what it would be like to have you here always – I imagine you coming downstairs in the evening to greet our friends, I see you at the head of my table as you ought to be, gracing my world, crowning my life ...'

The sincerity of his tone brought tears to her eyes. She put her arms round him and said: 'You're so good to me, darling. It's just ... It's such a big step to take.'

'But it's a step that's waiting to be taken, Margaret. It's time you started down that path. All I ask is that you think about it – don't shy away from it, face it and think about it. I've faith in your intelligence. In the end you'll see it's inevitable.'

'Nothing's inevitable. But I will think about it. It's only that ...'

'What?'

'It would be such a shattering blow to Jack. He has no idea that I'm even seeing you.'

'Don't you think you ought to tell him?'

'Oh, no!'

'I'd have thought your sense of honesty would drive you to it.'

'No, we always agreed, he and I, that we didn't need to "confess" to each other –'

'But that was only about passing affairs. We both know this isn't one of those, Margaret.'

She looked away, stifling the rejection that rose to her lips. She knew he was right, that they loved each other in a different way from casual lovers. Charles, seeing her pallor, left the matter there.

It was Friday evening. On the way home in the half-empty train, she tried to think of a way to prepare Jack for the news he would have to be told one day. That is, if she decided to leave him. Perhaps Charles was right. Perhaps she ought to prepare the way by confessing their liaison. How could she begin on a topic like that? 'By the way, Jack, I've been sleeping regularly with Charles Vernon.'

274

Impossible. She shook her head at herself. But if the words had to be phrased differently, perhaps she should be thinking about alternatives, for she might actually have to utter them one day.

When she got indoors, Laurie was nowhere to be seen. Jack put his head round the living room door and said: 'He's gone to bed. He was dropping on his feet – but tomorrow's Saturday so he didn't mind because he'll have you all day.'

'I see.'

'Dinner? I kept a slice of meat for you, and some salad?'

'No thanks, Jack, I've eaten.'

'Okay then, coffee in five minutes.'

She went upstairs to take off her dress and shoes. The day had been clammily hot; she showered briefly and put on a loose caftan. As she came downstairs the smell of real coffee wafted up to her. Real coffee?

She went into the living room. Their good coffee set was on the low table. Propped against it was a postcard, and attached to that by Blu-tack was a cheque. She picked it up and looked at it. It was for two hundred pounds and made out to J. D. Durley.

Jack appeared from the kitchen with the coffee pot.

'Jack! What's this?'

'My first fee as a landscape-constructor.'

'As a what?'

'You see in me,' he said, pirouetting, 'A master craftsman, whose work can extract fees of a hundred pounds or more from nutters who run model railways.'

'I beg your pardon?' She sank down on the nearest chair.

'Let's have some coffee. You look as if you need it.' He poured, and handed hers to her. She drank, enjoying the strong, hot mouthful. 'Now,' Jack went on, 'you remember that evening I'd taken Laurie to an exhibition at Central Hall, Westminster?'

275

'The one we had the –' She broke off. She was going to say, The one we had the row.

'The one we had the chicken and chips,' Jack took it up, laughing. 'Well, I took Laurie there as a celebration. I'd just earned a fiver that morning, digging Mrs Moore's garden for her.'

'What?'

'She saw me one day struggling to get out the old fly honeysuckle in our front garden, paused to say she'd got one she wished she could get rid of, and I offered to dig it out for her. She said it was hard work, I said I didn't mind, she said she'd insist on paying, and the long and the short of it is, I got five quid from her. I took it,' he said, with a darting glance of amusement, 'because I felt I damn well deserved it.'

'I should think so!'

'Well, after I'd washed us both off – because of course I took Laurie along to supervise while I did it and we got filthy – I thought, here I am with five pounds I didn't expect to have, why shouldn't we treat ourselves to something? You know, since we moved in, we haven't been anywhere, really – except the park and the market.'

'That's true,' she nodded.

'So I looked in the paper and saw this exhibition was on, and thought the kid would like it. *Well . . .*' he paused for dramatic effect and poured more coffee for himself. 'There were all these guys with train layouts, as earnest as circuit judges. You could see masses of money had been spent on them. And some of the so-called 'scenery' was awful – unrealistic, tatty, badly made. So I says to this here bloke, I says, 'Listen, mate,' I says 'I could make you a better landscape than that with one hand tied behind my back.' And one thing led to another and in the end he gave me five pounds for material and a promise of two hundred quid if I could make him a model of an Alpine mountain scene. Which I did.' He picked up the

276

card with the cheque, and waved it. 'The labourer is worthy of his hire. Not many men can say they constructed the Alps for two hundred pounds.'

'Jack, I can't believe it!' she cried, jumping up and hugging him. 'What a stroke of genius! Two hundred pounds? It's such a lot of money!'

'Isn't it just? Of course, I'm not going to earn that every week. We can't retire to the Bahamas on it. But this bloke – he runs a shop in Marylebone Road and he's put the lay-out in his window – he says he can get plenty of orders from his customers, and they all seem to be nutters willing to spend money on their hobby!'

She stood away from him and looked up at him. 'And that's what you've been beavering at in the spare room all this time?'

He nodded.

'And I thought you were . . . Oh Jack, I was so mean to you that day!'

'Yes you were, and you never gave me a chance to explain,' he agreed, but totally without rancour.

'I'm sorry, love. I was a bitch.'

'Quite true and if a beautiful lady train enthusiast comes along I may very well run away with her. But what do you think, eh? Not bad?' He waved the cheque again. 'You see, I can do it at home. I can do it at my own pace. It's fiddly, of course, and I suppose they won't all be as easy to please as Wilf – Wilf's the shop-owner, Wilf Krantz. He says some model enthusiasts ask for difficult scenery lay-outs. But it can't be worse than working for film directors.'

'It's absolutely wonderful!' she breathed.

'And I'll tell you another thing. I'm not expecting to work full-time on things like that, but I've got a second string to my talented bow. What do you think? I'm a gardening expert.'

'Well, I know that, because you – You mean,

277

somebody else wants to pay you five pounds?'

'Not exactly, but Mrs Moore has asked me to give a couple of hours a week to keeping her garden tidy, and old Mr Faraday heard about it and wants me to go in and get his Virginia creeper off his wall because it's making the house damp, and the long and short of it is, I can do about a dozen hours a week in the neighbourhood if I want to. I haven't settled a proper price for it – do you think two pounds an hour would be about right?'

'Two pounds an hour?'

'Too much? It's quite hard work, you know –'

'It isn't enough! Two pounds an hour? If you were doing the normal forty-hour week, you'd only be making eighty pounds. And I suppose you're supplying your own tools and equipment?'

'Oh, I ... er ... I don't look at it like that. I mean, they're our neighbours. I think two pounds an hour is enough, eh? I can take Laurie along with me, you see. Can't make out I'm a big business whizz-kid if I've got a toddler at my heels.'

Suddenly Margaret collapsed against him and began to laugh. 'Oh, Jack, Jack, where have you been all these weeks? I've missed you so!'

'Ha?' He put his arms round her and held her close. 'Where have *you* been, miss? All shuttered inside a complete stranger, seems to me.'

'I'm sorry. I ... I've had a lot on my mind.' She pressed her cheek into his shoulder. 'I've been a pain in the arse to live with, haven't I?'

'Well, financial worries and a long period of unemployment aren't exactly conducive to sweetness and light. And of course, I'm not claiming I've solved all our money problems by earning the occasional windfall for modelling a lay-out. But it'll help, won't it?'

'Oh, it will! It ought to mean we might have a holiday later in the year.'

278

'A holiday? Where? Not Mombasa, for instance.'

'Hardly. But the firm will have things to offer. Would you like a cut-rate week in southern Italy?'

'Sounds great.' He grinned. 'I was afraid we were going to end up spending a week with your parents.'

'We must invite them here soon, Jack. Do you think you can get the spare room ready for them?'

'Alas, no,' he said with evident pleasure. 'I'm going to need that room for my work. If they come they can't stay overnight.' He paused and added, 'It'll please them no end, won't it? Me bringing in a bit of cash. Gainfully employed – that's what they've always wanted.'

She had to agree it would improve Jack's standing with them. Their frigid attitude since they had to sell the house in Sussex had made it plain they thought their son-in-law was entirely to blame.

And to tell the truth, it improved his status with herself. She knew it was wrong, illogical – but the fact that he could use his talents to bring in a few badly needed pounds made him seeem less lightweight. It was simply a matter of status; a man with earning power has more status than one with none. She scolded herself for thinking so, but the view of society had moulded her outlook even though she'd thought otherwise.

They talked long into the night, in a way they had missed. The silences that had grown between them recently were utterly done away with. At last they washed up the coffee things and put out the lights, then went up the stairs together, arm in arm. They made love with renewed delight, carried away by passion and the pleasure of finding each other again. Next day was Saturday. No need to set the alarm, no need to rise early and hurry to work. The weekend stretched before them, with its leisure to be together in the way they always enjoyed so much – friends, companions, lovers.

If now and again her thoughts went to Charles, they

never lingered with him. There was too much to do and say with Jack and Laurie.

She returned to the office on the Monday morning with a new outlook on the world. Her marriage, which seemed to have been drying up and blowing away in a bitter wind of disillusion, was revived, refreshed. And as she applied herself to the pile of booking slips in her in-tray, the unoccupied part of her mind went over the things Charles had said to her on Friday.

There had seemed to be truth in them. He could give Laurie material advantages that were outside the possibilities she and Jack could provide now. But, although he was a good and kind man, he could never be to Laurie what Jack was. Laurie was Jack's son in a deeper sense than with most men; Jack was the mainstay of his world.

So that was accepted. Laurie and Jack could never be separated. And the next question was, could she ever leave her son so as to be with another man?

No. She knew it was out of the question. When she had refused the job in Buenos Aires, it had been because she would have to leave Laurie behind. Jack's disapproval was a strong factor but the clinching factor had been that if Jack didn't go, neither did Laurie. She wouldn't leave her son. Not even for Charles.

She loved Charles. She also loved Jack. Was it possible to love two men at the same time? All day, part of her mind was busy with the problem. She came to no very useful conclusion, except that she would have to tell Charles she couldn't contemplate a divorce. She couldn't – didn't want to.

'Didn't want to' sounded an odd way of putting it. But it was the truth. Her marriage had weathered the storms. Bonds that had been forged in tribulation held her to Jack. Laurie was one of them – the most important but only one of many. Jack and she had years of the past in common: shared amusements, interests, troubles, hardships. If one could weigh such intangibles against her feelings for Charles, they had to be balanced against Charles's conventional views and ambitions. And of course his money and the use he made of it.

It was impossible to take a dispassionate stocktaking. The two men were so different, with a strong appeal to different sides of her nature. But when you came right down to it, Laurie was the clinching factor. So she 'didn't want' a divorce.

That was unfair to Charles. She had been recalling echoes of his words to her: 'greeting my friends, at the head of my table' ... He wanted her to grace his household, entertain for him. That was only fair; the wife of such a man must be a credit to him.

But she found herself wondering if he would really like seeing her go out to work? Certainly he wouldn't approve of Mercury Travel – it was far too small-time for the wife of Charles Vernon. He would subtly arrange better opportunities.

She couldn't blame him for those actions if he took them. He would be trying to do what he thought was right. But where was independence if she could only work in surroundings that pleased her husband? Was it selfish of her to want to handle her own career? And, in the long run, would Charles want her to have one? The house in the country, good school for Laurie – and perhaps for a child of his own. Did Charles see her as a more conventional wife and mother?

She knew her thoughts were self-centred but after all it was important. It was certainly clear that Charles would want a different kind of wife from Jack. She would have to change if she chose to marry Charles. Did she want to change? Was she capable of it? Her life, such as it was, had been of her own making so far. Intuition told her that Charles would want far more say in her actions than

Jack. Selfish though it might be, she didn't want to change. The year that had just passed, for all its hardships, had made her more genuine, more real to herself. She had made mistakes but she had learned a lot. The Margaret Durley of today was someone she could accept. Charles's Margaret would be a different kind of woman altogether.

At lunchtime she went into St James's Park, bought a beaker of take-away coffee, then sat down on a bench to eat the sandwich she had brought from home. Wholemeal bread made by Jack. She smiled as she unwrapped it and felt a sudden surge of affection for him.

She couldn't leave him. Think it through, weigh it up, look at it from all angles – it was all nonsense. She couldn't leave Jack. With all his faults, with all hers – they were a pair.

She must tell Charles. It was wrong not to be honest with him. 'I'm never going to leave Jack and Laurie,' she said, almost aloud, causing the elderly man sharing her bench to glance at her in alarm.

She threw a few crumbs to a questing Khaki Campbell duck. The duck gobbled up the bread. 'Good, isn't it?' she said to it. 'My husband makes it.'

He made other things too. Clever models for railway enthusiasts, productive gardens, talented sculptures. A happy home, a happy little boy. Why was she always belittling Jack even when she defended him to others? Why had she so often compared him unfavourably with Charles, by giving part of her love to him.

She must break it off.

The stark thought caused a shaft of pain. Charles was so dear to her. He was her lover but he was also her friend. Yet in the end, what could come of it? If Jack ever learned of the affair, he would never forgive her. Charles Vernon was the only man he feared, because he knew how close she had been to marrying him in years gone by. He had sensed then how close the communion of minds had been – a joining of minds as well as bodies. Mere physical attraction he could discount: anyone can feel a momentary arousal for an appealing physique. But Jack had always sensed that Charles drew Margaret for other reasons – and they were reasons he couldn't contend with.

She shook her head to herself. The man on the bench said dubiously: 'Is anything wrong?' Pulling herself together, she gave him a smile and got up.

Nothing was wrong. Nothing that she couldn't put right by having the courage to deal with it.

When she got back to the office she found it in a state of near-panic. Olive Jones, junior 'associate' in charge of public relations, had failed to come back from lunch because of a headache. 'Again,' muttered Mary Groves, with no liking for the snooty young woman who, by a small monetary investment, had hoisted her position from executive in charge of correspondence to something like board level.

'She's gone off on a shopping spree, that's all,' Mary growled. 'And left O'Dowd with four noisy Italians to handle – and you know how poor his Italian is.'

'Who are they?' Margaret inquired.

'Hotel owners. You know – that new tour we're going to offer next year to archaeological sites on the southern Adriatic ...'

Margaret sat down at her desk, automatically picking up the first document in her in tray. Then she paused. She sat for a moment in thought. Then she picked up her phone and dialled O'Dowd's office. He was clearly too busy to answer, for he let it ring a long time. She was on the point of abandoning the idea when he picked up his instrument.

'Yes?' he barked.

'Mr O'Dowd ... I gather you're in a bit of a difficulty.'

'What the devil do you mean by interrupting like this –? Is that Margaret?'

'Yes, Mr O'Dowd. I just wanted to remind you ... I speak very good Italian.'

There was a pause from him, during which she could hear chattering Italian voices in the background. Then O'Dowd said in a tone of relief: 'I'd forgotten that. Get in here right away.'

It was an agreeable afternoon. The four noisy gentlemen, delighted to have an attractive woman to talk to instead of the flustered O'Dowd, sparkled and joked in competition for her attention. They begged her to go out with them that evening to dine. 'Show us London!' they begged. She excused herself on the ground that she had a little boy at home expecting her. All respectful understanding, they made her promise to come to lunch next day.

'You were a marvel,' O'Dowd said when he had put them in a taxi for the Dorchester. 'By lunchtime tomorrow let's hope you can get firm prices for accommodation out of them.'

'You ... er ... want me to handle that?'

There was a long pause. Then he said, 'I begin to think you're wasted on the booking files, Margaret.'

'Thank you, Mr O'Dowd.'

'See here, if we're going to be a team handling those southern bandits tomorrow, don't you think you should call me James?'

She smiled, nodded, and looked away. No need to rush into using his first name. She could come to that tomorrow, while helping him with the price nego- tiations. He was a decent sort, keen to make his firm pre-eminent in its field, a little over-zealous about efficiency.

On the way home in the train she was telling herself it

284

wouldn't be hard to improve her situation at Mercury Travel. Olive Jones didn't really care about her job; she thought having a little money in the firm justified a lot of skiving. If she cared to exert herself, Margaret could probably take on all the work she neglected and earn a considerable promotion.

Did she want to? Did she want to put her foot on the rungs of the promotion ladder, at the start of the climb to the upper echelons of the business world?

Problems, problems, she said to herself with a wry smile. But these were better problems than those she'd had to face this time last year. Last year she'd been facing redundancy. Now she was contemplating an improvement she could make in her career. She could think it all through in the next day or two. For the moment she sat back in the dusty carriage watching the suburbs of London slipping past and thinking she was a very lucky woman. She had a husband she loved and who loved her, a fine little boy, a home, and a job. The past year had taught her to value these things. That was another reason to know she was lucky. She had come to an understanding of what was really important.

There were issues to be dealt with, certainly. But not at this precise instant. As she made her way from the station to the bus stop, she gave herself up to the more immediate pleasure of thinking about Laurie as he'd run to meet her when she put her key in the door. She would tell Jack about the Italians. It was the kind of thing that would make him grin. And probably he'd have something to tell her – about his day's work as a jobbing gardener, for instance.

Little pleasures in a little life ... Yet it was the little things that she had come to value. If she had lost a lot in the year that had gone by – her status as a top level businesswoman, the hopes of another child – she had gained much, too. She had learned to take nothing for granted. Very little is 'granted'. Almost everything has to be earned.

So she would earn her right to happiness. She would work at it. She was, after all, a working woman.